Adam Melrose

The
Determined
Widow

A Matthew Holland Mystery

REFRACT SPEECH PRESS

First published in Great Britain in 2021
First published in the USA in 2021
This paperback edition published in 2021
****

****

Paperback Edition

ISBN 978-1-3999-0252-6

A CIP catalogue record for this book is available from the British Library

A record for this book is registered with the eCO, Library of Congress

www.refractspeechpress.com

To A,A,J,M and everyone who came before.

With love.

Thank you all for everything you have
taught me about life and living.

PROLOGUE

When he saw the message on his phone, his heart stopped.

Pete Stone, a battle-hardened man in his mid-thirties noticed his hand was trembling. As he replaced the phone in his pocket, he heard one of the work vehicles approaching across the gravel. He closed his eyes and prayed it would pass on by.

As the van slowed down, the stabbing pain in Pete's stomach doubled. The vehicle came to a halt. Pete kept his eyes closed. He inhaled the fresh summer air, trying to regain control over his body's fight or flight response.

'Alright Pete?'

'I'm good mate, you?'

'Yeah fine,' said Ned. 'The boss just radioed to tell me to drop you off at the site. Hop in. I'll give you a lift down there.'

A tingling sensation was now powering down Pete's arms. His boss was one step ahead of him, he could not just run. He could not be sure that if he ran, they would not go after his wife.

They set off to meet the boss, winding through the small Cotswold country lanes. Neither of them spoke. The only sounds were the engine and the long grass reaching out from the verge making its usual loud thwack as the grass-heads made contact with the plastic casing on the van's mirrors. The two men sat in silence. Pete began working out whether there was any way of escaping what he felt was coming. Try as he might, he could not come up with anything.

Ned turned the van off the tarmac and onto a dirt access road. Pete undid his seatbelt.

'Let me out here thanks. I could do with the walk up.'

'The boss said I was to take you up there.'

The two men had never liked each other.

Pete gave Ned as withering a look as he could, '*What am I?* Twelve years old? I think I can manage.'

Pete's facial expression had the desired effect. Ned hauled on the brakes. As he did so the resultant dust cloud blew into the van. Pete could feel the particles coming to rest in his mouth, instantly making it feel dry and uncomfortable.

'*Get out then.*'

Pete climbed out. He was glad Ned was so easy to annoy. It might buy the lifesaving time Pete required. Ned sped off back up the road.

Pete composed himself. He crossed the road, down some steps and under a bridge. He had an idea; he would call the police. The shooting pains were back in his arms and he struggled to hold the phone steady. No Service. Outsmarted by his boss again. They must have shut his phone service off. Of course they had.

Pete decided his best bet now was to reason with his boss. It was not like his employers were killers. He turned around and walked back up the path towards his rendezvous. Approaching the entrance to the works, Pete quickly emptied his pockets and placed a couple of items in a pair of disposable gloves he had to hand. He tucked them in a bush near the water. It was all he could manage to come up with at such short notice. If he was about to meet his maker, hopefully the police would find these and use it to piece together what happened to him.

He carried on his journey and before long he was deep inside the works facility. After the familiar walk along the damp concrete corridors, the staircases and several large grey metal doors, Pete had reached his destination, the final grey door. It looked like something that belonged in a submarine. He reached out to open it, his hands and arms shaking uncontrollably again. Taking a breath, he walked through the door. Although he did indeed see his boss was standing there waiting for him, Pete was delighted to see it was only the two of them. Pete relaxed dramatically. Internally he laughed at himself for being so melodramatic. It really was not like him to get so stressed. He approached his boss.

For the next twenty minutes they argued. Pete assured his boss that he was not about to betray any confidences about what went on here, and that he had only been mouthing-off in anger when he had threatened to earlier in the week. His boss did not seem convinced.

At some point during their argument his boss dropped a pen and bent down to pick it up. Before Pete realised what was happening, he felt a vice like grip on his ankles and a power forcing him up and pivoting him over the railing. Pete died the instant his head hit the concrete floor some thirty feet below.

The boss walked over to the phone fitted to the wall, coughed a couple of times and practiced a panicked, odd and high-pitched voice out loud before dialling.

'Evelyn de Varley here. Come quick. There has been a *dreadful* accident. Pete Stone has fallen over the railings; I think… *I think* he's dead.'

CHAPTER 1

16 Months later – May – Present day.

Matthew Holland was making his way across London from his flat to his office. Apart from an odd incident with a bald man in a boat, his holiday had been a perfect antidote to his struggle with his mental health. He re-read yesterday's text message on his phone.

From Ava:

Matt, hope all is good? Are you still back in the office tomorrow? Max has a case for us and has arranged for the initial client meeting for tomorrow at the office at 9:30 a.m. The referral is Max himself, and the client is his ex. Her husband was found dead. Official line is nothing suspicious; ruled as misadventure. Client insists otherwise. Issue over missing tattoos. Just thought I would give you a heads up.

Ava x

As the bus pulled up outside the building that housed the office of his private investigation agency, Matt slipped the phone into his pocket and hopped onto the pavement. The building in question was called Franklin Blake House; its location was on Fleet Street in central London, and it was a testament to the sort of money a tech firm could realise on becoming financially successful.

It was headquarters for the mysteriously named Refract Speech Ltd. This particular tech firm pioneered some early AI technology. In doing so, they had been able to generate some serious revenue, and here about ten percent of that wealth rose high into the sky; its glass and stone façade gleaming in the morning sunlight. As Matt passed through the outer courtyard, the combination of high walls and the sound of water splashing in the fountain provided its usual antidote to the frenzied hustle and bustle of the street outside.

Back when Matt was freshly out of the Army, he had a chance meeting with the Refract Speech CEO Oliver Scott, who was a distant cousin. This had resulted in Matt helping to solve the disappearance of one of the company's chief software architects. Matt and two friends had found the software genius just in the nick of time when no one else was able to. This had led to Matt's new and unexpected career; and ultimately the creation of his new investigation company called Scott and Munro, which now had a total of six full-time investigators.

The CEO of Refract Speech had been so grateful

for their help, and so impressed with how they managed to recover his valued employee, that on hearing of the official formation of this new company, he had insisted that he put his cousin's firm on retainer should he have any further need for them. Part of that generous retainer was the provision of some decent office space; way more than a newly formed investigation company could have afforded.

As Matt headed past the security station that sat in the middle of the entrance hallway, a man of similar build and stature to Matt turned and smiled.

'Morning Sir.'

Matt gave an equally effusive smile back, 'Morning Ian, how was the weekend?'

'Good thanks, nothing to complain about.'

'Happy days.'

Matt moved over to the reception desk to double check his client was on the visitor list. There were only two people waiting to be signed in. Everyone else had their own pass and was filtering through the automated barriers. Matt joined the queue behind the two visitors. The shaved headed man in front began to move off in the direction of the elevators whilst fixing his badge to his jacket.

Just the woman left to sign in, then I can get upstairs for a quick catch up, Matt said to himself. His inner monologue was interrupted by something in his brain tuning in to what the woman in front of him was doing. Her shoulders were just lifting and dropping a little. She must be listening to some music, Matt thought. He scanned as subtly as he could to see if there were some earphones hanging out of her ears. He envied people who could move comfortably to music in public; he was way too self-conscious to manage such a thing.

The woman in the queue was now lifting her left hand up and brushing it across the left side of her face and sweeping it back. At that moment Matt saw traces of moisture on the back of her hand; tears – she's not dancing you idiot, she's crying.

As this realisation dawned on him, the woman's small shoulder movements became more pronounced. This person was clearly in distress. The receptionist leant as far over the front of the desk as she could, and offered the crying woman a paper hanky from a small box of corporate branded tissues. The woman took one. This distressed soul was clearly not coping with whatever had happened to her.

The woman in question was about five foot five inches tall, with a slender build and coloured dark red hair. She wore a pair of slim fitting faded jeans, and a white blouse with dark vertical pinstripes. What finished the look off where the different coloured trainers that she wore, black on the left foot and dark blue on the right. Matt had always liked those traditional American ones with the white toe.

Matt caught the attention of Ian, and beckoned him over. By this time the receptionist had come around the front of the desk to join the still unhappy soul.

Reading the situation at once, Ian suggested to the woman that they take a seat in some of the chairs that were laid out in a row against one of the walls. She nodded her agreement, and the four of them headed in that direction. Matt instinctively grabbed a cup of water from the water dispenser to offer up.

The woman, now drying her eyes, and clearly embarrassed at all this attention politely declined the water, and was doing her best to sit up and apologise for causing a fuss. Matt drank the water, and placed the empty cup in the bin before returning to the two women who were now talking to each other.

'Who is it you're here to see? Let me phone them and get them to come down. Would you like to wait in our small meeting room?' The receptionist motioned to a door set in the wall just to their left, but the woman shook her head.

'That's very kind, no thank you, I'll be *fine*. I am *really sorry* about this, I have no idea what has come over me, this is not normally how I behave in front of strangers.'

'*Hey* there's nothing to apologise for. Are you able to tell me who you are, and who you have come to meet?'

The woman looked down and began reaching into the purple shoulder bag that she now had on her knee. 'My name is Bella Stone.' Her voice drifted off as she became more focused on what she was looking for. A set of keys jangled, followed by the sound of plastic cases clicking off each other and sliding along the lining until the searching stopped, and Bella Stone pulled out a yellow piece of paper with some handwriting on it, 'The company name is Scott and Munro... yes *that's* it. I'm here to see a man called Max Ingram. Is it possible to let him know I'm here, or should I wait? I'm not due until nine-thirty, but I found myself here early.'

The woman's voice was speeding up, her stress clearly not yet under control.

'I wanted to stay *busy* you see, so I left things as late as I dared precisely so this wouldn't happen. I had planned it so I would have no spare time to sit and think, but I got my calculations all wrong and arrived here way too early.'

Matt unbuttoned his suit jacket before lowering himself into a squat position in order to make direct eye contact with his new client. He also didn't want to tower over her as he spoke. As he saw her face for the first time, he saw the trickle of tears and droplets forming on her cheek, magnifying her flawless complexion.

'I can take you up to see Max. My name is Matthew Holland and I work with Max at Scott and Munro. I can take you up right now, if that's OK?'

The woman managed a clear nod of the head. Matt and the receptionist exchanged looks that signified a mutual agreement to the plan, and Matt motioned to Bella to follow him through the open security barrier. He took her off to one of the free elevators that had just opened its doors. Turning round whilst selecting the required floor button, Matt gave a nod to thank Ian and those who had stood back to let them take the elevator alone.

The elevator car began to rise. Realising it was better to give this distraught soul a few moments to compose herself Matt decided to say nothing. That was probably a more decent thing to do than make small talk. Things were going to get worse before they got better; Bella was going to have to recount the events that had brought her here to the doors of Scott and Munro. The process was necessary to allow the team to understand what they were getting into when taking on a new case. The downside was that although this was unavoidable, it was nevertheless a painful experience for the client which the whole team hated witnessing, and it did not seem to be getting easier with time.

The elevator came to a halt. The doors slid back, and before them lay an open-plan office with lots of natural light that was complimented by a lightly coloured beige carpet. The welcoming ambience was further enhanced with the smell of fresh coffee percolating in their general direction.

Standing by the elevator, ready to greet them, in a smart pair of dark blue coloured jeans and an open necked blue shirt with sleeves rolled up was a tall, elegant man with a very warm welcoming smile. As Matt and Bella stepped off the elevator, Max stepped forward, he and Bella put their arms around each other and hugged tightly.

In that instant, Bella suddenly felt safe for the first time since Pete had died. She breathed in through Max's shirt; he smelt the same, and she remembered that scent with fondness. Despite her best efforts, Bella let go and began to cry. Months of trying to control her grief whilst she fought the authorities to get to what she believed was the truth about her husband's death had finally caught up with her. Now she felt she was no longer alone. The relief at even the hint of some support from people that might be on her side was enough to lift the latch on the door she had locked all her emotions behind in order to go it alone; now out it all came, and she couldn't stop it. Matt caught Max's eye and signalled he would head off and wait in the meeting room. Max gave a gentle nod, still holding Bella.

'We'll be there in a moment Matt,' his voice was soft but deep, and Bella could feel his chest vibrating through his shirt as he spoke. She hugged him tighter.

After a couple of moments had passed, Max and Bella instinctively pulled themselves apart.

'Hey kiddo, how are you managing?'

'*They killed him* Max. He *didn't* die accidently. For sixteen months I have been trying to prove my husband's death was not accidental, and I keep being met with official people telling me in gentle tones that there is nothing suspicious. I'm afraid I need your help to find out what really happened to my husband.'

'Of course we will; *well,* we'll do our best.'

'That's *all* I'm asking.'

Bella forced a smile. Her brain was releasing happier chemicals now that she was with Max, but they were going to take a moment to outwit the bad ones. She stepped back and dried her eyes with the now damp hankie.

'Is there somewhere I can freshen up and sort myself out before the meeting?' Bella glanced at the clocks dotted around the walls of the office, it was nine-fifteen. 'I know you guys will be busy, and I don't want to keep you waiting.'

Max smiled, 'There's no rush, we allow half a day for these meetings; it's your meeting, your time. Come with me, I'll show you where you can freshen up. Just take as long as you want OK? We'll start when you're good and ready, not before. This meeting is going to be tough on you; there's *no* way around that. So like I say – *no* rush, just come over to the meeting room when you're ready.'

As Max led Bella across the office, his thought was that there really wasn't any pressure for time with this particular meeting; he had already looked at the relevant information she had forwarded to them. The coroner's report found that there was no evidence of foul play; it was just an accident, or misadventure to use the official jargon. The only troubling issue was the subject of the missing tattoos, though there was no doubt a very simple explanation for that aspect of the case. The real difficulty with this case was going to be how and when to assure a grieving widow who was convinced of foul play, that her husband's death was actually just a very unlucky accident.

They stopped outside a pair of large brown doors.

Max pointed to a room on the other side of the office; the wall of which, on this side was all glass.

'We will be in there, when you are good and ready.'

Some ten minutes later, after composing herself and freshening up in the bathroom; it was Bella who took in a deep breath, pushed on the glass door, and walked into the meeting room. She managed to get her head up high and smile.

As she did so, Bella gave herself one last talking to. I may not be able to get through this meeting without crying, but I sure as hell am going to start it with dry eyes and be professional. They need to believe I'm being rational and level-headed when I tell them my husband was murdered. I need them to help me, and they will only do that if they genuinely believe me.

Max stood up and came across to meet her.

'Ready for this *then*?'

'I think so, *yes*.'

Bella was rooting around in her bag for something. Her hands were still shaking a little. Max thought it would be a good idea to distract her with a trivial question for a moment and get her mind off what was coming, and then once she was distracted, just jump straight in.

Max gave Bella a moment more to rifle about in her bag, then he took his moment to divert her mind, 'I meant to ask how you knew I was working here?'

The trick worked. Bella stopped searching through her bag and looked up at him.

'*Err...*' she gave it some thought then her face lightened; she had obviously remembered, 'A flyer came through the office mail from you guys advertising your services, and I recognised your name. My boss threw it in the bin, so I took it back out and kept it in my drawer just in case the authorities screwed up their investigation into Pete's death; which they did, and here I am.'

Max replied after a moment, 'OK, cool. I'm just sorry it is under such unpleasant circumstances.'

Before Max could suggest beginning the meeting, Bella lifted her shoulders up tall.

'*Right...* I *think* I'm ready... thanks.'

She gave a knowing look that let him understand she appreciated his thought and concern; they had been separated for a good couple of years now, but it had ended amicably and by mutual agreement. Their connection was still there, they could still read each other at least.

Max walked forward into the room towards the table and Bella followed.

CHAPTER 2

Max cleared his throat to get everyone's attention and began the meeting.

'Right, good morning. Bella this is *everyone...* *everyone*, this is Bella Stone. Don't worry about names Bella, as things progress you'll get to know everyone and what they do.'

Bella looked around the table; including Max the team consisted of six people in total. She made sure she nodded to each one in person. They all smiled back, and there was a 'Hello.' or 'Hi.' or 'Welcome.' from each of them.

Bella was put at ease almost at once.

'Bella, why don't you just tell us in your own words why you are here, and then provide the back story for us? Leave nothing out. I know you've provided us with some very detailed notes and a report on the case, but it helps us to hear it all first hand from you.'

Bella nodded.

'We may interrupt at any point just to clarify something. We find it is easier to ask straight away rather than leave it to the end, especially whilst the point is still clear in your mind. At any time you want a break you just say so. OK?'

Bella nodded again.

As she tried to speak she felt the back of her throat instantly dry up. Before beginning she picked up the glass of water and took a drink; all the time telling herself she had nothing to fear here, she was amongst friends. She let the water linger in her mouth, its coolness and wetness providing a much needed natural tonic. Bella put the glass down on the table, looked in the direction of the middle of the room, smiled, swallowed, then took a calming breath and began.

'Hi everyone; firstly, *thank you very much* for seeing me. Right I will jump straight in… I met my husband three months before we were married, and we were then married for three months exactly to the day I saw him in the morgue. Apart from the end, those six months were some of the most magical months I have ever enjoyed in my life.

'We met at a fashion event. I was working there in my role as a PA to the head of a model agency. Pete was there in some security capacity, I forget what. We just got talking and didn't stop.

'I had to get back to work after a while so Pete left me alone. When things calmed down and I had a moment I went looking for him, but I couldn't find him, and no one seemed to know who he was or who he worked for.

'It was the following Friday, when I was leaving the office at the end of the day that he approached me in the street with some flowers. I was totally blown away; we then spent a bliss-

ful weekend together and more
that.

'We both knew it was rash
soon, but the weird thing was I didn't ᵻ
by anything related to him; even though noᵻ
mally I'm a cautious person when it comes to big
decisions. That total lack of fear told me I should
go for it and to hell with the consequences.'

Bella tried to subtly look around the room and
carefully gauge whether she had everyone's attention, and whether these people seated before
her would give any indication as to whether they
would believe her and take on her case. The momentary glance told her that she did indeed have
everyone's attention. Good, she thought.

'Probably we should have found out a lot more
about each other's backgrounds before tying the
knot, but the simple fact is we didn't, and I do
not regret that for a moment. The marriage cere-
mony was just us and the required witnesses in
a registry office. It was great; we could just focus
on each other. We then had a short honeymoon
in the Channel Islands on the Island of Jersey. To
keep costs down we stayed in this amazing pink
country house as guests of the elderly owner
who Pete somehow knew. We then came back,
and I moved into Pete's flat. It was bliss; we felt
like we had known each other our whole lives.
We then slipped back into our daily life routines.
Pete went back to his security job in Reading, and
I went back to my work as a PA.'

lla was about to continue when a man's voice opped her in her tracks.

'Hi Bella, I'm Bruno. Sorry to interrupt; you say Pete worked in security. Can you elaborate on that for us? *Who* for example? *Whereabouts* etcetera.'

Using this breathing space to take a sip of water from her glass, Bella then turned to face the owner of the voice; a lithe framed man with sandy coloured windswept hair.

'I *don't know* much really. He said it was a large tech firm based in Reading or just outside; I forget which. We had been so wrapped up in our romance that we didn't talk about work much.'

Bruno continued with his questions.

'Do you know for sure it was around Reading that he worked, did Pete tell you that or did you just assume it for some valid reason?'

Bella's stomach began to tighten a little. Was she losing them? Answer calmly, she told herself.

'Yes, Pete *specifically* told me, and I have seen a couple of petrol receipts lying around the kitchen that have a petrol station with a Reading address on them.'

Bruno nodded, 'OK, thanks. Please carry on.'

'Other than that, the only remarkable thing about life for the following weeks was that it was very unremarkable in the day-to-day element of it. We were both pretty blinkered by each other, so nothing has stuck in my mind as odd or suspicious. I have been over and over it in my head.

I can't come up with anything that stands out as odd.'

Bella proceeded to provide some day-to-day information of places visited, jokes shared and other memorable moments from her short time together with Pete. Bringing everyone up to date did not take long given that their time together had been so short.

It was now the turn of an elegant looking woman with raven hair sitting on the same side of the table as Bruno to chip in, 'Hi Bella, I'm Ava. I just wanted to ask; *why* are you so sure that this was not an accidental death?'

Bella's stomach felt like it had been instantly struck with a large bat. She nearly doubled over. It was a very valid question and asked nicely, but it still nearly floored Bella, such was the grip of terror in her mind that these guys would not take her case.

Smiling at Ava, Bella felt all her hopes and wishes were pinned on these next few sentences. 'I'm *afraid* this is where I need and *hope* you will take me at my word. I say that because I have no physical proof or eyewitness testimony to offer up to you, I just have my intuition and my knowledge of Pete and his consistent behaviour.'

Bella paused for a moment to draw breath and to pace herself before continuing.

'If Pete was one thing in the time I knew him, he was consistent. If he said he *would* do something, *he would*. If he was going to be late, he *would* let me know. We had made plans to go out for supper the day he went missing. If his plans had changed, he would simply have called me to say we had to take a rain-check. I know he would've known that I would've been alright with that; so he *would've* had no reason not to let me know.'

Again Bella paused in order to deliberately regulate her rate of speech and to let what she was saying sink in.

'Pete not calling me *didn't* fit with the nature of the man; it changed his narrative, and his narrative *didn't* change *once* in any other aspect in a very intense six months. I work with models in the fashion industry; I'm good at looking under the image a person presents and seeing the real person. For six months I saw the same man day in day out, no change. That lack of a short text or phone call just *does not track;* it's an exception to the norm, so it's *wrong*. Also; my gut says so. Sometimes you just know a thing's wrong *without* clearly knowing why it's wrong. His body was found sixty-something miles away from work in the wrong direction in a place he had no business being; if he had a legitimate reason for going that far out the wrong way on a night we were going out to supper he would have let me know. His *not* letting me know tells me he was taken there *against his will* and that something bad happened.'

Bella took a moment for her information to

sink in before continuing.

'One other point; there is *one thing* I believe to be the *real* key that will unlock this whole mystery. I haven't told the police because after their ignoring the tattoo business, I know they won't give it the relevant consideration it deserves, but I *will* tell you. I only ask that you give what I'm about to tell you the attention I feel it rightly deserves. I wanted to wait to be face to face to tell you.'

Bella looked around the table making sure she had everyone's full attention. She did.

'It's something I heard my husband say to his work colleague a couple of times when they were talking on the phone. On the surface it will seem to be nothing, but it has to very much be something, or else it's been said out of context, and if that was the case, it would make no sense and everything Pete said *did* make sense, so this needs to *also*.'

Bella paused to take another look at everyone in turn. They were still giving her their full attention. She was worried she was talking too fast. She tried to calm herself down once more.

'On more than one occasion I heard Pete say, "OK mate, I'll see you at Underworld." He would then laugh and finish the call.'

As silence filled the room Bella spoke gently to herself. There, I've said it. However stupid the word Underworld sounds, it is out there and I can't unsay it. I've been honest and said part of this is just my gut. If they won't help me then they won't. I have done my best.

A sense of relief washed over Bella, she had said what she was afraid to say, and with that, any fear about whether to say it or not vanished the instant she had uttered those words.

'I have a question Bella.'

The next voice in the room caught Bella off guard. It sounded like Max and then again it did not. Bella turned to look in the direction of the confusing voice. On seeing who it was, Bella's eyes lit up. It was Joe. In all her trying to hold it together and introductions being a blur, she had not looked closely enough to recognise him. Furthermore, it had been a fair few years, and even then they had only met a couple of times. Joe was Max's twin brother. They were not identical looks-wise, and yet you could tell they were brothers.

'Hey Joe.'

'Hey Bella.'

Joe continued, 'I'm sure I speak for all of us in saying thank you for that detailed walk through your time with Pete. That can't have been easy, but it does help us a lot, *thank you*. I appreciate that you provided us with some very detailed typed notes and history, but nothing helps like hearing things first hand.'

'Firstly, do you have any idea what Underworld refers to? Is it a joke or a code?'

Bella folded her bottom lip in under her top

one and gave a gentle shake of her head.

'No Joe, I'm sorry. I have wracked my brains about it, but *nothing* has come to mind. The only thing that I can come up with is I guess it's a nickname they have given to something.'

'Why do you say that?'

'*Because*,' Bella paused for a thoughtful moment, 'Pete said "Underworld". He didn't say "The Underworld" so it *must* have been a name of a place not *the* place. I just assumed it was something to do with work. I'm guessing she would know.'

'...*She* would know?'

'Sorry, didn't I *say*... the person he was talking to on the phone.'

'Why do you assume the person he was talking to was female?'

'Because he used her name.'

'You heard him call her by her name?'

'Yes ... might that help?'

'It might, what was her name?'

'He called her Sharon.'

Joe sat up in his chair, 'You *heard* him say Sharon?'

'I did,' nodded Bella, 'He said, "I'll see you at Underworld" there was a pause when I assume she was speaking, and then he finished with "OK Sharon." he laughed and then hung up. That was the last call I remember like that. Does it mean something?'

Joe shook his head, 'I thought it did, I thought a

lightbulb came on in my head when you said Sharon but...no it's gone. It's probably nothing.'

Matt was next to talk, 'So Bella, you think this reference to Underworld is the key because it must be linked to the only other unexplained things with Pete, namely his missing tattoos, and how he died? Is that correct?'

'Yes Matt, that and the missing tattoos have to be where the truth of what happened to my husband lies because everything else was normal and explained; there were never any absences, odd calls, odd people or holes in any of his stories. Everything except the odd references to Underworld and the tattoos vanishing fits together. Only these two odd things stand out, so to my simple logic, they must be connected to the third odd thing; my husband's death. However insignificant and trivial they seem, they *must* be relevant, because nothing else is.'

'OK Bella, we hear you, thanks.'

After a moment, Bruno spoke, 'I would like to address that other odd thing as you describe it, namely this business with the tattoos. So, you don't think they are as important a key to solving your husband's death in the way the mention of Underworld is?'

'*No*, I don't.'

'Can I ask *why* not?'

'It's mainly because he had them, I saw them daily and so I know them to be real. Everyone knew he had them, so I don't think there can be any mystery in a thing when everyone knows about it. Therefore if it holds no mystery, then it probably holds no clue. The only mystery is *why* and how they were removed; but as everyone knew about them, their removal can't hide anything. It may seem an odd thing to say, but I don't think it's going to be the key to unlocking how or why Pete died. That said of course, it strongly proves to me that his death wasn't an accident.'

Bruno made some notes on his tablet, 'Can you give us a quick overview of the tattoo situation then?'

'It's very simple and it's totally unexplained. From the first day I met Pete he had a half tattoo sleeve down both his left and right arms from his shoulders down to his elbows. And when I went to see him in the mortuary, *both* his arms were free of tattoos. It was a real shock. If my husband's death was accidental his tattoos would *still* be there. It is completely *negligent* of the authorities to ignore this fact. They either have something to hide, or they think I am a liar. '

Bella was a bit more confident now and looked around the room. What she saw was various expressions of surprise and perhaps confusion.

'Hi Bella, I'm Norton.' The man identifying himself on the left hand far side of the table had short blond cropped hair and brown eyes and was dressed in the same style of blue shirt as the others. Bella thought he had a very safe looking face.

'When you say your husband's tattoos were missing, do you mean they had been removed? As in someone had removed them with a laser, so there was still some ghosting?'

Bella could feel all eyes in the room settling on her. She had to take a moment to remind herself these people were friends considering if they could help her, and not a pack of wild animals circling their prey.

'No, I mean they had completely gone; no trace whatsoever.'

Norton continued, 'You're saying they were totally gone; as in the skin had been cut out or sanded down?'

Bella's face instantly went a couple of shades whiter at even the slightest thought of such an occurrence.

'*No*, I mean it was as if they had never been there in the *first place*.'

The room fell into silence. Bella looked at the people seated around the table. There were various looks of confusion and brains processing information.

Norton spoke again.

'So, just to be one hundred percent clear, his arms were fine apart from the damage from being in the water for so long, and otherwise they were unmarked and all was good? It just appeared as if he never had any tattoos in the first place; have I got that right?'

Bella felt all eyes on her yet again, 'Yes, that's

correct.'

Norton raised his eyebrows.

Bruno chipped in, 'So, how do *you* explain it?'

Bella's answer was pretty short.

'I *don't*... I mean I *can't*. I *literally* have *no* idea. The official investigation did look in to it when I made such a fuss, but could find no evidence of any tattoos ever being there so they just put it down as unexplained. There was no trace of them ever having been there so despite what I was saying, they just took it that they never had been present. As they didn't find any connection between the missing tattoos and the cause of Pete's death it was barely referenced. It didn't help that I couldn't find any photos of him showing his bare arms and his tattoos.'

Norton raised himself up in his chair a little, 'Moving on if we can Bella; have you or Pete ever been out to the area where his body was found? I mean *ever*?'

'No never, neither of us knew that part of the world, we were both London born and bred. We didn't make it out to the countryside very often, and if we did it was never that far from the city. I love it here and Pete had been abroad so much with work over the years that he liked to spend any time he had here rather than go off travelling again. To this day I have never been to the Cotswolds. I wanted to in the hope of finding some peace, but I just *couldn't* face it.'

Norton nodded, 'So you haven't been out to

where he, *well*… where his body was discovered?'

Bella looked at him, her eyes moistening a little and a micro quiver began appearing on her lip. Her face turned a little red, '*No*… no, I *wanted* to, but as I say I just couldn't bring myself to visit the location of his death. I got as far as Paddington Station a couple of times, but when it came to it, I just couldn't bring myself to board the train. I began to feel sick, so I took that as a sign not to. I turned round and came straight home.'

Norton took a moment to contemplate Bella's answer; nodded to her, and then scribbled something on the screen of his tablet.

Silence began to fill the room once more until Matt spoke again.

'Bella, would you mind giving us a moment. If you are happy to wait out in the main office, we won't keep you more than a couple of minutes.'

'*Of course.*'

Bella left the room and closed the door behind her. Matt swung round on his chair to face everyone still sat around the table. He was about to speak when Bella poked her head around the door.

'I would just like to add that Dr Edward Brett the pathologist has been really helpful through these last few months and has said I can pass his contact details to you. They are in the file I have given you. He said he would do *whatever* he could to help… Did I tell you that *already*? I can't remember.'

Bella then proceeded to ramble on about how Pete could not swim, so would never have been near the edge of the quarry where he was found. She had blurted this all out in an instant, and before anyone had time to say anything she promptly left the room again, closing the door behind her. Through the glass everyone could see her take a seat at one of the empty desks. She looked exhausted.

Matt spoke first, '*Right* – so I'm guessing we are all prepared to at least go and visit the site where they found Pete's body and have a nose around. We have nothing else on the books at the moment and I'm guessing we are all happy to do this for Max if not for Bella. It's clear she needs some closure to this, and we can give her that if nothing else. Let's give it one night and two days, and if as I suspect we find nothing; then Max can gently break the news to Bella and hopefully she will be able to find some closure and we will rip up her invoice for any work done. *Agreed*?'

The only person to speak up was Norton.

'I *don't* agree... *no*. I'm sorry Max, don't get me wrong, I am happy to go for a poke about, but she is clearly *lying* to us. I'm not sure she is going to find any closure because there is no way that's the full story. I just want to register that now before we embark on this escapade.'

Max looked down at the table. His twin Joe and Matt both threw Norton an angry look. Joe began to speak, but was silenced by Matt raising his hand in Joe's direction. He then turned to stare directly at Norton.

'A word Norton… *now.*'

Matt got up and walked out of the room and Norton followed. As Matt passed Bella he gave her a confident smile.

'We will be with you in two moments *OK*?'

Bella nodded. Matt wandered over to the far end of the room and round the corner to the small kitchen. Once Norton had caught up, he waved him inside, walked in and closed the door.

'What *the hell* was that?'

'Since *when* are we not allowed to give our considered opinion when looking at taking on a case?'

'Since the client is sitting on the other side of the glass and you *know* she can hear *every* word spoken in a normal voice, and *unlike* me, you spoke in a normal voice.'

'Sorry, yes I should have thought of that, *but…* I think we are being played and it annoys me.'

'Did you *misunderstand* what is going on here? *There is no case*; we are trying to help out Max, who is in turn trying to help his ex find some closure. She's clearly confused and exhausted. Her initial call to Max said the tattoos were the main clue, now she is saying its Pete's phone calls to his work colleagues. She just needs some support and direction. This is an exercise in friendship, not a real case. You get that, *yes*?'

'I do boss, sorry.'

'*Good,* well let's say no more about it, get back in there, and support them both and *do* the decent thing. If there was something to this tattoo business, the police would not have ignored it. It's clearly an accidental death, so let's *help* her find some closure.'

'*Sorry.*'

With the conversation being over, Matt and Norton returned to the meeting room. Matt then explained to Max all was good, and everyone was in agreement.

Max smiled, stood up and opened the door, inviting Bella to come back into the room. Her face looked frozen in terror as if the next few words spoken to her would shape the rest of her life.

'OK Bella,' said Matt, 'Thanks for waiting; we won't keep you in suspense. We *will* look into your case. That said, I just need to make the following statement to you, not because I don't think you understand the situation, but for my own peace of mind. Then I know that we have played it straight from the start in terms of realistic expectations for this case. I don't want to feel in any way that we have misled you about the chances of getting anywhere with this investigation.'

Bella instinctively sat down in the chair closest to her. Matt waited for her to settle before continuing, 'The chance of us finding anything new is *incredibly* slim. Given how long ago this happened, how long your husband's body was in the water before it was discovered and the fact that the police have carried out a thorough investigation, and that there has been an official inquest means there is only the remotest chance of us turning up anything new or helpful.'

Matt paused again for a moment before continuing, 'Add to all that, if your husband *was* killed deliberately or accidently by someone in passing rather than someone he knew, then there will be an even smaller chance of any success, because any thin pieces of evidence that connected the two will most likely be long gone.'

Matt counted to six slowly in his head to give Bella time to process what he had just said.

'Before you spend any of your money, and potentially get your hopes up, I need you to be aware of all of that. I wouldn't be doing my job properly if I didn't clarify this with you.'

It was Bella's turn to pause for a moment. She wanted to be equally clear in her response. She needed Matt and his team to be one hundred percent committed to this project with no concerns. How best to phrase this, she thought.

'*Matt,*' Bella sat forward in her chair and established clear and focused eye contact with him, 'I do appreciate all that you have just said and *why* you feel the need to explain it. I really do; *but...* I need to be *one hundred percent sure* I have tried every single avenue open to me in order to find out what happened to my husband. I won't be able to get on with my life if I have any doubts.

That's why I am willing to try this despite the low chance of finding anything new. Not only is this about genuinely finding out what happened to him, but it's also a form of closure for me, even in the event we find nothing.'

Bella lent forward, grabbed her glass and took a drink of water. She still felt she needed to show calm composure to gain their full trust. The more she could show a strong element of calm, the more they would trust her.

'I do get this is not *even* a cold case, it's a *closed* case. That said however; I think despite everything, there is a small chance there might be something that everyone has overlooked, and I need to be sure. Until the odds counter is down to zero percent I want to continue. I accept it is probably only at one percent now, but that leaves me with a chance, and that last little chance is what I want to explore.'

Matt also waited for a moment. He stood up and began to smile. As he rose to his full height he stretched out his hand in Bella's direction.

'In that case Mrs Stone, we look forward to working for you.'

Now it was Bella's turn to smile. She positively beamed.

'*Thank you.* I just can't believe there isn't a *single thread* hanging out there for us to find; and that when we pull on it, the curtain that I personally think is shielding the truth should start to unravel.'

Matt smiled back. He didn't need to say anything. He just hoped there wasn't too much more disappointment lying in Bella's future. It was clear she had had quite enough of that.

'So, Max, are you happy to give Bella the relevant paperwork to sign, and then show her out?' And everyone, we all leave from outside here tomorrow morning at 0900 hours. That gives us a chance to miss the worst of the rush hour traffic, especially as we will be heading out of London. I'll arrange parking for both cars in front of the building for tomorrow morning.'

Various forms of yes were given from everyone. They all began to get up. Max was the first out of the room and walked towards his desk with Bella.

Max and Bella reached his desk as everyone else spilled out of the conference room to their various desks. A day's worth of admin would need to be done so that they were free to concentrate on laying Bella's mind to rest for once and for all.

Tomorrow, the Cotswolds.

CHAPTER 3

The entire team was in the office by seven-thirty. Matt buzzed Max's phone extension.

'Good morning boss.'

'Morning.'

'Was Bella OK yesterday when she left? Sorry I didn't get a chance to ask you with all the paperwork I had to catch up on.'

'Yes thanks, she's very grateful that we're going to take a look.'

Matt swung a little on his chair. 'I had a feeling she was going to try and meet us up there; she *isn't* is she?'

'No, she wanted to come, but I explained we were better going alone and working from her notes. I think it took a lot of effort on her part not to push to come, but she's going to wait at home until we get in touch.'

Matt began leaning in towards the phone, 'Great, I have a couple of things to do, then I am good to go.'

'Same.'

'Oh and by the way, I have put all our diving gear in the cars and some radar equipment I borrowed from the lab; just in case we want to get into the water at the quarry.'

'Good plan.'

As soon as he had replaced his handset Max shook his head, picked up the handset, dialled and Matt's phone rang.

'Sorry, I meant to ask; did you have a whole load of fliers done for the business?'

'No I didn't. We are just going on word of mouth like we agreed. *Why*?'

'Bella said that's how she knew I was doing this and how to find me.' Max could see Matt frown a little.

'That's odd. Oh *wait – no* I did get a firm to draw up some flyers for approval to discuss with you guys; they said they had printed them up and sent them out by accident. I think Norton handled all that. I've forgotten exactly what happened, but they never charged us, so I just let the matter go. It was probably one of those.'

'Cool, thought it would be something like that. Cheers.'

For the next couple of hours the team focused on getting various admin tasks out of the way. At 8:50 a.m. both cars were in the courtyard waiting for the team, fuelled and ready to go. Everyone grabbed their go bags and headed towards the elevators. A few moments later, all six members of the Scott and Munro team were assembled in the courtyard, standing around the vehicles. Both the dark grey Audi A6 Avant and the black Range Rover Vogue had their tailgates open; go bags and some other equipment were being packed securely.

Joe threw a small black rucksack towards Max shouting, '*Heads up.*'

Max swung round, stuck out a hand and caught it.

'Is this one going in Bess or Dougal?'

'Whichever mate, it is only spare towels.'

'Bess or Dougal. *Who* are they? I thought there were only six of you?'

Max pivoted around to face the direction that the voice was coming from. Everyone else stopped what they were doing and looked.

Max's voice broke the silence, '*Err*, morning *Bella.*'

Bella walked towards him, carrying a white cardboard box about the size of two shoe boxes.

'I... I *wasn't sure* what to bring you guys as a good luck charm, so I brought you these. It's a box of assorted Krispy Kreme doughnuts.'

She handed the box to Max, who thanked her, and placed them on the back seat of the car nearest to him.

'And here are the papers you asked me to sign for my officially engaging you etc.'

Max took the papers, zipped them up in a leather folder, and put it back in the car.

'Thanks.'

Everyone else carried on with what they were doing while Max stopped to talk to Bella. She repeated her question sheepishly, as though she was not sure if she should be asking; but the drive to be involved in any way possible was too strong to resist.

'So *who* are Bess and Dougal then?'

Anyone else and Max would probably have swerved the question but not Bella; it might make her feel involved which would be a good thing, 'They're over there.'

Bella looked in the direction that Max was pointing, but all she could see were the cars and some other people passing by. No one was standing out per say. Bella gave a quizzical look.

Max pointed to the Range Rover that was sitting to their left, '*This* is Bess,' he then pointed to the Audi on their right saying, 'And *this* is Dougal.'

Bella beamed. Max had been right, that had brought a much needed smile to her face.

'You *are* kidding *right*? You *name* your cars?'

'No... I'm not kidding, I'm serious. You never know who's listening in to any communications when you are out on an operation. You don't want to say anything that identifies a vehicle that you intend to use in your escape. That's why the cars have nondescript code names.

'Ah I see; that makes a lot of sense.' Bella then gave both cars a once over.

'So I suppose these two aren't standard?' Bella looked at the number plates.

'That Range Rover is a P38 model, a 2001 Vogue and that Audi is a 2007 model; that's a fair age for vehicles in this line of work surely?

Max gave Bella a knowing smile, ' In answer to your first question, nothing major. Just maybe not quite as they left the factory.'

'But why so old? The *cars* I mean; *surely* newer would be better?'

'Both of those cars are pretty much as capable as the more modern versions, but being older they blend in easier to all surroundings. Their age stops people giving them a second look, which in turn gives us the added advantage of blending in. If we had brand new ones, they would stick out like a sore thumb in certain environments; it's a deliberate strategy to have the older ones.'

Bella gave a thoughtful nod.

Max noticed both cars were now loaded up and ready to go.

'Bella thanks for the doughnuts that is very thoughtful. We should probably get on our way.' He began to turn towards the cars.

'We will be in touch once we have checked things out.'

Bella chased up behind him and gave him a hug.

'*Be safe,*' she whispered.

'*We will.*'

Bella stood back as both cars drove around the fountain, across the courtyard, then under the archway and headed out into Fleet Street. In a moment they were gone, merging into the traffic.

Suddenly she felt alone. Bella followed the car's direction, under the archway and out into the London throng as the large gold and black vehicle access gates closed behind her. Their sheer size meant they had a gong like sound as they locked against their fastenings.

'For whom the bell tolls.' Bella could not help thinking there was something symbolic there. This was probably her last chance to find out what really happened to her husband. Suddenly she had a dreadful sense of foreboding.

CHAPTER 4

The two cars headed along the M4 motorway away from London and towards the Cotswolds; an area encompassing parts of several counties including Wiltshire, Gloucestershire and Oxfordshire.

The Range Rover with Matt at the wheel and Joe and Max aboard was in front. Following closely behind was the Audi, with Ava at the wheel and Bruno and Norton for passengers. A proprietary system from Refract Speech had been fitted to each car, that included an AI computer system designed to offer help where it could; and an advanced and encrypted communications system that allowed the occupants in both cars to talk and hear each other as clearly as if they were all in the same vehicle without the signal breaking up.

As they headed towards the junction with Chieveley Motorway services, it was agreed they would pull off and grab some coffee to go with the doughnuts. Whilst Ava and Matt went in with the drinks order, the others milled around the cars making small talk.

After a few moments, talk turned to the case; Norton looked at the ground and kicked the tarmac with his toe.

'Would we really take this case on if Bella weren't a friend of Max's?'

No one really wanted to have this conversation for the sake of Max's feelings, so it took a while for an answer to come.

Joe spoke up first, 'No, in truth probably *not*, but when we find nothing odd, we can be the ones to break it to Bella as gently as possible and help her find closure. It seems to me like my brother, and now all of us are doing the decent thing here. This particular case is more about helping a friend out than anything else. We can afford to make an exception to our criteria for selecting cases as far as Bella is concerned.'

Norton was quick with his reply.

'I *actually* think the opposite; I *think* we *are* going to find something, and I *think* there's going to be a nasty surprise waiting; that's why I am asking.'

Max spoke next, looking straight at Norton, 'What do you mean *something*? What do you think we're going to find.'

'I don't know Max, but something's off with her story. That rushed bit at the end of the meeting, the bit about him not being able to swim. That's what caught my attention. Why blurt all that out. It just doesn't fit with the rest of the story. She told it in a different way. I can't put my finger on it exactly, but something's off.'

Without looking at anyone in particular Max

spoke again.

'Does anyone else agree with him?'

Bruno was next to talk.

'I have to say I got the same feeling when she came back into the room at the end of the meeting. I just didn't buy that part of her story, and I'm a bit confused over the tattoo business, but I *did* buy the rest of it. I think she's a very sad woman, desperate to find reason in something totally unreasonable. I don't mean I think there's something sinister going on; I just think she will say *anything* to get us to look into this. I think she was simply having a last throw of the dice and possibly she was just trying to entice us with a small white lie. I don't hold that against her; she's desperate, *and desperate* people do *desperate* things. You, and by extension now us, are doing the right thing by her Max.'

Bruno turned to look directly at Norton, 'We have taken the case Norton. *Get over it.*'

Max lowered his head and seemed to be thinking deeply.

Norton broke the silence.

'Yeah but all I was doing was gauging how you guys felt; I'm not for a second saying this isn't worth checking out or anything. I was just saying I think, *well...* I'm not sure what I think. Forget I said anything.' Norton noticed Ava and Matt coming back with the drinks. He lent in through the open window of the car, grabbed the box of doughnuts and began walking towards the grass area. The others followed. Norton felt that perhaps he should not have said anything.

He decided to brighten things up and backtrack to support his team.

'Look I shouldn't have said anything; we have taken this case, and I for one am delighted to dig out the truth - whatever, like we always would; and treat this just like any other case and investigate thoroughly.'

Norton put his free arm around Max's shoulders and gave him a one-armed bear hug, then let go. His effort paid off, the awkwardness evaporated, and the usual break-time chat ensued for the next twenty minutes.

Soon they were back on the M4 heading west towards their destination; a disused and flooded quarry. That quarry was one of two things. It was either, as the majority of those familiar with the case believed; the setting for a deeply tragic accident that took the life of a newly married man; or it was the site of a deliberate and wilful drowning that had a solitary advocate.

Less than an hour's drive further on, and the two cars pulled up at the gates to the quarry. It was time to try and find out what had happened here for once and for all.

CHAPTER 5

Everyone got out of the cars. Ava walked over to meet a very cheery looking man who clearly worked outdoors. He had a beard and was wearing a baseball cap. Ava guessed he was in his late fifties. The man was removing a large metal chain and padlock that had been holding the gates shut. As she got closer, he began to swing one of the tall green metal gates open.

'Mr Collins...? Mr *Ralph* Collins?'

'Morning, yes that's me, you must be Ava?'

'That's correct, Ava Scott from Scott and Munro. Thank you for opening up for us.'

Mr Collins made some small talk with Ava for a few moments, about how the gates used to be left open, but with increasing volume of traffic from opportunist visitors; the boss had decided they should now stay permanently closed. There was a pause before Mr Collins scratched his arm and continued chatting.

'Of course there was the coincidence that we actually had *two* problems happen on the same day that the body was discovered.'

Ava looked at him in such a way that Mr Collins was in no doubt that he had her full attention and should continue.

'Well it was just that when I came to open the gates that morning, the lock was jammed shut on the padlock, and I couldn't get the key in. *Nothing* could get the little hatch open in order to insert the key. In the end I just cut the padlock off and fitted a spare new one. I was *sure someone had glued the key latch shut*, but *why* would anyone do that? I gave up thinking about it and, as I said, I fitted the spare.'

Mr Collins could tell Ava was giving what he had said some serious thought. He was enjoying the attention considering he spent most of his working days alone.

By now everyone had come over to join Ava.

'These are my colleagues Mr Collins.'

Various versions of 'good morning' were given back and forth.

Mr Collins looked at his watch, 'Right, do you want to drive up to the quarry or walk. No one else is due, so you can leave your vehicles here by the gates if that suits.'

Ava spoke up, 'There was no vehicle found in relation to the body being discovered was there?'

Mr Collins shook his head, 'No.'

'Then I think if it's OK with you, we will walk in on foot and assume that's what the victim must have done too. Do most people come in through this way if they're on foot, or is there another route in?'

'We leave the chain locked but slack on these gates, so that those determined to get in on foot, come this way and therefore don't damage the high-security fence that surrounds the site. So to answer your question directly, this is the only way in without cutting the fence.'

'And the fence had not been cut around the time of the discovery of the body?'

'No.'

Everyone had their electronic tablets out and had begun orientating themselves with the site. They were looking at the map Bella had drawn up from what the police had told her.

Joe spoke next, 'Did you find the body then?'

Mr Collins swung round to make eye contact with this new voice.

'*No* young man, I am glad to be able to say *I did not*. It was the environmental guys that I had let in that morning that found the body. I had let them in at the gate, but didn't come up with them. They come here every four weeks to poke about and measure things like water quality. I just left them to it as normal.

'I was only just back at the office on the out-skirts of Cirencester when my phone rang and one of them sounded deeply distressed, gabbling away about a body. I could tell they were terri-fied so I just headed straight back here. I assumed I had misheard when they said body, I thought they meant body of water. I wasn't really listen-ing; I was looking forward to my cup of tea. As I say, it was the tone of terror I could hear in his voice; you just know something is *very* wrong.

'Well, as I say, I came straight back expecting to find one of them floating in the water, or their rubber boat having sunk; but their boat was back on shore, and they were both dry, yet seriously agitated. They told me that they had found a bloated and severely damaged looking body, that they were quite sure was that of a man. They had already called the police by the time I got back here. The police were not a long time behind me.'

Joe spoke again, 'Sorry to be morbid, but did they give you any description in relation to the corpse or say anything that you thought odd or out of place?'

Mr Collins took a good few moments to think, 'Oh, you mean like *missing tattoos*?'

Everyone stopped what they were doing that instant, and looked at each other briefly, before attempting to disguise their surprise, so as not to tip off Mr Collins that tattoos were exactly what Joe was referring to. It had been an instinctive long shot and Joe had certainly not expected such an instant and positive response.

'*Yeah*, or *anything else* that struck you as odd.' Joe decided to play it very cool.

'No, nothing, they were so shocked at finding a body in the first place. All I asked was if they were OK and if they were sure the man was definitely dead. They said that although for both of them it was their first dead human, the state of the body left them in no doubt he was long dead. I caught a glimpse of the body when they brought him ashore, *God rest his soul*, I saw what they meant. I have never seen anything so... *so grotesque* I think is probably the word.' Mr Collins shuddered.

Joe spoke again as he wanted to be crystal clear on this specific point.

'Did you see *either* of his arms at all?'

'I saw his arms, *yes*, but he was wearing a dark coloured top with the sleeves rolled down. No skin or tattoo was visible to me or anyone else unless they tried to roll up a soaking wet sleeve.'

Joe gave Mr Collins a moment before continuing.

'What made you mention missing tattoos just now?'

Mr Collins gave a knowing smile. He seemed to be enjoying his involvement with the investigation.

'Well, that's what you meant *isn't it*. That's what *she* kept going on about.'

Joe and Max both spoke at the same moment; their voices sounded equally unnerved.

'*She*?'

Mr Collins smiled again.

'Yes, the woman with the red hair. She's his *widow isn't she*?'

Now it was Norton's turn to speak.

'His widow has been *here*, asking about missing tattoos?'

Something in Norton's voice resulted in Mr Collins smiling a little less.

'Yes. She has been up here a lot since the body was found, and then later she tracked me down and was asking all sorts of questions like, "Was I sure I had not seen his arms?" I'm afraid I lied to her and said I hadn't seen anything of the corpse at all.'

Bruno looked up from his tablet.

'Why did you lie to her?'

'I lied to her because as I have just explained, the state of the body was horrendous. She didn't need to hear about that from me. If she was to see her husband's body in a Chapel of Rest or some such place, then fine, but it certainly wasn't my place to tell her how horrendous her husband looked; especially as I only witnessed the bloated corpse just as it was being removed from the water.'

Bruno was still looking directly at Mr Collins.

'Yes, I would have done the same thing.'

Joe leant towards his brother Max and spoke in a hushed voice.

'I thought Bella said she had never been up here?'

Max closed his eyes and drew in a breath, then breathed out long and slow.

Matt was the next to speak to Mr Collins, 'Could you take us up to the quarry now?'

Mr Collins nodded and began to walk on with them all following.

Joe looked down at the hard-core road they were walking on.

'I don't suppose you remember what the weather was like on that day, or had been like in the week or two leading up to the discovery of the body?'

Mr Collins slowed his pace a little as they wound around a slight bend in the road. There were tall grasses and elder trees, whose sweet scent filled the air. These were interspersed with some stunning buddleja plants; their purple flowers nodding in the warm summer breeze.

'I *do* as it happens. It had been massively dry for several weeks. This track was the same then as it is now.'

'So, it wouldn't be possible to tell if any illicit traffic had been up and down this road?'

Mr Collins came to a complete stop.

'*Not a chance* of being able to tell for sure. I remember the police asking me that at the time. The padlock on the gates was locked when I let the environment guys in, so there couldn't have been any traffic in before us. The key latch on the padlock was jammed; and as mentioned to Ms Scott, I had to cut it off, but the gates were closed and locked.'

'Thanks.'

Joe made some more notes on his tablet.

Mr Collins moved off again and everyone began to follow. A few moments later they came to a halt on the water's edge. In front of them lay a body of water that seemed to take a shape more fitting to a natural lake than a flooded quarry. It was beautiful. From their stand point the team could see pretty much the whole quarry site. Some of the banking was grass, there were three separate reed beds complete with tall rushes, and at one point a stunning weeping willow hung over the water's edge. Then there was the cliff-face. It seemed to be trying to cast a shadow over as much of this beautiful place as it could.

Bruno was the first to speak. 'What a stunning place.'

Mr Collins nodded.

'Isn't it, especially the willow. That was there when this was just a field and luckily it stayed.'

Ava pointed to the reed bed closest to them.

'Is this the reed bed that they found the body in?'

Mr Collins was taking in the lake as if it was the first time he had seen it. He did not take his eyes off it as he answered.

'That's correct, the one closest to the cliff-face.'

Ava scrolled through something on her tablet, 'And the boat the guys used, that was theirs and they brought it with them?'

'That's correct.'

Matt was looking at the cliff-face. 'That's an odd feature; it doesn't seem to fit with the land-scape.'

Mr Collins nodded, 'No, it doesn't. It's where the rock changed type, so they stopped quarry-ing and just left it there when they landscaped the quarry at the end of its working life.'

'And that is where they think Peter Stone fell from – those cliffs, what are they twenty or thirty feet from top to bottom.'

'Apparently. They think he fell, died and then rolled into the water.'

Now everyone was looking around. There was no way there was going to be anything left for them to examine that the police and authorities had not already looked into. More than a year had passed, so they did not expect to find anything but until they saw for themselves, they couldn't have been sure. Everyone had made the same assessment and had decided it was time to walk back. It was Norton who was the first to stop in his tracks.

'*Hang on,* I've just been looking through the copy of the autopsy report from Dr Brett that Bella sent us. It mentions finding concrete of some description in the head wound that was deemed to be the cause of death; but I can't see any concrete structure here. If that's the case, then why did the police accept this as the location of the death? That doesn't track; they wouldn't have done that if the concrete couldn't be explained, and that looks like dirt, not concrete at the foot of the cliff.'

'I can actually answer this for you.'

They all turned to look at Mr Collins once more. He waited until he was sure everyone was paying attention. He rarely got to be part of something like this, and was going to make it last as long as possible. These guys would soon be gone and he would be back to working on his own.

'What I doubt you have in any of your paperwork is that there has been a break in here; one that happened a good few days after the body had been found. We couldn't believe it; the theft happened about a day or so after the police had packed up and left.'

Bruno followed quickly on the end of Mr Collins's sentence.

'OK. You think this is relevant?'

'*Yes*, I think it is, *because* of what we had stolen during that break in.'

Matt was also quickening his replies. He had a bad feeling about where this was going, and he wanted to get to the punch line as quickly as possible.

'*Please* Mr Collins, *tell us*; what was stolen?'

Mr Collins was milking his attention for every last drop.

'You'll *never* believe it; you just *won't*.' He then noticed a sudden lack of smiles across the faces of his captive audience. Something told him he should probably get to the point.

'Our concrete staircase by the water.'

'*What*?'

The confusion on Bruno's face spoke for the whole team.

Mr Collins was beginning to get the feeling that he was going to push his solo performance too far. He decided a concise summary may keep his audience grateful. Pointing towards the closest reed bed he spoke, 'Over there beside that reed bed below the cliffs, there was a set of concrete steps that went down into the water. The owner of this quarry uses it on occasion with his family and has a boat. He had the steps put in so that they could get in and out of the water that way, rather than scrambling up the banks in the mud. Well they've been *stolen*. *Stupid* I know but there we are, *they've been stolen*.'

'Can you give us a brief description of how the steps were constructed Mr Collins?' asked Ava.

'Sure, it was a concrete set of steps that sank half in and half out of the water. The top three steps were out of the water, and the bottom three steps were in the water. The top step was much longer than the others, so it produced a sort of concrete platform heading back from the water towards the cliff. It just meant you could walk from the grass embankment onto the top step and down into the water, avoiding the muddy section of the bank.'

Ava made some notes, 'And how were the steps fixed in place?'

'They had four metal feet under the steps that were all under the water level and sunk into the bank.'

'Thanks Mr Collins.'

Matt's voice was becoming more earnest.

'Did you report this to the police?'

'Yes I did as it happens, it took me a while to

get them to take it seriously, but they did come and have a look. They couldn't find any evidence of how the steps were removed from the site and again, the padlock on the gates had not been cut off. The younger copper said he reckoned they were lifted by helicopter. It was at that point I realised they weren't taking it seriously. I told the boss and he said just to leave it.'

'Hmm yeah I can see that. Sorry Mr Collins do you mind if we have a moment?'

'No of course not, I'll just wait over here.' Mr Collins took a few steps away.

'Thanks.'

Matt beckoned everyone around and spoke in a hushed tone.

'Is anyone else here thinking what I am thinking?'

Joe nodded first, 'You're thinking the steps went *down*, not up.'

'That's *exactly* what I'm thinking. Here's the plan. Ava can you and one other bring the cars up here. Then decide which two people are going into the water. Get hold of the underwater portable radar from the car; let's see if we can locate these missing steps. I'll go and see if Mr Collins can get his boss on the phone and secure us permission to enter the water.'

'Then can someone get on the phone to the pathologist and confirm there was a match found between the concrete on the steps and the concrete in Peter Stone's wounds. Also; ask him if we can email him a close-up photo of the concrete on the steps, would he or one of his team have a quick look and see if there is any obvious discrepancy between our sample from today and theirs from the time of the investigation.'

Matt left the team to their discussions and walked towards Mr Collins.

'Mr Collins, is there any chance you can get your boss on the phone for me right now?'

Within two hours, permission had been secured to enter the water, the equipment had been brought from the cars, and Bruno and Norton were in their diving gear. They were ready to enter the flooded quarry and begin searching for the missing steps. Contact had been successful with Dr Brett the pathologist. He confirmed that they had matched a sample from the concrete steps to the concrete in Pete's fatal head wound. He also explained that he remembered something about one of the concrete samples apparently going missing, but it had just been misplaced. He had also confirmed that they could have a preliminary look via photo under magnification, and if there was enough of a difference in the concrete, he would be able to tell today.

Everyone waited for Bruno and Norton to complete the sweep of the section of the quarry floor that they had mapped out. Matt's hunch was the steps wouldn't be far away given their size as described by Mr Collins, and hopefully not in the much deeper water.

Soon Bruno and Norton were out of the water and sitting on the bank. They were uploading the printout from the portable radar unit that they had on loan from the labs at Refract Speech. The steps had not been very far down, so they had also managed some photos and had found what Matt expected. The steps had been deliberately destroyed. It turned out that they had been built very cheaply, which was not surprising as they were only there for occasional family use. Someone had cut through all four of the legs, with what had to be some form of underwater heavy-duty kit given all four metal legs were always under water.

There was enough mobile phone signal to send the pictures to Dr Brett and await his reply. It was now past three p.m. and they had done all they could here. They decided to pack up, thank Mr Collins, head to their hotel and check in.

They dropped Mr Collins off by the gates at the edge of the main road. Ava grabbed a bottle of malt whisky from the boot of the car and handed it to Mr Collins. He was genuinely delighted.

'Glenmorangie, that's my favourite drink, but I don't have it too often. *Thank you.*'

Ava smiled back, 'No Mr Collins, *thank you*, your help has been invaluable today. If you ever think of anything else, or want to ask anything, you have my number.'

They made their goodbyes and with everyone on-board, the cars began to roll towards the main road. As they did so Mr Collins came back towards them. He seemed to have something he wanted to say before they parted ways.

'Please solve this for his widow; the dead man's I mean. I have hated seeing her so upset and consumed with grief. She seems like a lovely person, this is all such a shame. Closure would really help her I think. Good luck.'

Mr Collins tapped his hands twice on the open window ledge of the front passenger door and turned to walk away. As he did so, Norton lowered the rear passenger window and partially lent his head out.

'She hasn't been here in ages though?'

Mr Collins stopped his departure and turned. He looked sad for the first time that day.

'She was here yesterday afternoon I'm afraid. She didn't see me, but I saw her. I just left her to her grief.'

Norton was still leaning out of the window.

'*You're sure*? You're sure it was *her*... Bella Stone?'

There was a slow nod from Mr Collins.

'I am. It was the red hair that I recognised; and I know of no one else who wears different coloured trainers – it was *her* alright.'

Mr Collins began to turn away from them and as he did so he began to slowly raise his right arm as a goodbye salute, the left hand still holding the whisky. The cars rolled out of the entrance, the crunch of gravel giving way to the softer sound of rubber turning steadily on tarmac. A palpable hush filled both vehicles for the short journey to their hotel. The same thoughts were in all six of the team's minds.

Should they have gone anywhere near this case? It was the first day on the case and already they had discovered their client was lying to them.

CHAPTER 6

The hotel sat on the edge of a beautiful lake. All the buildings were wooden in construction and had an American lodge hotel feel to them. It was very comfortable and everyone was welcoming. By chance there was a small wing at one end that had seven bedrooms along one corridor with a locking outer door to the rest of the hotel. Ava had been able to secure all the rooms, and exclusive use of the corridor. The code had been changed and they each had a key. They would not be troubled by other guests. The seventh room, a large suite with balcony was made into the Operations Room.

Everyone had been quiet. They had all unpacked, showered and were just meeting up in the newly renamed Operations Room. Matt was getting everyone a drink. Although the mood inside was sombre, the late afternoon outside was warm and pleasant. The wide balcony doors were fully open, and a warm summer breeze was blowing in across the room, gently lifting the curtains.

Matt suggested they had an hour or so to discuss their thoughts and where they wanted to go next with this investigation; then they could go down and enjoy a pleasant evening meal in the restaurant, and put today's events to one side; for a couple of hours at least. His main concern was Max. Max was strong, both emotionally and physically like the rest of them, but this had to be having an extra strain for him.

Matt sat down with the others. He decided he would lead the discussions. Normally they would discuss the most important aspects first; which in this case would be the fact they had discovered Bella had lied. Matt did not want Max feeling pressured though, so he made the excuse that he wanted to try a different approach. He wanted to address the relevant topics of interest in a random order, starting with the padlock situation.

After much deliberation, the team decided that on balance the padlock situation was most likely a wilful act of vandalism, totally unrelated to Pete's death. But, if it was connected, then the only reason for tampering with the padlock that the team could come up with was that someone wanted to disguise the fact they had been up to the quarry with a vehicle; perhaps to dump a body – perhaps. The distance between the gates and the steps was too far even for two people to carry a life-less corpse.

If Pete's body was driven to the quarry, and the scene of death there was staged, then it looked like Bella might be onto something. At the very least it pointed to Pete dying somewhere else first before being moved here, which begged the question why; and suggested something suspicious. They decided they wouldn't try and answer that aspect of things for now. It was far too early in the investigation; and a possibly tampered with padlock on its own was not enough to warrant too much time looking in that direction.

They did discuss the fact that it was a well-known trick amongst the type of person that breaks and enters, to case a targeted place first; especially if the stakes were high. If it is discovered that the place they want to gain access to is secured with a padlock, a new identical padlock is purchased first. The culprits break-in and when finished, on the way out they fit the new identical padlock. They then glue the hatch shut, or pour glue into the lock. A Police Constable had explained to the team on an earlier case that this was done to buy the culprits some time. If security patrolled the site and looked at the door or gate, they would see the padlock in place and locked. Unless they had reason to try and open it, and hence discover a problem; they would have no reason to assume there had been a break-in. PC Smythe had explained that the more time between the break-in and the discovery of the break-in, the less chance of getting caught. Indeed that was apparently the same for most crimes.

PC Smythe had explained that many owners or security patrols would just assume the padlock was the original one, and when they could not open the hatch or get the key in, they would simply assume it had seized or jammed shut. The glue ensured they could never discover their key would not fit, so they would not learn it was a different padlock. This meant there was an increased chance no alarm was raised until much later; sometimes never. The problem was just put down to a duff padlock mechanism.

Finally, it was decided that as far as the padlock situation was concerned, two of them would head back to the quarry gates tomorrow, and just walk about with a metal detector for a while on the off chance the old padlock was lying around. It was a long shot, so they would not invest too much time on it, but the exercise was worth an exploration. Whilst they were there, they would ask if Mr Collins knew of a second issue with any padlocks around the time the steps were sunk.

They all took a fifteen minute break before discussing the next topic. During that break they had an email from Dr Brett, confirming that the original sample of concrete from Pete's head, and the original concrete sample from the steps were a match; and that his brief examination of the magnified photo the team had sent him today, showed their concrete from the steps was also a match. It was all the same concrete. He reconfirmed that at the time of the investigation, they thought someone had stolen one of the samples, but it was found to simply be misplaced. He finished his email by saying he would call tomorrow or the next day when he had a moment.

Next to be discussed was the curious case of the sinking of the concrete steps. Again, it was agreed this could be a wilful act of vandalism; but the effort and the specialist kit needed meant that in the case of the steps, that was much less likely. Again, they explored how this act might relate to Pete's death.

In light of such little evidence to go on, the team had to hypothesise as best they could. It would be guesswork, but as this was the first day on the case that was fine; also, it was all they had to go on. At this stage it was more about getting a feel for things and what might possibly be going on, rather than cold hard facts. For arguments sake, assuming there was foul play and not just two coincidental acts of vandalism, and one accidental death in the same place; the only series of events that the team could accept with any plausibility were the following.

Pete died or was killed elsewhere. Then for some reason, his body was dumped in the quarry and the place was staged to appear as if this was where Pete accidently died. Furthermore, that whoever did this knew about the comings and goings at the quarry, and the brand of padlock used on the gates etc. They then managed to orchestrate the swapping of the concrete samples to ensure it appeared as if Pete's fatal head wound occurred on the steps. Then in order to keep things tidy, whoever had staged the death, sank the steps once the police had left.

The timing of the sinking of the steps proved to be the stumbling block to the team's solution. Why wait to sink the steps later? By then the crime scene investigators had been everywhere and taken all the samples they needed. So why sink them at all? There was no obvious benefit.

It was Bruno who solved the issue. He pointed out that in their enthusiasm; they were trying to create the perfect, tidy crime. He reminded them all of what they already knew, but were forgetting. Crimes were rarely perfect. There were always issues and problems to deal with just like any other aspect of life. Given that angle, they thought about it again.

Max was the one to settle on the most plausible plan they could come up with for now. Namely that whoever was behind this needed the police to find the steps, and yet not find the steps. On the one hand, they needed the police to identify the steps as the site of where Pete fell and died; but on the other they needed them not to spot any fresh wound in the concrete that showed where the culprits had taken a chunk out of the steps to use in his sample swap. It would be fresh and stand out. It wasn't perfect, but then as Bruno had just pointed out, murder rarely was. Whoever was behind this had to take a chance, and that was the chance they took; but as soon as the samples were taken and the police left, the steps were sunk to hide the fresh damage, and increase their chances of getting away with murder.

Not only would the steps be hidden underwater, but the fresh concrete exposed in the sample area would tarnish and blend in with the rest much quicker when under water. Should some bright investigator come back to check a theory like that out, the steps would be gone, and whoever was behind this would be safe.

There was nowhere else to go with the steps for now; though they all agreed that if there was anything validating Bella being correct, it was the sinking of the steps. That was just too odd and required too much effort. Something that odd needed more consideration.

The first day on the case was over, and on balance, most of them thought the official verdict would still prove to be correct; but they were developing an alternative. Pete's death may well have been accidental, but there was a chance it had occurred somewhere else and his body had been moved. If that was the case, there had been a sleight of hand played that pointed to a more suspicious death. The various official reports that Bella had got hold of for the team showed there was no foam around Pete's mouth and no water in his lungs, so he had not drowned. That meant he had been dead when he hit the water. The relevant reports had also shown that the blood spatter on the steps and damage to Pete's head was consistent with a fall. The height from the top of the cliff to the concrete steps was consistent with Pete's injuries. It did all tie up. That was the main thing keeping their thoughts in line with the official findings for now. It was time to give their brains a rest.

Matt got up and began pacing whilst he talked.

'Well I think that's a good place to stop for now let's go and eat; our table will be ready.'

They all headed down for what turned out to be a pleasant evening meal and a few drinks, which led to a good decompress over the rest of the evening. It passed quickly, and the next morning everyone was refreshed and ready for the meeting scheduled with Detective Chief Inspector Edward Stimpson, the Senior Investigating Officer for the case of Peter Stone's death.

Max couldn't quiet the words playing over and over in his mind since last night.

Bella is a liar

You are being played

Max shut the words out of his mind as best he could.

CHAPTER 7

Bruno walked in to their Operations Room, 'Morning.'

Various versions of good morning came back from everyone.

'What time and where are we meeting the SIO; Stimpson did you say his name was Matt?'

'Morning, yes, his surname is Stimpson. We are due to meet him at nine-thirty at the Safe Harbour pub. It's just at the other end of the hotel grounds, so no distance at all.'

Bruno nodded and grabbed himself a coffee.

'What's Stimpson's reputation like; any intel on that?'

'I called a mate who has worked with him in the past. Stimpson has a good reputation as a thorough copper, and a decent and incorruptible man. I don't think we have anything to worry about as far as he's concerned. That said though, like any policeman, he isn't going to welcome us snooping about in case we find something he and his team have missed.'

Matt turned towards where the twins were sitting.

'Max, Joe, would you guys be happy to grab the metal detector and take one of the cars and go back to the quarry? I want you to scan around the gate area and see if you can find anything of the old padlock. It's a long shot, but if you did find anything, then at least we can confirm we are on the right track as far as that is concerned. Ava should be getting you permission now; she's on the phone to Mr Collins.'

Max stood up and walked towards Matt.

'Actually Boss, I would quite like to meet the SIO and weigh him up myself if you don't mind.'

'Of course, *sorry* I should have thought of that. Norton, are you happy to go with Joe?'

'Sure thing.'

Matt made some notes on his tablet.

'OK then, I think everyone is sorted.'

At that moment Ava walked in from the balcony, having just got off the phone with Mr Collins.

'He will meet whoever is going over to the quarry at nine-thirty and let you in.'

'Right then,' Matt called everyone to attention, 'OK so Joe and Norton, you are heading to the quarry gates; I would not give it more than an hour. Everyone else with me to the pub to meet the SIO; the hotel has said they will bring a pot of coffee and tea over. We can sit out on the veranda. The pub is not open until after eleven. Then we can all meet back here.'

The team milled about, chatting and drinking coffee and tea until it was time for the respective groups to head off.

By the time Joe and Norton pulled up to the

gates at the quarry, there was a white pickup parked across them, signalling Mr Collins was already here and waiting. As they got out of their vehicles, Mr Collins gave a 'Hello' that was as welcoming as it was when they first met. Mr Collins lent against his pickup and took out his phone.

Joe replied, 'Morning Mr Collins.'

Mr Collins gave a second welcome, 'Morning lads.'

'Thanks for this, we won't be long. Can I just ask you something first?'

'Sure you can.'

'Great. When the police arrived and took over the quarry, did they use your padlock to lock the gates at night?'

'No, they used their own padlocks I guess. Then when the quarry was returned to us a couple of days later, I came down and the gates had been closed, but they weren't locked.'

'Ah OK, so anyone could have got in here then?'

'Yes, pretty much. Now we know the steps were sunk, I guess that's how whoever did that got up to them with all the equipment they would have needed.'

'Yeah, I think so. Right, thanks, we had better wave this metal detector around and see what we find.'

Their plan was indeed a good one, because it took them less than twenty minutes to get an alert from the detector. They found the padlock. Although it was rusted where its metal casing had been in long term contact with the damp soil, it was still very clearly a heavy-duty padlock that had been cut. Norton having been careful to photograph it where it lay then picked it up with an evidence bag. Out of another pocket in his jacket, Norton took a moisture absorbing bag, broke its air-tight seal, and dropped the bag in with the padlock, sealing the evidence bag shut.

When they got back to the cars, they showed the evidence bag to Mr Collins.

'I'm really sorry, yes that is indeed one of our padlocks. I now feel rather stupid for not looking for it on the day.'

Joe gave Mr Collins a friendly smile.

'You've nothing to be sorry about; you had a fair amount going on that day to deal with. I am guessing the padlocks don't look that different, if you can remember the original one?'

Mr Collins held the evidence bag.

'No, as you can see, that is the type we use; that's what is on there now.' He pointed to the open gate, its large chain and heavy padlock.

'It's the brand our local DIY store sells, so I guess it is not surprising that they used the same make.'

Joe and Norton agreed it was not.

'Thanks again Mr Collins, Joe and I will be off and let you get back to work.' The three exchanged pleasantries, and having got Mr Collin's permission to keep the padlock, Joe and Norton headed back to the hotel to join the others.

When they parked up, they noticed the rest of the team still waiting on the veranda; Stimpson the SIO was a no-show. Matt looked up when he heard footsteps on the wooden veranda.

'You guys didn't take long.'

Joe smiled, 'No we didn't need to; we found the padlock.'

Norton was holding the evidence bag with the padlock in it and passed it to Matt. He in turn passed it around for everyone to have a look. There was clearly some solid glue showing on the edge of the latch. The bag eventually came to rest on the table. From behind them a voice spoke up.

'Good morning, I'm Detective Chief Inspector Edward Stimpson; sorry I am running a little late, I got delayed interviewing a suspect.'

A man in his mid-forties, with a very official bearing, and a well-fitting suit leant forward to shake everyone's hand in turn. They all made their introductions and offered him some coffee. Matt motioned to him to take a seat. DCI Stimpson was doing his best to present an unruffled, calm persona. He had checked up on these guys, so he was aware they got results.

'Well Mr Holland; as I said on the phone there is not much I can tell you. Nothing we found points to anything other than an accidental death. Obviously, I could not discuss the details of the case with you normally; but in this case I can talk to you as Mrs Stone has told you everything I have told her. I'll summarise it for you.'

'A call was made to the emergency number with reports of a dead body found floating in a disused and flooded quarry. The caller made it clear that the body was heavily bloated, and death had occurred some considerable time ago. They explained even someone with no previous experience of dead bodies could tell that.

'On arrival the first officer on the scene, who is quite a new lad could not ascertain whether this was a result of misadventure or a deliberate attack, so he treated the body and the scene as a category one death and quite rightly so. As a result, everything was preserved. As we went through the investigation over the next few days, it was downgraded to a Category Two death by me as SIO, having liaised with the Pathologist and the Coroner.

'The Coroner was satisfied that the concrete found in the fatal injury to the head matched the concrete sample taken from the stairs. It would match with him losing his footing at the top of the quarry cliff and landing on the concrete stairs. There was no grass or debris found in the wound as you will have read; but that is deemed to have leached out from the wounds whilst the body was in the water. Being forced in deeper due to the impact, and being heavier, the concrete particles remained in the wound.

'We could find no good reason for him being in this part of the world; we looked down every possible avenue, but there just weren't any. Nothing came to light at all. There was no vehicle, his company car was in Reading where it should be, as was his own car. His wallet and phone were missing and never traced. After considerable time and a lot of effort from everyone an inquest was held; in pretty quick time I might add, and the only conclusion that could be drawn was drawn; "Accidental Death or Misadventure".'

Norton leant forward as if to speak. As he did so, he caught Matt's stare. Matt calmly but clearly shook his head slowly enough that Norton knew to sit back and keep quiet.

Matt spoke instead, 'So you visited his place of work?'

'I did, a house in the countryside outside Reading. He was head of security there. Place is apparently owned by some absentee tax exile who is never there. The place is stuffed with amazing furniture, and a large collection of valuable cars, so it needs protecting.'

Matt and the others all instinctively glanced at each other.

'And you found everything there to be in order?'

'We did, yes. Why?'

'Oh *no* reason, I just wondered.'

Stimpson began talking again, 'As I say; I'm sorry if I seem to be being unhelpful, but I have shared all the information we have, there is nothing else going on here, I'm sorry if you have had a wasted journey.'

Matt looked thoughtful for a moment.

'Of course, we understand that. I am guessing that if we should find anything amiss, you would like us to let you know though?'

Edward Stimpson was beginning to get up.

'*Yes*, please do. I don't think we have missed anything, but I'm not a stupidly proud man; if somehow we're wrong, then I certainly want to know about it. If there has been foul play I will certainly want to apprehend the culprit or culprits, and I will want to see them prosecuted to the full extent of the law. It's just that in this case I don't think there is anything amiss. We don't have unlimited resources to spend endless time on every case, but we were and always are thorough.'

DCI Stimpson was about to make his goodbyes and leave, Matt nodded to Norton; Norton cleared his throat and spoke.

'DCI Stimpson, you might be interested in this then.' He pushed the evidence bag across the table. Stimpson didn't hesitate in moving forward to pick it up.

'Ah, so it *was* tampered with.'

The team realised at once how sharp minded this particular policeman was. They were talking about one closed case, when he must have plenty more open current cases in his head; and yet on seeing the padlock, he had instant recall and understood its significance.

Nevertheless, Norton wanted to be clear that they were all on the same page about one thing.

'If you look carefully at the small flap where the keyhole is, you will see a hard clear substance stuck to its outer edge.'

Stimpson looked closer and agreed, 'I *do*. I see the blob of glue. Can I hold on to this for now then?'

Matt and Norton both murmured a 'Yes.'

Stimpson slowly looked round the table, his facial expression open and inviting, 'Have you found anything else?'

For a moment or two no one said anything. Various versions of the same thought were going through the minds of the six team members; namely that Stimpson had played it straight with them and wasn't warning them off; so on balance, there seemed to be no reason to keep anything from him.

Ava was the first to break silence.

'It's just that we have found out the concrete steps at the quarry have been destroyed; the ones that are identified as the ones that resulted in Peter's death. Someone has used some underwater equipment to cut through the metal stakes holding them in place.'

Stimpson gave Ava's comment a moment's thought before speaking.

'Yes I remember; we were told about the steps going missing. A very diligent young officer thought my team should be made aware of the incident, given how it seemed such an odd occurrence. My colleague and I gave the situation some careful consideration; we pondered what motive could have led to the steps being moved, and wondered if the concrete sample could be the concern. I checked with the lab though, and the concrete sample was where it should be, and had already been a match to the steps; so, we could see no logic to it. We put it down to a unique act of vandalism.'

Stimpson paused for a moment, 'Well if you have nothing else; I'll be on my way.'

Matt got up to walk with Stimpson as he left, and thank him for taking the time to speak to them. They had not always met with such an open and accepting fashion by the officials they had encountered on previous investigations.

CHAPTER 8

As Matt and DCI Stimpson walked off one end of the veranda, someone approached from the other end. It was Bella.

'Hi everyone.'

Max had to catch his breath with this unwelcome surprise. What the hell was she doing here? He had stuck his neck out to help her, and she had repaid him by blatantly lying. He wasn't sure how best to handle this; he had wanted time to plan how to confront her properly. His mind was desperately trying to remember why she was his ex, had she done something? Did he break up with her? Why could he not remember? That was not like him.

'Hi Bella.' Everyone was welcoming, though they all looked deeply surprised to see her there.

Registering the surprise on everyone's faces made Bella panic slightly; perhaps she shouldn't have come. She wondered if she was pushing her luck, so thought it best to quickly explain.

'As I've *never* been here before, I thought I would come and say hello, look the place over and see if there was any update. I'm *sorry* Max, but I *couldn't* keep away.'

Max looked directly at Bella and smiled. Bella thought the smile lacked its usual power; perhaps he was tired.

'We were all heading back to the Operations Room we have setup; would you like to come with us, and we can update you?'

They all stood up in unison and headed along the veranda and down into the car park. Max smiled and said 'Good morning' to the two members of hotel staff that were passing them. They smiled back, but they looked at the group strangely.

Once they had passed the group, they stopped and turned round. The one with blonde hair spoke first; her accent was Eastern European.

'*Bella*… It *is* Bella Stone, *yes*?'

Everyone stopped dead in their tracks. Bella's previous sentence began to repeat in Max's mind before it trailed off. "I've *never* been here before…"

The repeat of Bella's sentence was interrupted with a sentence of Max's own that conveyed exactly how he felt. A very short sentence as it happened; just one word in fact, and he was careful to only mutter it under his breath so that no one else heard: '*Shit*.'

CHAPTER 9

Bella looked genuinely puzzled, 'I'm *sorry*, *have* we met?'

Max was watching Bella's reaction like a hawk; specifically her body language, especially her eyes. His gut still told him she was the decent woman he had always believed her to be, but he could not rationally discount the increasing number of pointers towards this no longer being the case. At the very least she was lying. She could be lying for good reason though, he thought.

Both women moved closer towards Bella. The other member of the couple spoke now.

'No, you have never met us, but we know all about you. We have seen your photo. We know; I mean we *knew* your husband Pete pretty well.'

Bella's whole body gave a visual jolt. It was so noticeable that the other woman instinctively put her hand on Bella's shoulder in sympathy.

The woman quickly clarified her last statement.

'No, *not biblically*; he was our *friend, that's all.* He used to come and spend his lunch breaks with us on occasion. By us I mean the hotel staff. Ten of us got permission to turn a disused bar into our break-room. Your husband would come by and eat lunch with us on occasion. Turns out one of the guys who works here in the grounds knows your husband from way back.'

'*Mary*,' the other girl looked aghast, 'I don't think Mark meant us to tell anyone that; *remember* what he said.'

Mary was quick with her response.

'Oh *don't* be silly; she's his wife, Mark won't mind.'

Mary paused for a moment before continuing.

'Why don't you come over and say hello to whoever is in the break-room. I'm sure they would want to pay their respects; your husband was liked by everyone, very much indeed.'

Bella looked to Max for some input. Matt had just joined them having said thank you and goodbye to DCI Stimpson. Max thought they should all go in. He was hoping they may well learn something to their advantage.

Mary looked hopefully at the group of people standing with Bella.

'Of course that invitation is to you all.'

Max smiled and took the lead on behalf of the group.

'Thanks, we would like that.'

Mary looked happy to have them all coming too.

'Well come on then, this way.'

The group of nine crossed the end of the tarmac, and walked over some undulating and very short grass. The group passed through a small copse of willow that had been allowed to grow up, and once on the other side saw the building the women had been referring to. A run down and smaller version of the smart pub they had just left. Mary noticed the various expressions of surprise on the group's faces.

'This was the original pub that was here when the quarries were being worked. It's too small to be practical for the hotel, but it is part of the area's heritage, so they don't want to pull it down. Until they decide on what they are going to do with it, we can use it. Coming here feels like we get away from things during our break times.'

Mary climbed the steps and pushed the door open whilst beckoning everyone inside.

The main room had been decked out with some sofas. They looked like the ones in the hotel and Matt guessed they were furnishings that were considered past it for continued use in the hotel, although they still looked like they had plenty of life left in them.

'Please take a seat; can we get you all a drink?' Mary said.

Matt thanked them.

'Some water would be great.'

The team fanned out and looked at the printed photos that were on the walls. All around the room, stuck to the walls were photographs of the same people laughing and joking in different poses. The photos were printed on cheap printer paper. What they lacked in presentation they made up for in jollity and happiness.

Bella froze. There in an A4 sized photo of two men laughing was her husband.

'It's Pete *and* with his tattoo's.'

The team came closer to have a look. It was indeed Pete sitting with another man. Both had polo shirts on and both had tattoos showing on each arm.

'*Look*,' said Bella, 'I wonder who that is with my husband. They seem to have slightly similar looking tattoos.' Still looking at the photo on the back wall, Bella continued talking, but to no one in particular, 'I would really like to meet this man.'

From behind Bella a deep and unfamiliar voice provided a reply, 'You *can*, I'm right here.'

Bella swung round quickly. Before her stood the other man from the photo.

'I'm Mark.'

Bella walked towards him and shook his hand. He was about five foot eleven inches tall and thick set. He had brown eyes and short cropped brown hair.

'I'm pleased to meet you Mark; I'm Bella, Pete's wife.'

'I know. It's nice to finally meet you Bella. Please everyone, take a seat.'

They all did. Water was passed around.

Bella caught herself wondering what she should say, so she decided to introduce who the team were, and why she had hired them. The hotel staff waited and listened while she did so. Mark in turn briefly explained that he and Pete had worked together long ago, and that he saw Pete in the hotel car park one day. They had a good catch up and ever since that day, when Pete was up this way he would pop in and see them. After that, the conversation did not have any real path to follow so it went silent for a moment.

Bruno noticed Mark had tattoos on his arms and had a sudden idea to try something. Seizing the moment and making eye contact with Mark he made a nod towards his arms.

'Nice ink you have there, it looks similar to Pete's.

Mark shook his head, 'Well yes and no. Pete didn't have any tattoos.'

'*But…*' Bella had gone red in the face and her eyes were as wide as they would go. Before she could get going with her protestations, Mark interrupted her.

'Yes, I *know*… You saw them. Well, you *did* and you *didn't*. What you saw were removable tattoos, did he never change them in front of you?'

Bella's eyes were wide once again but this time with delight not concern. Was she about to finally get one of her most pondered questions answered?

Mark continued, 'Pete and I were in the military together. I'm not going to talk details about where we were or what we were doing as it's not relevant, and more importantly, I can't. Suffice it to say, there were four of us, and when we had succeeded in what we had set out to achieve, we all wanted to mark it with something memorable that we could have around us every day that had meaning. We settled on tattoos.'

Mark took a drink before continuing.

'We found this brilliant tattoo artist who designed all our tattoos to be part of a set. The key feature of the design is when we are together in t-shirts or polo shirts, the story of our mission together is told across our eight arms. Whenever we are together, our story is complete. We liked that idea a lot after what we had been through. That sentiment summed up how we all felt about each other and the bond we had after all we had been through together.

Mark paused for a moment, 'You obviously were aware of the large number of pretty sizeable moles on both your husband's arms Bella?'

Bella shook her head, 'No I'm afraid he never told me his tattoos were fake. He never took them off in front of me, so I have never seen his bare arms. Maybe he wasn't as open with me as I thought he was.'

Mark gave Bella a knowing smile.

'In all the years I have known your husband; I have never seen him *so* happy... *never*. He was *so* much in love with you. He was probably embarrassed at wearing fake tattoos and was wondering how to tell you. That's all.'

Bella's eyes were showing signs of tears. Mark

did not want to cause her distress. They looked at each other as Bella reached into her pocket and withdrew a hanky.

She dried her eyes, '*Thank you.*' she whispered.

Mark thought it best to continue.

'Well, we formed such a brotherhood on that mission that Pete was determined to be part of the inking. He did lots of research into how safe it was to tattoo over his moles. The consensus was you shouldn't, and the tattoo artist strongly advised him against it. The artist suggested a design for Pete that worked around his moles; but Pete wanted his to be part of our story, and not stand out as different. We were all heading on to new lives, and Pete happened to mention he had landed a job working on a massive hydroelectric dam construction project somewhere in Europe; and that consequently, he would be spending much of his time underground in very damp, humid conditions for the next six months. The tattoo artist also strongly advised him to wait or not bother on the grounds that the scab would not heal. He was told he stood the very real chance of a serious infection.

Mark paused to clear his throat.

'We were all sat in the pub and Pete looked very downhearted. It was one of the lads who just told him to stop moping, and pointed out that with his engineering brain, Pete should easily be able to come up with a solution. A couple of months later, and he had. He had found some clear tubular breathable plastic that was used in some laboratory or medical process; it shrinks and binds to the skin. Then somewhere in Asia, he found a firm that would print or transfer the tattoo designs onto the sleeves. The only problems were, they would fade over time and need replacing, so he used to carry a spare sleeve for both arms in his pocket; and if they were wet for a long period of time; days not hours, they would slowly dissolve. Thing is, they are so cheap to manufacture he just ordered a couple of hundred every six months, or earlier if needed. Also, he couldn't ever see a time when he would ever be days in the water.

'That was just typical of your level headed, intelligent husband. The things he could engineer and adapt; well, it never failed to amaze us. He saved all our lives a few times with his mad contraptions.'

Matt allowed a moment to pass before he changed topic.

'Did Pete ever tell any of you why he was up here?'

Mark spoke first.

'I did ask him, and he said best I didn't ask again, so I left it. I assumed his telling me not to ask, meant he was doing some sort of private security job.

Matt moved his head to look straight at Mark.

'So it *was* work then?'

Mark nodded.

'I assume so. Pete was a very easy going guy, he liked the simple life, and he was very much in love with Bella. I know that much, so he wasn't up here for anything other than work.'

Not looking at anyone in particular Mark spoke out loudly, addressing the entire gathering, making sure that he was heard even in the back room.

'Anyone know anything about why Pete was up here?'

One of the younger women who had come in when Mark was talking stepped forward.

'I don't know what he was doing up here, but I do know where he was going when he was up here. It's on my way home, so I have seen him going in there a few times as I passed by.'

Ava spoke in a conversational tone so as not to alarm the woman.

'Are you happy to tell us where it is?'

The woman nodded, 'Yes, he was turning down a single-track country road that only led to the manor."

Ava looked up, '*The Manor*?'

'Yes, that's right, Nalebury Park; it's the big house for the village of Upper Nalebury.'

Ava looked up again, 'Thank you, that's great.'

The woman nodded and smiled.

Matt stood up and put his glass down on the makeshift table-top, which was a disused fire door.

'Well we should let you guys get about your business. Thank you very much indeed for giving us your time, it has been invaluable.'

Everyone got to their feet.

'Yes, thank you so much,' said Bella, 'I have deliberately not held a wake for Pete yet. I will do when the mystery of his death is finally solved. I would like you all to come. Can I get hold of you here via the hotel number?'

Mark acted as spokesman for the group.

'We will be here Bella, and I think I can speak for everyone; we would love to come.'

Since the team's arrival in the pub more members of staff had come in for their break. Every single person in the room nodded. Bella was delighted to see how well liked her husband was.

Max looked back towards the group as they headed out of the old pub.

'Shall we go back to the room and make a plan? Bella are you coming? I would like a word with you anyway.'

Matt said he thought that was a good idea and Bella smiled and nodded. She was beginning to hold herself a bit higher now. Max noted this steady, continued improvement and hoped the necessary talk he was about to have with her was not going to put a dent in her happier spirit. He had decided to listen to his gut, and give her one last chance to explain herself. He felt with everything she had been through on her own, her behaviour could be explained away. He would see what she had to say.

They were half way across the car park when

the woman who had given them the info about where Pete was going came running after them. They all stopped and waited. As she ran towards them, the woman did not pay attention to a large green car that was leaving the car park. It had to swerve and brake. The driver glared out of the windscreen at the woman. She apologised and continued until she made it to the group.

'Sorry,' she said a little out of breath, 'I should have added; a friend of mine worked up at the manor I have told you about. I thought I should just let you know, they are *not nice people*, in fact they are *very nasty* people. The man there, the owner, he is *exceptionally* rude and ungracious to his staff. Anyway, I just wanted to let you know before you went in there.' With that, she turned and began to walk quickly back towards the old pub.

'*Thank you.*' Ava called out.

The woman raised an arm in a gesture of no worries, then reached the willow coppice and was gone from sight.

The seven turned back towards the hotel and continued their journey to the room in silence. Seven brains were engaged in analysis of what they had learned. It was certainly food for thought.

When they got back to the room, Norton was the first to speak.

'So should we inform Detective Chief Inspector Stimpson of our findings?'

There was some discussion, but they decided after ten minutes of talking it over that for now, they would hold off. Stimpson made it clear he already had his mind made up, and any information or evidence that was going to change that would need to be substantial. Bella agreed, that they must continue; she Max and Matt discussed terms to which they all agreed. Bella felt it necessary to explain that she had some life insurance money from Pete's death; and that she could think of no better use for it than getting to the bottom of what happened to her husband for once and for all. It was agreed that Bella's being there had actually been very beneficial. Both Matt and Max were convinced the staff at the old pub would never have told the police any of what they had shared with the team that afternoon. Probably, if Bella had not been there, they would not have shared it with the team either. Them all meeting like that had been a serious stroke of luck.

They agreed that tomorrow, Bella would return to London; and the team would focus on finding out who Pete really worked for, what he was doing up here in the Cotswolds, and what the deal was with his supposed work location being in Reading. They would give the case another two days, then re-assess.

Before it got too late, Max wanted to get his conversation with Bella out of the way.

'Bella, can I have a quick word?'

Bella's stomach lurched; something in Max's voice was different. She had thought everything was going well, they had just as good as confirmed that. What could suddenly be wrong. Max walked out on to the balcony; as Bella followed him out through the door, she saw he had walked to the far end, and out of earshot of the others. Her pulse was quickening.

'I'm sorry Bella, but you and I need to have a *serious* conversation. Before we get any deeper into whatever it is that's going on here, I need to know *why* you have *explicitly lied* to me and the team. We know you have, *don't* deny it. Just tell me *why*.'

Bella fell against the balcony railing and grasped it for support.

'*Shit* Max, I am *so genuinely sorry*. I shouldn't have denied coming here I know. I have begged you for help, and then lied to you, it's *unforgivable*, and I don't know what to say.'

Max looked out over the water without turning around to face her; his voice was steady and professional.

'The *truth* Bella...*you tell the truth*.'

'There's *no* excuse... I know; *but* the genuine truth is that for some reason, I felt Pete's not being able to swim would add enough of a hook to get you to investigate the case. It was just an afterthought; I couldn't gauge how well the meeting had gone, I was desperate, *I admit it*. I'm *sorry*.

Bella took a moment to compose herself before continuing.

'And about not having ever been here; I lied about that because I thought if you knew how much I'd been down here, it might make me look obsessive. I didn't want any of you to think of me as obsessive when I was asking for your help. Once again, *I am so sorry*.'

Max turned to look directly at her.

'And you give me your *absolute* word that's why you lied, and that you are not hiding anything else?'

Bella hung her head in shame.

'I didn't *exactly lie* about Pete and the swimming. I don't know whether he could swim or not; but yes, I *solemnly promise* that's why I lied, and that I have not lied to you about anything else; there are no more secrets.'

Max's body language softened.

'OK then, fine, thank you for your honesty. I will have to tell the others about this at some point; you do understand *I can't* keep *anything* from them?'

Bella nodded, 'I do Max.'

Max made a motion towards the door.

'In that case, let's all go and eat.' He was glad she had mentioned the two subjects she had lied about without prompting. Max had deliberately not said what the lies were that he was referring to in case she disclosed another one. His stomach had been tight at that point in case she had exposed more lies, and his relief when she had not was palpable. He could now be confident the matter of Bella lying was closed.

As they headed back into the room, Bella smiled to herself. Her heart had sunk when the missing tattoos were explained. She was tired and fragile from the last sixteen months, fighting everyone, a lone voice against the official machine. The simple practical truth that the missing tattoos probably just dissolved, and there was nothing more to that particular aspect was shattering. She knew if she was still on her own, it would have been the last straw, she would have given up. It was all too much; but she was not alone, Max and his team were with her, supporting her, and they didn't seem to think the tattoo explanation was the end of the story. The nonsense with the steps was enough for them to consider it worth pushing on with for now. Bella smiled again.

She headed down stairs and booked herself a room for the night. Max updated the team on his conversation with Bella. Everyone said they were fine with the apology and agreed to move on, even Norton which Max was not expecting given his performance since the initial meeting with Bella. Still, Max was emotionally knackered; for tonight at least, he would take the win of Norton's support, and give Bella the benefit of the doubt one more time.

They all headed down stairs, met up with Bella,

and enjoyed a pleasant evening meal in the restaurant; buoyed by the fact they were, for now, making some progress.

As they all entered the restaurant and waited to be seated, Bella had a thought. Is that a ray of light I see at the end of the tunnel, or just a synapse misfire in my brain? Please let it be a ray. Please.

CHAPTER 10

The evening was still light when they had finished eating. Norton excused himself and went for a wander around the hotel lake to walk off some of the calories he had just consumed. There was also someone he wanted to call.

Once he was out of sight of the hotel, he took a phone from his pocket and dialled the number stored in his contacts. It was answered quickly.

'Hi, how's things? All good?'

'Yes, I know we agreed I wouldn't call whilst we are down here, but you are going to want to hear this…'

'I *think* you are going to get a visit from the team in the very near future…'

In one ear Norton could hear the lake water lapping against the shore; the other his friend's voice was talking in a concerned tone. Norton realised he was tuning out of the conversation; all he wanted to do was give his friend a heads up. It was late and he was tired, he didn't want a long drawn out discussion. He waited for a break in the talking before butting in.

'It wasn't anything I said, I promise. That *bitch* of a wife of his turned up; *uninvited* I might add, and was spotted and recognised by some of the hotel staff. It was one of them that told the team about you I'm afraid. Yeah of course I will keep you posted. Which reminds me, she mentioned Pete's calls to Sharon at work. Yup, I know... if they pick up on *that* clue we have a *major problem*; but they won't, not a chance – you know that, you know why. Chill, *just*...chill. Trust me; Matt and I have grown up together since we were kids. It's not like I am a new employee to be suspicious of or anything. I have sown enough seeds of doubt about *Bella bloody Stone* to be going on with. Like I say, trust me, none of them suspect at thing...'

Norton hung up his phone, wishing he hadn't bothered making the call in the first place. He looked out across the lake and the setting sun, the warm evening breeze washing over his face. He tried to feel the warmth and happiness that others talked of when experiencing such evenings. He thought there was a flicker of a memory from his childhood where he could connect with such feelings, but the flicker vanished as quickly as it came; simply to be replaced with the disconnected emptiness that seemed to have taken up a permanent residence in his soul. Norton turned and began walking back to the hotel.

CHAPTER 11

Everyone had passed a pleasant evening, and breakfast was an equally social affair. They all ate at one of the tables in a bay window overlooking the lake.

As everything workwise had been discussed on the previous night, the conversation was light and consisted of pointless, but pleasant chat. It was the perfect antidote to the previous heavy couple of days, and the morning's meal passed quickly.

It had been decided that Bella would return to London. Ava and Norton would work from the hotel, researching into where Pete was supposed to be working. They would also see what they could discover about his employer.

Ava gave Bella a lift to Kemble railway station. They walked towards the Range Rover. Bella smiled, 'Are we going in the Nobility Scooter then?'

Ava let out a loud laugh, '*The what*?'

Bella explained, 'A friend of mine has a habit of renaming things for fun. She decided to re-name Range Rover's as Nobility Scooters on account of their history of shipping posh folk about. I thought it was funny, and so it's kind of stuck in my head.'

Ava laughed, 'I think that will stick in my head now.'

Within the hour, Ava had dropped Bella off at the station, and then returned to the hotel, joined Norton, and begun their research.

Meanwhile, the rest of the team were heading towards Nalebury Park to see what they could discover. They were looking for something that might explain Pete's regular presence sixty-five miles in the wrong direction from where he officially worked.

Matt started the car, and before long they were rolling out the car park. They headed towards Cirencester.

'So Matt, what's the plan?'

Matt glanced into the rear-view mirror whilst talking to Max.

'I think we'll drive as close as we can; have a look around, and if we can see any livestock, we'll use our old 'Just trying to find the farmer to let them know their sheep are loose.' trick to justify a preliminary snoop around the manor, then go from there. You guys alright with that?'

Max, Bruno and Joe all nodded. It was only twenty minutes before they found themselves on the road heading towards the manor. The fields left and right contained exactly what the three had hoped they would. They contained sheep.

Matt turned the Audi up the narrowing road towards the manor. They arrived at a set of grand and extremely tall stone pillars. A set of equally large wrought iron gates sat open; their black and gold paint steaming in the morning sun as the early morning dew evaporated. Chiselled into the stone on one of the pillars were the words Nalebury Park.

They drove through, and on up the drive; gravel now crunching under the wheels. The enclosed feeling from the tall hedges on the side of the road gave way to a large sweeping lawn that rolled down towards fields. In front of them sat a large stone manor house. Everything was well manicured. They pulled up outside the front door. Matt hopped out and put on a colourful plastic coat he kept for such occasions. The idea was to look as much from the town as possible, so hopefully look the part of a concerned tourist when coming face to face with the landowner.

That was not to be the case on this occasion though. Four separate doorbell presses over a five minute period brought absolutely no one to the door. He nodded back towards the car and headed off around the side of the house. Arriving in the courtyard at the back of the building, the neatness continued. The concrete standing was brushed clean, the gravel was raked in circles and up against the garage wall, logs and blocks of peat were stored in neat, methodical rows. Again though, there was no sign of life. Some moments later he was back, removing his bright coloured coat and getting in the car.

'Well that was a busted flush.'

Joe was leaning forward from his back seat, 'Nothing at all, no one about?'

Matt shook his head looking at the three of them in turn.

'Quiet as the grave, very odd.'

Bruno chipped in next, 'What shall we do now then?'

His question had been loosely directed at Matt, but it was Max who answered it.

'There's a pub up the road, perhaps we should go there; always a good place for a fact finding mission. I have cash, so we can be anonymous.'

Matt started the car, headed back down to the main road and with directions from Max; they were soon outside the pub. The pub was not yet open. Bruno hopped out and went over to find out when it would be. They would have forty-five minutes to wait. As Bruno walked back towards the car, a metallic creak came from above. Looking up, he saw the pub sign was swaying gently in the breeze; in old English font it had the words, The Wellspring written large.

When the landlord opened up; Matt, Joe, Max and Bruno made sure they were loudly talking about how much they had enjoyed their walking holiday so far. From the table they had taken over, Bruno suggested that they should go back to that big looking house and take some photographs. Other customers had also arrived at the pub despite the early hour, and the team's hope was that some of them were locals, who might hear what they were saying and comment. That particular ploy had worked before. They were in luck this time too; an elderly gentleman, already installed at the bar swung round and advised them most earnestly, that they should not do that.

Seizing the moment, Matt got up to get in a round of drinks, making sure to include their potential information source. To Matt's delight he accepted not only his offer of a drink, but also the invitation to join them at their table. Matt felt it would be worthwhile trying to make the man as welcome as possible. He risked pushing things too far by suggesting food to the others, who intuitively knew to agree; however little hunger they were experiencing. As he arrived at the table with the tray of drinks, Matt caught the eye of a short, elderly lady who looked exhausted and had just come out of the kitchen.

'Can I ask, where would I get some lunch menus from?'

The woman looked up at him; her face broke into a warm smile.

'I'll bring some over in a moment sir, five for lunch is it?'

'Thanks that would be great. Yes five.'

The pub was cosy and welcoming. It had been freshly decorated.

Over the next hour, the team played their roles of innocent ramblers and managed to extract some gossip about the owners up at the manor. It largely backed up what the girl at the hotel had said in reference to lack of popularity and unpleasantness; but some extra gaps were filled in. Most importantly, they learned the owner's name was Evelyn de Varley. He owned the manor, the pub, several houses, several cottages and about four hundred acres of the surrounding land. He very rarely came to the pub though.

The team had learned early on that their new friend was known as Old Fred. There was no sign of New Fred though, as Bruno ran through the options of who that might be.

Fred, now liberated from any verbal restraint, thanks to the several pints he had consumed, confirmed only that he recognised Pete by description, and had seen him from across the lawns a couple of times at the manor. He had then moved on to some irrelevant personal revelations about Mr de Varley. It turned out Old Pete worked for two and a half days a week in the grounds. Today was his half day, he worked in the afternoon. Fred had started at the manor as a boy, and had been kept on by Mr de Varley when he had purchased the place back in the eighties.

The conversation continued to reveal how little the man was liked locally. Old Fred was about to continue when the waitress returned to clear the plates. She spoke before Fred could.

'Come on now Fred, we best *not* speak ill of the landlord, and your boss. We are in his pub after all. Hadn't you better be getting to work?'

Fred bowed his head and went very quiet, 'Yes um.'

Feeling slightly guilty, Matt and the team offered to drive Fred back to the manor and one of them would follow in his car. Fred was very grateful for this offer and once Matt settled the bill they all got up to leave.

The waitress appeared from the Kitchen and came over.

'Come on Fred, I will drive you to work. This lot will get you *fired*.' She then led Fred out into the car park.

The team left the pub and wandered across the car park and sat at a couple of tables. Matt spoke first, 'So what have we learned?'

'We've found out the owner's name, what he does, and the fact he is not liked much by the locals we've met so far. We've also found out that someone who works in the grounds has seen Pete a few times, but has not confirmed he works at Nalebury Park.'

Joe gave a slight nod.

'Yes well we're further on than we were, but still no clear explanation of why Pete was up here so often, and no proof he worked for Mr Evelyn de Varley.'

Matt walked towards the car.

'Let's go back to the hotel, meet up with Ava and Norton, and discuss where we are with all this.

CHAPTER 12

Matt managed to get hold of a whiteboard on wheels from the hotel's conference room.

'Right, so let's just have a re-cap on where we are, and what we know.'

The marker pen protested in a squeaky fashion as Matt jotted down a summary of where the case was so far.

Matt spoke as he wrote.

'We have a death ruled as misadventure that only the deceased's spouse seems to disagree with. We have some oddities that might suggest something is afoot; namely missing tattoos, though that might now have been explained. An odd conversation with a reference to underworld, someone found dead miles from anywhere they have any business being, and a crime scene that might have been tampered with on two separate occasions. None of these on their own prove anything; but taken together as a whole, it certainly points to the beginnings of a possible alternative explanation for what happened to Pete.

'We have the tattoo's explained, is everyone happy with what Mark said?'

Bruno pointed out that you could buy novelty tattoo sleeves that looked believable until closely examined. He added that it was not much of a leap to believe that someone with Pete's apparent talents could perfect the design so that even when close, it was difficult to tell they were fake. Everyone accepted the tattoos had simply dissolved from their extended time in the water, so ultimately offered no clue as to how Pete died.

Matt paused for a second before continuing with the next subject. 'OK, I don't think we can do anything with the underworld conversation just yet. I am guessing no one has had any thoughts in that direction?'

Everyone intimated that they had no ideas on that for now.

Matt moved on, 'Ava, what did you and Norton manage to find out about where Pete worked?'

Ava put down her glass, 'We didn't find out anything conclusive, but the company that is listed as Pete's employer is definitely not a UK based business. It's an offshore company based out of the Cayman Islands.'

Matt turned to face Ava, 'How does that work from an employment perspective for a UK resident? Do we know?'

'No, it's not the easiest set of rules to clarify for sure without consulting an accountant; but I spoke to Bella, and she said Pete was definitely employed through a UK employment agency, which to my mind would get around any legal issues.'

'Ah OK, that makes sense. What else did you

find?'

'His ultimate employer, Towers & Hurst has no UK offices, and there is certainly nothing around Reading, but there is a private residence near Reading called Hurst Towers. That ties in with what DCI Stimpson said. Remember he explained Matt was working for security, guarding a country house. There is no large business there though, so he can't have been guarding anything else. I initially thought the similar name was just a coincidence. It was only luck I found it. Someone has had it removed from the maps.'

Joe looked surprised, '*You can do that*?'

'It's not easy to make an existing house disappear. From what I can understand, it means someone would have had to mislead the relevant government bodies. I think they would have had to say it had been demolished or something; and it would at the very least involve creating some false paperwork to get it successfully removed from all the maps.'

'OK, good work. So, it looks like someone is going to some considerable lengths to obscure ownership and what is going on at Hurst Towers then.'

'It certainly looks that way, and someone who is happy to bend the law.'

'OK, and you think this is where Pete was going?'

'Norton and I both theorised that assuming the guys we met are right, and Pete works up here, then perhaps whoever he really works for wants to disguise the fact by making it appear he works at Hurst Towers instead. We can keep digging for now and hope to find some further proof.'

Matt continued writing on the board.

'That's great; yes, if you have any ideas, test them out. That would all fit with what we discovered, which is that a gardener from Nalebury Manor also said that he had seen Pete there. The place is supposedly owned by a guy called Evelyn de Varley. Let's see what we can find out about him. It would be good at this point to see if we can identify anyone who might have wanted Pete dead.

Bruno lent forward and placed his tablet on the table.

'Slightly different tangent boss, and just a thought, but if we are struggling for who, either with Pete's death or the other stuff, perhaps we should try looking for the where, that might then give us the who... It's just a thought.'

'Oh... go on with that thought Bruno, I like your thinking.'

'Well, it's just if we can't find a person to focus on; then assuming Pete was killed elsewhere if the quarry was staged, then perhaps we should try and work out where that other place might be. If we found that other place, it might give us some suspects to look at. It might shine a light on people we don't even know about yet.'

At that moment, Matt's phone rang. He put

down the pen and walked out onto the balcony to take the call. The others all talked about Bruno's idea. About twenty minutes later Matt walked back in.

'That was Dr Brett. He has triple checked; all three samples do match. That's the sample from Pete's head wound, the original sample from the steps and the photographic one we sent, so that's a dead end for now.'

Norton looked up.

'So it's not looking like foul play then.'

'Officially *no*, *but* he did have something interesting to say. I told him what Bruno had said about a different location. He remembered they did find a different type of concrete in Pete's boots. The granules of sand that make up the concrete in his boot treads are of a different size, roughness and they contained quartz.

'As the other two samples for the head wound and the steps were matched, placing the scene of death in the quarry, this different concrete embedded deeper into his boot treads was not an avenue that was explored further. But with this new information I think we should follow Bruno's plan of where rather than who, focusing on this different concrete in Pete's boots. Dr Brett says they will send over what they have by the morning.'

With that they all went down for an early meal, they then had coffee in the Operations Room before turning in for the night.

Matt ran over his outline thoughts for the morning.

'Shall we all meet here say nine am and do some office-based research. Mostly on looking into Evelyn de Varley and about Bruno's where Pete might actually have died. Of course he may still have died accidently; it's possible someone moved the body for a reason unrelated to Pete's death, unlikely; but it is possible.'

They all passed a reasonable night's sleep and before long, they were back in the Operations Room. The whole of the morning was taken up with a slew of phone calls, and internet surfing, emailing and compiling and printing reports. Mostly based around what they could find about Mr de Varley and going over what Dr Brett had sent over about the different type of concrete. In what felt like very little time at all, it was four p.m. and they were gathered around the white-board.

Matt began.

'So, Mr de Varley is the owner of Chantmarle Capital, a hedge fund operating out of London, but with affiliated companies in... The Cayman Islands, the address is on the same street as the Towers and Hurst business. It took ages just to find that out, but for now we will note that as a relevant coincidence. Ava, what about Dr Brett's information?'

Matt sat down as Ava got up to present what they had discovered.

'So we went through Dr Brett's information that he sent us this morning. His team provided a detailed breakdown of the differences between the matching original concrete samples, from Pete's head and the steps and his boots, as well as the different concrete type buried deeper in the treads.'

Ava handed out copies of the one page summary.

'It references various elements such as fine silica and quartz dust, but the upshot is, there is no doubt from the lab that these are two quite different types of concrete. The two original samples from the steps and Pete's wound is a standard concrete, nothing special. That is what you would expect given the fact we were told they were put there simply to avoid getting muddy.

Ava paused for a moment to double check she was quoting things properly.

'The interesting bit comes with a more detailed analysis of Pete's deeper boot sample. It has shown to be a specialist type, referred to as an Ultra high-performance concrete. It's used in areas of extremely specific engineering, such as bridges and dams. There was reference to metal fibres being present; which apparently goes further to point towards a substantial structure construction project with some extremely specific engineering requirements; this stuff is not used in the building of normal houses.

Ava now paused for a moment or two in order to let the info sink in and register before continuing.

'The *really* interesting point that might help us narrow down where Pete actually died was in what one of Dr Brett's assistants said. They re-read the reports and found mention of Pete's trousers being quite ingrained with mud and soil, so they found their original analysis and guess what. It's quite a *rare* soil type, something called f*uller's earth*; it's used in stuff like kitty-litter because of its ability to absorb moisture. Given that it is quite rare, we looked to see if there was anywhere around here that was known to have fuller's earth deposits, and to see if there was any large-scale engineering close to that deposit. We're in luck. Not far from here there is an area of fuller's earth, and what appears to be a disused canal and tunnel. Our initial research shows that both the canal and the tunnel are much older than the invention of this super concrete, but they could be using it in repairs. All that and the fact it is basically behind Mr de Varley's home means we think it is worth a look.'

There was more silence as everyone processed the information, and what it meant for this investigation into Pete's death. There was still nothing substantial enough to persuade the team the original verdict was wrong; but it was becoming increasingly difficult to completely dismiss the growing elements of this other potential version of events. Was Bella right all along?

Matt spoke next.

'Right then, if it's local; there is no time like the present; shall we go and have a poke about?'

They all agreed, and soon were heading out to the car park. As they approached the cars, Norton took Matt to one side.

'Sorry boss, do you mind if I just follow a hunch for the next thirty minutes unless you need me with you?'

'No Norton, we don't all need to go. You go and follow your hunch.'

'Cheers Boss.' Norton headed across the car park towards the old pub.

Matt addressed the remaining Scott and Munro employees.

'Right everyone, Norton has just gone to check up on something so we can all go in one car. We will take Bess; hop in, I'll drive. Ava, you keep me right on where we are going.'

'Ahead of you Matt, already forwarded the location to both Bess and Dougal's Satnav systems. We should be good to go.'

CHAPTER 13

En route, whilst looking at the map, it was decided the team would park up once they had driven across the bridge. They would then approach the last section of the journey on foot; along what was the supposedly abandoned towpath. They came through the village of Upper Nalebury and began the decent down into the valley where the tunnel, or to give it its proper name, the Nalebury Portal lay.

Joe suggested that they just referred to it as 'The Portal' from now on. Agreement was swift and unanimous on that matter.

Once down the hill, and having found an unofficial parking space by the side of the road, Matt pulled over, and everyone disembarked. The team all stood looking around. The ancient trees that surrounded this place were stunning; mostly consisting of beech, with some oak. The bright sunshine, the blue sky and the brilliant green of the tree's leaves were electrifyingly vivid. It was as if someone had asked Mother Nature to turn the contrast setting up to full in order to show the place off to its maximum beauty.

Adding to this majesty was the fact that the trees were standing on a large man-made bank.

This resulted in the top of the tallest trees towering over one hundred feet above where the team stood. The whole effect instilled a feeling that you were standing in some magnificent arboreal cathedral.

Ava took out her tablet computer and brought up her notes. The tablet's screen turned red and the machine froze, it had never done that before. Ava rebooted the device, and whilst it was initializing, she took the footpath down underneath the bridge with everyone else following.

The team took a background briefing about a new location on-site if they could. It allowed for context, which was an obvious assistance in knowledge retention; but had also been proven to help with spotting key clues on a couple of previous cases. In this case there was not much to impart, just some background history on the old place.

Once everyone was gathered directly under the bridge they stood still. Below them in the canal, there was a wooden dam in place to keep the water in. The bridge's architecture meant that even normal every day sounds had an unworldly element to them; and the sound of the water pouring over the dam echoed around them loudly.

Facing into the canal, with the bridge wall to their backs, it was a story of two very different halves. To the left; above the dam, although now somewhat narrower than it's originally intended size, lay a very well-kept towpath. Someone was clearly tending to this place, although there didn't appear to be anyone about at the moment. Mother Nature was being kept in check; paths were clear, banks were tidy, and the stonework that made up the canal walls was in good order and showed signs of recent repairs.

Not exactly abandoned then, thought Bruno. Despite the fresh air and the warm weather Bruno, the battle-hardened man noticed he was feeling a little uneasy about being here. He looked around taking in the atmosphere; it was warm and sunny; why did he feel uneasy? No answer came, so he tried to shake the negativity from his mind.

Below the dam and to the team's right-hand side, there was a few feet of murky water. This gave way to a muddy canal floor that in turn gave way to grass and reeds. The whole canal bed appeared as if it was slightly raised up. Here the canal walls had long gone, and the area just resembled a pit. It was clear by looking around that no one was caring for this section, and clearly no one had for a long time.

They stood upstream from the dam and gazed into the deep water. Any sizeable debris had been cleaned out; all that was left was a sand-like sediment on the bottom. As a result the water was gin-clear; it was almost like discovering a swimming pool out in the middle of nowhere. Indeed there was certainly a blue hue to the water that mirrored the sky above; it looked very pretty and inviting.

Ava and the team moved to the left a few more feet and stopped just outside the bridge's structure where sounds turned back to normal. The air temperature rose and as their skin reacted pleasantly to the warmth; their nostrils filled with the smells of warm summer woodland. Although they stood on what looked like solid ground, it had a certain spring to it. The sort of cushioned feeling you get when walking on years and years of accumulated leaf mulch. Above them, several feet further up the bank, a small line of twigs, sticks and leaves ran horizontally in both directions as far as the eye could see.

Ahead of them, they could see the gin-clear water of the canal snaking around the corner and out of sight. The ground and vegetation on both sides of the canal looked as though it had been swept to within an inch of its life; so much so that nearly all the leaves were pointing in the same direction on all the shrubs and bushes.

The whole team felt that they were now stood in an ancient, but cared for garden belonging to some grand and elegant mansion house that was just out of sight. So herculean were the earthworks, plantings and sheer energy that must have been required to create this bizarre place; that it was not difficult to imagine God had personally been involved with, or at the very least directly consulted in, its design and creation.

The towpath had been reduced in size, and was relatively narrow; the team walked silently apart from the hollow crunching of beech nut husks under foot. On rounding the corner, they walked through an invisible wall of cold air. Everyone stopped dead in their tracks. They collectively shivered and drew a clichéd, but in this case warranted intake of breath.

'Is that really sitting there, or am I seeing things?' Joe said breathlessly.

They walked on a bit further until they stood face to face with what Joe was referring to.

The building that was now sitting silently before the team and commanding their full attention could probably be described as resembling some ornate ancient temple. Given this was England though; it was probably more accurate to describe it as the front elevation to some grandiose country mansion, where the stonemasons had been given free rein to go completely mad on the creation of its appearance.

The way the grounds around the portal had been created meant that during this part of the day at least, in contrast to the cold air surrounding the team; the sun's rays fell warmly against the mellow Cotswold stone from which its façade was constructed. The sunlight imitated the way a spotlight might shine on an actor as they made their grand entrance on stage.

Two enormous oak doors sat open, resting against their respective stops on opposite sides of the canal; badly rotten to a point they would no longer move as intended. The rot was highlighted by the odd angles at which they now rested; their days acting as effective wooden sentries to this mysterious underground palace were long gone. Now they just offered a visual indication of decay and contributed to an atmosphere of death by exuding the faint odour of wet, rotting wood.

The stone archway these doors once protected was expansive, yet its design only permitted the daylight to penetrate a couple of feet inside, before the cool inky darkness came forward to meet it, and stood resolute; allowing no further trespass on its domain. From where the team currently stood, however much they squinted, they could see nothing inside.

It was a moment or two before the team could focus on the fact they were to begin the site briefing. This place was unnerving them. Taking his eyes back out of the utter darkness of the portal and back onto the exterior of the building, Matt could not help but marvel at it all.

The neo classical façade rose high into the sky; at points along the stone balustrade that ran the full width of the structure, there were stone finials and statuary in various states of crumble and disarray. The statues seemed to be of Greek Gods, but with the level of decay on the stonework it was difficult to be sure; erosion and time had blunted their fine features. The whole ensemble was finished off with rows of false windows. It was unlike anything any of them had ever seen before. This orgy of masonry was keeping everyone's attention longer than a building might normally do.

Joe was the first to speak.

'Why am I having *flashbacks* to my childhood and *specifically* drawings in books showing what the entrance to a dragon's layer looks like?'

It was Max who was the first to answer.

'Because from my memory of our childhood, that looks *a lot* like those drawings. Maybe the artist for that book knew of this place.'

Silence lingered amongst the team for just a moment longer than was comfortable.

Bruno looked at the building. His mind began to analyse what was off here, 'All innocent, un-emotional and quiet; built from solid stone. And yet, it elicited a great deal of emotion in those that lay eyes on it. The fact it is hundreds of years old means it must all be correct, or it would have crumbled and fallen... and yet... and yet, I begin to look closer and things don't add up, something is definitely wrong.'

A few moments of blankness passed as Bruno's brain scanned through everything it had witnessed.

'The proportions are all wrong, *yes that's it*. It is massively oversized compared to its surroundings. If you take it at face value it just doesn't make sense. I have never experienced that with a building before. All this crazy detail; it's to disguise how enormous this place is. If this were all only plain stonework it would be so obvious.'

Bruno slowly turned his head and then his body three hundred and sixty degrees, taking in every aspect of the place that he could.

'I get the feeling all this landscaping and majesty is very deliberate and there's more to this than just showing off. It's not just about visual pleasure.'

'Why, what do you mean?' Ava's question caused Bruno to jump. He thought he had been talking to himself and had not realised he had been talking out loud.

'It feels like from the moment you take the very first steps down off the road that your mind is being *played* with. Nothing is just there for practical engineering reasons. There are two reasons for every feature.'

Bruno looked up; everyone in the team was facing him and focused on his every word. He continued.

'What I think I am trying to say is, it feels like we have walked onto a stage or a set or into a theme park. Even the sunlight is harnessed and directed to light up the main character on stage. Everything is meant to look natural and free formed but it's the complete *opposite*. Your movements and what you see and think are all very tightly controlled. It's very subtle until you realise it. Then it becomes a bit more obvious. As a visitor here you are being manipulated.'

The team stood stock still listening to Bruno.

'Look at our journey since getting out of Bess. Once we were across the road and started to come down those steps, we are forced to see only from the narrow perspective and position the absentee director of this bizarre circus wants us to see everything from.'

'In what way?' It was Max's turn to look concerned.

Bruno continued.

'In the scheme of things here, look how narrow the path is. It counts for a surprisingly tiny percentage of the area, yet we are forced to walk down it with no alternative. We can't turn right or we will end up in the inviting, but deep water with steep sides and no easy way out. We can't go left; there is an incredibly steep bank that is clad in ivy and other slippery surfaces that dissuade you from even thinking about it. Then look at the trees towering above our heads. Specimens that tend to number in the tallest trees have been planted already high up on the banks.'

Bruno took a moment before continuing, 'That's my point really. All this majesty helps disguise the true size of The Portal. By the time we get here to The Portal entrance, our minds and imaginations are so overwhelmed by our walk up here that our senses cannot process much more without a rest. That is when we are presented with this profusion of carvings and details that themselves require time and space to process. All that allows this insanely large building to sit here hiding in plain sight.'

Ava spoke next.

'You are saying that it is larger than it needs to be for a standard canal tunnel, and that for some reason it was important to hide that fact. *Why bother though*? It *didn't* work for you.'

Bruno paused a moment before replying.

'Well *no* trick works on *every* audience member, I think any conjuror, illusionist or trickster will admit that. But it works *enough* of the time to fool *enough* of the people. I guess in this case, the aim is to create the illusion that there's *nothing suspicious* to see here. If the illusion infects enough of the group, then with human behaviour and group dynamics being what they are, the illusion will spread through the group *like a virus* until the majority finds it easier to buy into the illusion rather than fighting it.'

'Are you sure it is not *delusion rather* than *illusion*?'

Everyone smiled at Ava's remark.

'But like Ava says... *why*? Why go to all this effort to hide the fact The Portal is larger than normal.' Joe was looking all around as he spoke.

Bruno looked down at his feet.

'Well that's the million-dollar question, and to be honest I have absolutely no idea.'

Ava was next to speak.

'*OK*, should I read out the background facts

that I could find out about this place? That might make it seem a little less surreal and allow us to break any spell it might be holding over us.'

The chorus to that particular line was a resounding '*Yes*.'

'OK, so this impressive looking entrance to The Portal masks an even greater feat of engineering that lies behind it. At one point this was the longest tunnel in the United Kingdom. It runs for nearly three miles. It was begun in 1784 and opened in 1789; which makes it only thirteen years younger than the USA as we know it today. More than sixteen men were killed during the construction of The Portal. This was due to the fact the creation of The Portal section in this terrain required them to work at the bleeding edge of what technology they had at the time.

'It was such an amazing feet of engineering, that even King George the third visited it, and The Portal was quite popular with holidaymakers of the time. It has also featured in a Novel, one of E M Forster's. The largest distance in height between the Portal Roof and the ground above is 216 feet. It was closed in 1911 even though the owners had just spent thousands on repairs. It was very expensive and problematic to maintain given the geology in which it is sited. As well as solid bedrock, some of the ground is, wait for it... fuller's earth. When it swells with rain water, it pushes against The Portal walls, which has led to various collapses and expensive structural issues. Since closing, The Portal has been fitted with those ornate wrought iron gates to stop people travelling inside. Clearly, as you can see, they are currently open, which is odd.'

By now they had moved closer. Everyone turned to look at the portal and could see; just on the edge of the daylight there was indeed a set of enormous decorative metal black gates inside, that spanned the whole of the portal mouth.

Ava altered the angle of her tablet before continuing.

'Oddly I can't find out who owns The Portal.'

'Shall we take a closer look?' Everyone followed Matt down the stairs to the small harbour that was just by the portal mouth.

Bruno took off his shoes and socks, then slipped gently down the rest of the steps and into the water. It came up to his knees.

'There's a solid base under this silt, something like concrete.' He walked into the portal mouth.

'Matt, I sure as hell hope there isn't a large metal double door in there painted bright red, though I wouldn't be entirely surprised.'

Matt laughed.

'I don't think so Bruno, I don't think this place belongs to *them*... though that red door is only about twenty-five miles from here, so I wouldn't bet my life on it just yet.'

Bruno laughed and continued his explore. The others gave Matt a quizzical look that told him he needed to explain.

'I can't really elaborate guys; it was a job Bruno and I were involved with in our old careers. Let's just say the whole incident revolved around a large metal red door; that was in a tunnel as well, but that's about all I can say. But I can't say anymore, and we are not supposed to talk about it are we Bruno?' Matt jokingly raised his voice towards the end of his explanation.

There was another laugh from Bruno.

'No, we're not, and I didn't give anything away. Back to this place though, there is a small lip here in the floor.'

For a little way into the portal, the floor rose up like a small ramp. Bruno was not far in though before the water level started getting deeper.

'*Be careful mate.*' Matt made sure Bruno heard him.

'Will do boss, I'll go no further. I'll just take a couple of photos. *Whoa.*'

'You alright?'

'Yeah, I'm fine, this floor is insanely slippery. It's *really* odd. Just a few more photos.'

Bruno took some shots of the floor and then of the wall. He looked at his phone to make sure that the photos had come out, something caught his eye. Bruno slowly made his way across to the portal wall. Once there, he rubbed his hands across the wall. He stopped and repeated his action, not realising his mouth had opened a little.

He took a closer photo.

'The bricks on this portal wall; they *aren't* bricks.'

'What are they?' came Joe's reply.

'They are just painted on. They look amazingly lifelike, but when you touch the wall, it's made of the same smooth material that the floor is. *It's odd.*'

'Bruno, come out *now*.' Matt's voice didn't usually carry that level of severity; Bruno knew to follow the order.

'Coming back now, just give me a moment, I need to go easy.'

Matt's reply came quickly and with equal severity.

'Not a problem; take your time, but *come back*.'

Bruno was now out of the portal, and climbing up the bank, his head was level with one of the bushes. A blue object tucked inside the bush caught his eye.

'That really annoys me; there is no need for littering in the countryside in this day and age with bins all over the place.'

Matt swung his head round, 'Why do you say that?'

Bruno reached further into a small clump of leaves just inside a thick shrub that seemed to be flourishing on the side of the canal.

'Because someone has thrown away a disposable glove... no my bad... a pair of disposable gloves. They have gone to the effort of tying the ends shut on both and then tying them together, but can't be bothered to find a bin.'

He retrieved them and held them aloft for everyone to see.

'There is simply no need for that sort of behaviour. I'll find a bin somewhere and get rid of them properly.'

Now Bruno was sitting on the bank having dried his feet with a clean hanky; he was putting his socks and shoes back on. The team passed Bruno's phone between them, looking at the photos.

He grabbed the gloves and as he stood up, Bruno shared his thought.

'Well I don't think we need to go and look for any fuller's earth; this place would be my central focus for the special concrete, and I'll bet Pete's job had something to do with this bizarre fun-palace.'

Once they had all had a look at the photos, Matt took the phone and passed it back to Bruno.

'Right everyone, I suggest we head back to the Operations Room and make a plan, we're not equipped to explore this place properly. Shall we head back to where Bess is parked?'

Matt nodded his head in the direction of the car, and Ava took the lead. Matt would follow up at the back. He wanted to make sure his team were all safely back at the car as quickly as possible. This feat of fantastic science and engineering was giving him the distinctively unscientific creeps. At this moment, being within easy reach of a car that could get them all out of there quickly was very much his utmost desire. He would relax when they were back at the car, not before.

CHAPTER 14

Norton found himself a nice table on the terrace overlooking the hotel gardens. He decided he was going to take most of the day off and enjoy it. He knew his team trusted him, so he would be safe from being checked up on. Besides, it wasn't often that he had a chance to spend the day being pampered at a hotel and spa with two Michelin stars. He took out the two phones from his pocket. One he turned off. The second, he swiped through until he was dialling the solitary contact that was in the phone's memory. He would get this call out the way; then he would be free to relax.

'Hi, just another update. They have headed off to your abandoned tunnel. You might want to scare them off, or not – I just wanted to give you a heads up.'

'No worries, I get you are busy, I was just letting you know. Speak later.'

Norton turned towards the direction of the approaching footsteps and smiled at the waitress who was bringing him his coffee. As he did so, he ended the call and turned this phone off too.

'Thank you, that looks perfect.'

'Are you staying with us sir?'

'Only for the day. I take it your spa is open to

non-residents?'

'It is sir, yes.'

'Perfect, then I will enjoy this coffee and head over.'

'Of course sir. Enjoy your stay with us.'

Norton thanked the waitress, dropped his sunglasses into place and sunk into the comfortable chair. This would do very nicely. It certainly beat poking around some damp old tunnel. He would just say his hunch came to nothing and he would be fine.

CHAPTER 15

Before long, the team were climbing the steps back towards the main road. With each step climbed, more of the car came into view. Once back at Bess's side, Matt opened the tailgate, reached in and offered bottles of water to those who wanted one. The team stood on the edge of the country lane drinking water and admiring the view.

'Afternoon.'

Still slightly on edge from their meeting with the portal, the salutation startled them all more than it should have.

Everyone turned round to meet an older man who looked to be in his fifties or sixties. He was dressed in country tweed and wellington boots; on his head, he had the requisite flat cap. The man's face was weather beaten, and his eyes were a deep blue colour that matched the colour of the water in the canal; they beamed with a brightness more akin to new light bulbs than aging eyes.

Within a few seconds of each other, the team had managed their own greetings in return.

'Out for a walk are we?'

Ava tried to place the man's accent. It was a mix of well-spoken with some West Country drawl.

Ava put money on him being a local farmer. Visually, he certainly fitted the bill.

'We were just having a walk along the old canal up to that funny looking tunnel thing.' Matt was trying to play down them being anything other than some tourist types out for a wander. He had no idea who this person was.

In an instant the stranger's face shifted. A frown rolled across his face like some dark thunderstorm rolling across the prairies.

'*Well take a warning from me,*' he practically snarled.

'*You* and *your friends* just *keep away* from *that portal*. Nothing good has *ever* come from its existence. It should be packed with high grade Octogen and blown sky high. What remains of the structure should be removed and spread across the country and used as hard-core for building roads. Then maybe it will do some good.'

'*Spread across the countryside*?' Bruno's face was showing mild annoyance. Something about the stranger was really irritating him.

'Yes, its remains should be spread far and wide to kill any of its powers, and make sure it stays dead.'

Bruno wasn't in the mood for this.

'*Whose powers – what stays dead? What the hell are you talking about*? Not The Portal surely? That's *just* a structure. It *cannot* and *does not* have any soul or powers.'

This only seemed to anger the stranger more.

'*Now you listen to me*,' he growled, 'I have lived here sixty years man and boy, and I have watched this place consume lives. It took sixteen lives when it was born; *some say built*, I say born... this place *is alive*. Then there are the Shadow Tide deaths. Every now and again, a great well of water rises up from the belly of that portal and spews forth into this pretty little artificial valley, turning it into a metaphoric bloodbath. More than thirty people have lost their lives in these Shadow Tides since that portal was born, including an entire family out for a walk. That particular day it took four generations of one family, just because it could. The scale, size and power of these tides is unnatural, and the force behind it is ancient. Modern people don't understand what they are dealing with. If the portal had felt threatened by you whilst you had been walking there, you would have joined the ranks of its other victims. *Let me be clear*; if you know what's good for you, you will all *leave, and never return*.'

Once the man had finished his rant, Matt stepped in to calm things down.

'Sorry, I didn't catch your name?'

Matt half expected the stranger to say nothing. He certainly didn't expect him to share anything personal or revealing; but it was worth a shot to defuse things. Surprisingly though, the man had no issue sharing his name.

'My name is Alastor.'

'Nice to meet you Alistair.' Matt extended and arm in order to shake hands, but none was forthcoming from the other man.

'*Al-a-stor* – not Alistair.'

'My apologies *Al-a-stor*. Look, we are not here to cause any problems, there are no signs saying to keep out, and we didn't do any damage to anything. *So*, much as it's nice talking like this, we were leaving anyway; good day to you.' Matt had made sure to show a determined stance in bringing this conversation to an end.

As Matt turned back towards the car he caught a glimpse of Alastor's face. In that instant it relaxed and was warm and welcoming again. The facial storm seemed to have passed.

'No no, my apologies, that was too strong. It's not you causing it harm that worries me; it's the other way around. I just don't want to see any more death up there, and I just wanted to make you good folk aware of this place and what is capable of. Just do me one favour before you go back there. Read your history books, do your research. There is plenty online. Good day to you all.'

'Before you go – if you don't mind me asking; do you know why this phenomenon is called a Shadow Tide? I think that's what you called it just now.'

Alastor gave Matt and then the rest of the team a look that seemed to cross somewhere between anger and concern.

'You *really* want to know?'

'I *really* want to know... *we really* want to know.' Matt decided he would put on a tone of voice equal to Alastor's; they were not going to be yelled at for no reason, whatever this guy's issue was. It worked and Alastor moderated his tone back to a more conversational one.

'I do know that as it happens. I met one of the survivors. I think he found some sort of therapy in being able to recount his story and having lived to tell the tale. He had trespassed into the portal like you lot just did.'

Matt could see Bruno was about to object, but he caught Bruno's eye and gave an almost imperceptible shake of the head; an instruction not to interrupt which Bruno understood, and so went no further with his objection.

Alastor had failed to notice and was continuing with his explanation.

'The name Shadow Tide comes simply from the characteristics of the phenomenon. They were confirmed by this survivor I talked to. He was one of these... what I think they now call urban explorers. He had gone deep into the portal in a canoe, and after a mile or so he hit a roof collapse he couldn't get past. On his long way out, he put on his headphones to listen to some music and started paddling. He said he was quite close to the mouth of the portal when it felt like some giant creature breathed down the back of his neck. The boy described how the breath got in under his collar and he could feel the dampness working its way down the skin on his back. That's known as the harbinger breath. It freaked him out, so without wanting to turn around quickly and alarm whatever was hitching a ride on his canoe; he tried to look around subtly. As his eyes looked to the side of the portal walls he was mortified to see a long black shadow bearing down on him. The next thing he knew; his vessel and he were being picked up with such force that he said he felt his body flex and fold as if he no longer had a skeleton holding everything in place. Then it went extremely cold, then... *nothing*. He woke up days later in hospital. His description to the press was simple; a cold, damp breath on the neck, a shadow bearing down on him along the walls, and then a gigantic wave of ice-cold dark water that picked him up with an unholy force of power and threw him out of the portal. I may add, leaving the poor lad with internal bleeding, broken bones and lucky to be alive; oh, and a newly acquired terror of water and tunnels.'

Alastor abruptly nodded his head to indicate he was done talking; and with that, he moved through the group, and wandered off across the bridge, up the slight incline in the road, rounded the slight bend and vanished out of sight.

There was silence between the team for a moment or two as they gave thought to what had just been said. Then Ava walked briskly in the direction that Alastor had taken. She too rounded the corner not more than a few moments after Alastor had. Ahead there was a straight couple of hundred yards of road before it turned sharp left into an embankment and railway tunnel. There was no sign of the old man at all. Ava turned round to come back to the others; stopped, and turned round again to double check her eyes were not playing tricks on her. They weren't. There was no one there and she could see clearly to the end of the road.

A shiver ran through her whole body; she turned and walked back towards the others. She was a tough, battle-hardened woman and yet her walk back to the others was definitely that little bit faster than she had consciously intended.

CHAPTER 16

Once back at the car, Ava could hear something she could not ever remember hearing before. Joe, Max and Bruno were having a discussion that was increasingly becoming an argument. The source of this disagreement was even more surprising. They were discussing the supernatural. Bruno was adamant that there was no such thing, and Joe and Max being twins, had a more liberal attitude. Mostly, the twins believed what people today labelled supernatural would be explained by science in the future, probably quantum physics. They had a level of intuition between them that seemed to be greater than most non-twin people had, so they were open minded in this respect.

Ava interrupted the conversation, *'Where's Matt?'*

That short question did exactly as she hoped; it stopped them in their tracks. They all swung round to look at her. Joe was first to talk.

'I have no idea; he was here a second ago. He can't have gone far.'

Both Joe and Max shouted at the same time, 'Matt.'

'Over here.'

'I was wondering if there was a bin anywhere

around here, but it doesn't look like it. Here you are Bruno, a bag to put your gloves in. Not having any idea what their story is, I would rather not just leave them lying on the carpet in case they stink the car out.'

Bruno took the bag and placed the gloves inside, then tied the bag shut and placed it in one of the boxes in the boot.

'Thanks, I was thinking the same thing.'

Matt shut the lower and upper tailgates.

'Right come on everyone; let's get back to the hotel.

This place was getting under all their skins. Matt could feel his heart rate lower once they were all in the car and the doors were shut. His heartbeat continued to lessen with every mile they put between themselves and the portal until it returned to a normal resting heartbeat and they were back at the hotel.

CHAPTER 17

The warm, comfortable hotel room made for the perfect antidote to their earlier venue. Norton was back with them. He had explained his hunch had come to nothing. In turn, Matt had filled Norton in on the visit to the portal.

They were all getting a drink and taking five just to chill before sitting down and having an update meeting.

Max sat down on the sofa, then lent forward towards the glass coffee table. Instantly, he shook his head and got up again.

Ava looked inquisitively at Max.

'What's up?'

'Two seconds ago I told myself I would go and get the gloves out of the car and chuck them away. Then in no time at all, I forget and sit down with a drink. I must be getting old.'

Ava laughed, 'If forgetfulness is a sign of age, I'm way ahead of you there.'

Max shook his head, 'I'd argue I was worse than you, but that's not a race I want to win. I'll be back in a second. Boss, you got Bess's key?'

Matt reached into his pocket, removed the key, and threw it to Max.

'Thanks Max, I forgot about the gloves.'

Everyone milled about for a few moments,

waiting for Max to return before starting. When he returned a few moments later, Max had a perplexed look on his face.

'Everything alright?'

'Yes, it's just that there seems to be something inside these gloves Bruno found. There is one item in each. Given where we found them, I think it is worth a quick look before we throw them out. Bruno, they were your find, do you want to do the honours?'

Bruno shook his head.

'Thanks, but no, on you go.'

Max took the gloves over to the plastic trestle table that they had setup near one of the windows. He cleared a space, placed the bag down and carefully removed the gloves. Then, he placed them on a tray to catch whatever fell out. He began to cut one of the gloves open.

The expression on Norton's face was one of concern mixed with revulsion.

'I hope there is nothing disgusting in there. I hope these aren't going to turn out to be some juvenile practical joke.'

'Yeah... I *seriously* hope not,' said Bruno.

'I know what you are both thinking, but whatever is in here is hard like rock, so I think we will be OK.'

Max had now nearly completed his cut; the age of the gloves and the time they had been lying outside meant they had no fight left to give, and they succumbed to the knife instantaneously.

Before going any further, Max reached into his pocket and pulled out a pair of disposable gloves and put them on.

'I think this might be a wise move.'

He slowly emptied the contents onto the tray; they consisted of a small lump of earth, a small rock and what looked like clear plastic that someone had drawn or written on.

'What *the hell...*'

Everyone moved in for a closer look. No one was quite sure what they were looking at. Matt suddenly announced he was getting a tension headache, and was going to go out for a wander in the hotel grounds, and needed a few minutes to shake it before it took hold and lasted all day. He passed a quiet twenty minutes walking around the lake, the light summer breeze helping to clear his headache and relax him whilst he did his breathing exercises. Turning around and walking back, he heard a voice.

'Hello.'

Matt swung round to see the familiar face of Mark coming out of a side path pushing a barrow full of earth.

'Hi Mark, busy day?'

'Yeah, we are clearing out a ditch and have to move all the soil by barrow. It's hard work.'

Something drew Matt's attention to Mark's arms, he was wearing a short sleeved t-shirt and his arm muscles were tense with the weight of the barrow. The moment Matt noticed his upper arms, a flash of realisation dawned in his mind. He had to get back to the Operations Room quickly.

'Sorry Mark, I've just realised something important relating to work, would you excuse me, I need to get back to the hotel.'

Mark nodded, 'Of course no worries.'

Matt walked back to the hotel and up to their rooms. When he entered the Operations Room again, he went straight to one of the hotel phones dotted around the room, and called down to reception.

'Housekeeping please.'

Having made his call, Matt returned to the gloves and their contents. The others joined him, having waited for his return before doing anything else.

Norton leant in even closer, 'That is the most random assortment of stuff I have ever seen. What is it, some kids, a pretend treasure map?'

Matt shook his head.

'No, it's certainly not that. Besides, I don't think any parent in their right mind would let their children play near The Portal.

There was a knock at the door, Matt went to answer it.

'Hi, come on in. Thank you very much for coming up. Ah you have it, great, thanks.'

The girl was one they had met in the car park who had told them were Pete worked. She gave Matt a sheet of paper. He came over to the table where they all were.

'Max, can you try and unfold one of these plastic sheets of paper as best you can, and cut it down one side, then spread it out flat; if I'm right it will be OK.'

Max did as he was asked. Matt grabbed himself a magnifying glass from their mobile office toolkit. He came back and carefully laid the sheet of paper he had been handed close to the clear plastic. He then lent forward and compared the two.

'*I thought so.*'

Ava stood up straight, 'What?'

'I know what this clear plastic stuff is.'

'A cry for help?'

Matt handed Ava the magnifying glass, 'What do you see?'

She took the magnifying glass and examined the piece of paper, then the clear plastic.

'*Ah*, I see what you mean.'

Norton's voice was impatient.

'*What…* what does he mean, *what* is that sheet of paper that has just been brought in?'

'*That* sheet of paper is one of the photographs from the staff break room in the old pub. It's the one showing Pete with his Tattoos.'

'And they're a match. These plastic sheets with drawings are actually a set of fresh replacement tattoos, just like Mark told us about when we met him.'

'OK,' said Norton, 'I can accept that, but what's with the rock and the earth?'

'Well for starters, that's *not earth, well not technically* I guess. It would probably be better to describe that as a sedimentary material. It's *peat…*'

Matt was about to continue, but was interrupted by Norton.

'…And if that's peat, and another word for rock is stone, suddenly we really do have *one coincidence too many.*'

'Exactly, and the scales have firmly tipped in one direction.'

Matt turned to the woman who had been kind enough to bring up the photo.

'Thank you very much indeed for bringing this. I would keep it safe for now; the police might want to see it.'

The woman left the room.

CHAPTER 18

Moments later, Matt had wheeled the whiteboard back out of the cupboard. Everyone was seated facing the board.

'I don't know about the rest of you, but that is one coincidence too many for my liking. I know we still have no proof of anything, the case is still closed and all that, but I am now firmly of the opinion that we *are* dealing with foul play. There are too many pieces now that simply don't fit with the accidental death narrative. Just because we can't yet see how they all fit together, doesn't mean they don't.'

Joe was the first with a question.

'So, you think this was Pete asking for help then?'

'I do, *yes*. From the various reports we have access to courtesy of Bella, we know Pete had no phone on him, and to date his phone has never been found. So probably he had no way of communicating. We know he is resourceful and ex-forces. Again from the reports, we know he had no car with him. So if he was trapped and thought he was going to die, he would at least try and leave a clue. It's what we would all do when faced with no other options right?'

No one objected, so Matt continued.

'Right, so he can only work with what he has to hand. Joe, empty your pockets onto the table.'

Joe did as he was asked.

'What's the first thing you have pulled out?'

'A pair of latex gloves.'

'Exactly, we all have them when we are working; many people do in these modern times. It is certainly no leap, to imagine Pete did. Also, we know for a fact from Mark that Pete carried an extra pair of replacement tattoos, which are also present. And then there is the stone and the peat.'

Max was next to speak.

'The only thing is, where did Pete get hold of any peat from? That can't be easy to get hold of in Gloucestershire at this time of year, not readily at least.'

Matt looked a little sheepish.

'*Well yes and no*. I should have said something before, *but* I have seen a stack of peat already since we have been here, it was at Nalebury Park around the back. We know from old Fred that he had seen Pete around in the grounds, what if he had helped move it. It's not a great leap of faith to assume some ended up in his pocket.'

'So that places Pete at *Nalebury*. I think it's time we dig into Mr Evelyn de Varley in much more detail.'

Random acts of vandalism with no obvious benefit at a scene where the deceased was discovered, glued padlocks and gloves spelling out the name of the subject of their investigation when put together were all beginning to spell out a very strong case for an alternative solution to the mystery of Pete Stone's death.

'OK,' said Matt, 'The next question is, what do we tell Bella?'

Max felt he should take the lead on this one.

'We tell her the *truth*; we keep *nothing* from her. That's our only option. She is strong. We have been asked by our client to uncover the truth as much as we can, so I say that is what we do. We tell her, in such terms that make her aware what each step is, so she understands the difference between theorising and proving in legal terms for a case like this. Most importantly, we make her aware there is still no proof of anything, just too many coincidences and that is what we are looking into.'

Joe offered a thought.

'I think it would be a good idea to talk to Mark again. He might be prepared to offer some more detailed insight into who Pete was workwise. That might help us work out what he was doing up here and point us in the right direction.'

Matt cleared some of the superfluous notes off the white board and wrote down the two main tasks for the rest of the day. Speak to Mark and speak to Bella and update her.

Then he spoke.

'Max, you and I and Ava will talk to Bella to update her and make a plan. Joe, Norton and Bruno, can you track down Mark, and ask if he will share anything about Pete that might point us in the right direction of what he did for work up here. I think it was way more than a security job. There are too many smoke and mirror antics for whatever he was doing work-wise to be straightforward.'

Joe, Norton and Bruno left the room in search of Mark and decided to first try the old pub. Meanwhile Max, Matt and Ava worked out what to tell Bella.

Matt outlined his plan.

'I think we should still play this investigation two days at a time maximum. We have made some inroads, but we still have nothing – well nothing concrete if you'll pardon the pun. We tell Bella that we have some avenues to explore but – well I'm sorry Max, I don't think we should tell her any specifics. We still can't be *totally* sure why she has lied to us and she has appeared here without warning. I don't want her turning up at The Portal and putting herself, or us in danger if we tell her about it.'

Max nodded, 'Good plan.'

Ava was taking notes and adding to the progress report, but instinctively nodded her head in agreement also. She trusted Max's intuition that Bella was a good sort, but equally, she understood the anguish Bella was feeling, and knew just how far off course it could take a person who was suffering this much grief; she thought Matt was right to exorcise caution.

They updated Bella on the fact the case was progressing, and that they had a couple of potential leads to follow up. They confirmed that she was happy for them to progress and report when they had more findings or in two days' time, even if there were no further developments; and they would go from there.

The others had managed to track Mark down. It was his day off and he was down the road, enjoying a pint in the beer garden of a local pub. The pub in question was only a few minutes away, and they were there in no time.

Joe sat back in his chair and turned towards Mark.

'We appreciate you can't talk about what you and Pete did in your army days, but you mentioned that when you were all done Pete went off to work on a hydroelectric dam. Can you tell us anything about that? Bella seems to know nothing.'

Mark took a long drink from his pint, held it up towards the sun, and lowering the glass to the table nodded a thank you for the pint.

'I'll tell you everything I know, but there is not very much I'm afraid. He got a job working on a very large dam construction somewhere in Germany, I think it was. He has had a beer with a work colleague from that German dam project here at the hotel. I saw them a couple of times, said hello, and Pete introduced me to him, saying they had worked together there.'

'I don't suppose you remember this man's name by any chance?'

Mark gave it a few moments thought, 'Jeff... *Jeff Pyke*.'

'Thanks.'

Bruno was taking notes on his tablet, 'What was his job there; was it site security?'

'Good God no, Pete was a highly qualified engineer, heavy engineering and construction of things like dams and tunnels for roads and railways; that was his line as well as his military background. His degree was either in civil engineering or structural engineering. I forget where from though. I must admit, I thought it odd that Pete appeared to be doing a security job given his skill set, but guessed he had his reasons for doing it. Like I said previously, he said best not to ask so I didn't. That said though, I do remember that he said he undertook corporate security work from time to time in the past when engineering work was not available, if that is what you meant; but more along your line of investigations, rather than guarding a site against intruders.'

Joe's face registered a flash of inspiration.

'He was a structural engineer working on the construction of a vast hydroelectric dam?'

Mark nodded.

'So he would know about specialist concrete then, and probably be in close proximity to it for some of the time?'

Bruno and Norton looked at each other.

Mark looked at them both.

'I guess so Joe, I have never worked on a site like that so I *wouldn't* know for sure. Why do you ask?'

'We're just trying to find out what Pete was doing up here work-wise. We don't think it was just site security either.'

Mark stared down at the floor.

'*No*, I suspect not. If his job had been simple security, he would have told me as much; there would have been no reason to swerve the question. I probably should have pushed him a bit further, I might have managed to help more.'

Without looking up Joe added.

'I think you have already helped him to be honest.'

Mark looked up from his pint.

'I don't really see how my saying what little I have will help in finding Pete's killer. That was a while ago. Also, there are no big heavy engineering projects around here.'

'Not current ones, *no*,' remarked Bruno.

Mark looked towards Bruno, he was clearly thinking for a moment before speaking.

'The only large scale engineering project around here that I have heard speak of was the renovation of the old canal tunnel; but that's been derelict for years, and the project never came to fruition from what I understand. I'm not surprised; the restoration costs would be insane.'

'No, I *agree in principle*,' said Bruno, 'Though we

have been there for a look. There is something going on there, it's certainly *not* abandoned; I think the renovation project may actually have been underway for quite some time, and that Pete was involved somehow. There are a couple of things pointing us in that direction at the moment, and we don't have anything else, so will have to go with that for now.'

Mark looked surprised.

'*Why the hell* would anyone want to waste millions on renovating an old canal tunnel, there would be no commercial benefit.'

Bruno gave a nod, 'That's something we are going to look into, but for now, we have no more idea than anyone else.'

Mark said nothing; instead, he finished off the rest of his pint.

The conversation turned to small talk once more before Bruno, Joe and Norton headed back, leaving Mark where they had found him; enjoying his well-earned day off.

CHAPTER 19

Once again, they were back in the Operations Room. Ava had looked up the name Alastor online and found the only thing that came back as a name, other than for an animal was as that of a demon; specifically, one concerned with exacting retribution. She explained the other meaning was that of a baddie or scoundrel in ancient Greek, and lastly – it was the name given to one of the four horses that belonged to Hades. They had all given the matter of Alastor further consideration, and the consensus for now was that until there was evidence to the contrary, he would be viewed as a harmless old eccentric. Every member of the team had grown up in the British countryside and knew such characters to be relatively commonplace.

Matt noticed that Ava looked anxious.

'Are you *OK*?'

'I am thanks. But I think we need to take all this demon business seriously.'

Norton let out a loud laugh.

'You think we should take demons *seriously*?'

Ava's nostrils flared and she stared at Norton.

'*No*, I *don't* think we should take demons seriously, *but* I do think we should pay attention and respect how seriously the locals might take them.

Matt gave Norton a look that made it clear he was unhappy with his behaviour.

'Go on Ava, explain what you mean.'

'It's just that we are still dealing with a pretty ancient place. I think that sort of history demands respect. Especially given there have been a lot of deaths up there. We know about the ones when the place was built, and if Alastor is correct then there have been even more deaths recently.'

Norton gave a small shake of the head.

'*So what* – you're saying there *is* something sinister up there and we *need to be careful*?"

'*No, that's not* what I am saying. What I am saying is the place is steeped in history and associated with an abnormally high percentage of deaths. Factors like those feature very strongly in the psyches of the people living in close proximity to such places. It becomes part of their folklore – their narrative, and can have a noticeable psychological effect. *That's all I am saying*. It is important to respect the beliefs and values of the community you're based in, even if you are only there on a temporary basis. If you just trample all over everything – there will be consequences. That is what I am talking about – not spooks and the supernatural, but simple human nature in terms of the collective unconscious. *We ignore that at our peril*.'

'Thanks Ava,' said Matt, 'That's *good advice* and we *shall all* heed it. We don't need any more problems than we already have trying to get to the bottom of this case.'

Matt was swiping through his tablet and took a moment to think before continuing.

'Right, so on top of what we already know; I see from Bruno's meeting notes, that Mark says Pete was a highly specialist engineer, and that although he had done corporate security investigations in the past, it is very unlikely that he was doing a site guarding security job. I think our next focus needs to be on Evelyn de Varley and this Shadow Tide phenomena that Alastor character was on about. Norton, you and I will investigate de Varley, as I have an idea of who might be able to help; Joe Ava Bruno and Max, can you guys investigate the Shadow Tide subject, that would be great. Then in a couple of hours' time, we can all meet up and go from there.'

With that, Matt pulled out his phone and dialled a number, then got up and walked out onto the Balcony, 'Oliver Scott please…Ollie, its Matt, how are you? Good. I wanted to ask if you knew someone by the name of Evelyn de Varley…'

CHAPTER 20

After what felt like very little time, the team assembled to share what information they had managed to find out. On both subjects, there was very little online information. Matt updated them all on what extra he and Norton had managed to find out; namely that Evelyn de Varley seemed to have been the owner of a hedge fund which they already knew, was reputedly worth in excess of five billion pounds; also that he was single, and exceptionally secretive. The manor seemed to have been owned by an offshore company for the last thirty-five years, so it was not possible to establish how long it had been in Evelyn de Varley's possession.

In relation to the Shadow Tide side of things, the others could find no reference to them going back further than fifteen years. The official version of events was that The Shadow Tide phenomenon was a genuine thing. There had been six deaths in total, three individual deaths, and one family of three. In every case the bodies had been found along the tow path, their lungs full of water and their bodies battered and bruised. The dead were either children or older people. It appeared that the local papers were the first to use the name Shadow Tide after the second death, which led the team to assume it was the press that came up with the name. These small findings were enough to put the final nail in the coffin of anything Alastor had to say about Shadow Tides being ancient, and that there had been thirty deaths.

The real surprise had come when Ollie had told Matt that he did know Evelyn de Varley and that after speaking with him, Evelyn, who had somehow heard of the team's investigations had invited the whole team to dine at the manor.

Joe offered the first thought out loud on that news.

'Well either our Mr de Varley has everything to hide, or nothing to hide with an offer like that.'

'Yeah, either a genuine offer of help,' said Max 'Or an attempt to find out what we know and start a cover-up.'

Matt came back in from making another call.

'A courier company will be delivering our black-tie outfits from the office this afternoon.'

He continued, 'I think the plan is going to be to glean what information we can out of tomorrow night's dinner party. Be aware we might be being watched from now on. Let's not forget just how different the world becomes when you're a billionaire. If there is something going on, we are probably well out of our depth, and we probably won't be able to see the full game plan. Mere mortals like us don't see things through the same lens as billionaires.'

'Is their world really *that* different?' asked Norton.

'From what little I have witnessed of it, yes.'

'I saw something about this online,' said Ava 'That really put things into perspective. I cannot remember the exact reference, but it was using units of time to demonstrate the vast difference between a million and a billion.'

Ava checked her tablet.

'Yes here we are, so a million seconds is twelve days, whereas a billion seconds is just over thirty-one years. I am not sure if that is factually accurate, but it makes the point.'

Everyone widened their eyes in support of quite how wide the gap was.

'So, there we are guys,' said Matt, '*keep your wits about you*; we are entering another world, we should be on our highest alert. If some game is being played, the stakes will be extremely high indeed.'

Ava shivered a little.

'High enough to potentially warrant a murder.'

'High enough to warrant *more* than one murder; I'm afraid. Right, as tomorrow night is work, I strongly suggest you all get some rest, and have as relaxing an afternoon and evening as you can today. I need to go and call Bella.'

'Bella – *why*?'

'Because Max, Bella has also been invited to the party. De Varley has confided to Ollie that Pete did work for him, and he wants to meet and pass on his condolences to Pete's widow.'

'Would you mind if I made the call?'

Matt smiled and handed Max his phone.

'Tell her its black tie and please Max, impress upon her how important it is to keep calm, and not give away too much.'

Max put his hand on Matt's shoulder.

'I will make very sure of that boss, assuming she can come.'

Matt gave Max a knowing look.

'Something tells me *she'll be here*.'

'Hello Bella?... Sorry about that – its Max, how are you?'

Ava turned to the room.

'I think I am going to go and rent a pushbike from up the road, and go for a cycle, anyone fancy joining?'

There were no takers, Joe said he thought he would go for a swim in the hotel pool.

Before she left the room to change, Ava turned to Matt.

'Is Ollie coming to this dinner too?'

'He sure is. He is in Europe this morning, so will fly into the airport that's two miles from the manor, and he will meet us there.'

'Great, it's been an age since I saw him.'

The next 24 hours passed without issue. The team took some time to chill out and recharge their batteries. They all knew this dinner party had the potential to go one of two ways. Whichever of those two ways it went though, it would certainly be enlightening.

When the time came around the following evening, they all gathered in the Operations Room at 6:30pm for the briefing. Nothing new was imparted, just a reminder to everyone to be on their guard. Everyone already was. On some level, they all had a feeling that Mr de Varley was involved, or at least aware of what really happened to Pete. Everyone looked impeccable.

There was a knock at the door and Matt went to answer it.

'Bella good evening, come in.'

Max smiled at Bella when he saw her. She smiled equally strongly back at him and walked over to join him after saying hello to Matt. She was wearing a long black dress that fitted her perfectly.

'You still scrub up well Max.'

'Well so do you kiddo, you look fantastic, and that dress looks superb.'

Bella lent forward to mock whisper in Max's ear, 'One of the perks of working in the fashion industry; I get to borrow some dresses that often require a second mortgage.'

Max copied Bella's mock whisper, 'Well it suits you kiddo, definitely triple A rated.'

Ava wandered over to say hi to Bella, and they were both quickly commenting on each other's dresses. Ava also looked fantastic in a shimmering, but understated dark purple dress. The two quickly sank into more technical dress chat that went straight over Max's head. He asked Bella and Ava what they would like to drink and headed off to get what they both requested.

Bella watched Max head back to the drinks table once he had ensured everyone had what they wanted. She whispered in a conspiratorial manner to Ava.

'Wow, they are a good-looking bunch of men; they look good in their black ties.'

Ava looked around the room nodding.

'They sure do, not that I get to see many of them dressed up like this very often. It is very unusual indeed to have to dress up like this to talk to a client, it should be an interesting night. Has Max told you the plan?'

'He has Ava, yes. This Mr de Varley has admitted to being Pete's boss, and you all think he knows more than he is saying about Pete's death.'

'That's about the size of it. We are not sure what this grand gesture is all about, but we will find out by the end of the evening. Are you comfortable, got everything you need?'

Bella nodded, 'Yes thanks, all sorted.'

Matt clinked his glass.

'Right, I think it is time we headed out to the cars. Just to reconfirm what everyone already knows; the aim of this evening is just to find out as much as you can, without arousing any suspicion of our having Mr de Varley in the crosshairs. Whoever else is at this dinner party, don't trust them. You just don't know who they really are. I cannot over-emphasise caution over everything else. If we come away with nothing, but haven't tipped our hand, I will still be happy with that. Once we are in the cars, no discussing the case, keep to small talk. I'm sure there will be no listening devices on the manor drive etc. but such kit does exist, so let's assume nothing is safe until we are back here later. Any questions?'

Norton was the only one to speak out.

'So you say we are not to trust anyone we meet at the party, but won't Oliver be there?'

Everyone laughed including Matt.

'Yes OK Norton, we all know we can trust Ollie. He is family after all. It goes without saying we all trust each other.'

They headed down to the reception area. As they walked through reception and out into the car park, they drew plenty of admiring looks; the two women leading, the five men following up behind.

The party of seven split up into the two waiting vehicles, then headed off to the manor. Before long, the cars were pulling through the large black and gold wrought iron gates. They parked up and walked to the front door. As they reached it, the door slowly opened to reveal a fully uniformed butler beckoning them all inside.

'Perhaps he did it,' Bruno muttered under his breath. Those that heard stifled their laughs professionally enough.

Matt and Norton took up the rear. Nothing

could quite have prepared them for the interior of the house. Matt registered his surprise at the museum quality artworks dripping off the walls. Norton simply shook his head.

The butler had closed the front door and was now moving through the group, ushering them through some highly polished double doors into the drawing room.

As they followed across the hall, towards the drawing room, Norton nodded in the direction of a painting that looked quite modern.

'Is that a Jackson Pollock?'

Matt looked at the painting and shook his head.

'I wouldn't have a clue to be honest; I don't really know anything about art.'

Norton moved in to look a little closer.

'How do they even know if it's the right way up?'

'*Because* they have taken care to study the artist and his work, and they collect it for love. Your line *is* amusing... *somewhat clichéd* ...but amusing.'

The deep, powerful voice from behind them slightly startled Matt and Norton. They turned to face the direction the voice had come from. Before them stood a middle aged, very athletic framed, tall businessman. He was wearing an expensive suit.

The man to whom the voice belonged, smiled and seemed to genuinely being enjoying the encounter.

'You must be Matthew Holland, pleased to meet you, I am Evelyn de Varley.' He then turned to Norton. 'And you are....?'

'Norton Graey Mr de Varley.'

Evelyn de Varley shook hands with both Matt and Norton in turn.

'Please don't be formal, call me Evo, all my friends do. Come on in; let's get you both a drink.'

He ushered Matt and Norton further along the hall and on into the drawing room. On the right, a majestic staircase swept up to the first floor. The threesome entered the drawing room through the double doors where they joined the others. There was yet more museum level art in this room consisting of paintings, sculpture and furniture. The delicate furniture was placed around the outside of the room whilst in the centre there were three large comfortable sofas, and matching chairs.

Norton made his excuse and said he needed to freshen up, and wandered off back out of the drawing room to find the loo.

Good luck, thought Matt. Norton seems a bit confident he will find the cloakroom on his own. Then Matt's focus turned back to the room and why they were there.

The butler had already attended to the rest of the group who were all holding various drinks. The team all made small talk between themselves as Evo worked the room. There was another couple there also, an older couple looking like they had reached retirement age. Matt heard part of the conversation of them introducing themselves to Joe and Max. Matt reckoned Evo had deliberately invited these extra people to ensure he could not be ambushed with uncomfortable questions. He knew Matt and his team would do nothing to embarrass Ollie. Typical billionaire thought Matt, very forward thinking and determined to control everything to his ultimate benefit. There is no way we are going to learn anything this evening he doesn't want us to. Damn it.

Matt watched as Evo spent a good few minutes laughing and joking with Ollie and a third man who had grey hair and a natural looking tan. The three of them seemed to know each other quite well. At that moment, Norton re-entered the room, so had obviously got lucky with his search for the cloakroom.

Bella leant in subtly towards Ava.

'Who is that handsome man with Ollie and our host? The one with the grey hair.'

Ava studied the man as closely as she could without being obvious.

'I am afraid I don't know.'

From behind them an unfamiliar female voice spoke up.

'His name is Jonathan. He is a business associate and acquaintance of my boss. It was he who gave Mr Scott a lift on his private plane.'

Ava and Bella turned to face the voice. Their

eyes met a short, late middle aged and immaculately dressed woman who was holding an empty tray down her side in one hand.

'Thank you,' Bella smiled. 'I probably should not be so direct, but I was just very taken by his appearance.'

'Not at all ma'am.'

I am Bella and this is Ava, who are you?

'I am Eva Veresum ma'am. I am housekeeper to Mr de Varley.'

Before she could stop herself, Bella asked about the close sounding names.

'Your name is Eva and you work for a man called Evo, does that not get confusing?'

Eva's face drained of colour and any life.

'No ma'am not really, I wouldn't dream of being so familiar as to address my employer as Evo. To me, he is Mr Evelyn, Sir or Mr de Varley.'

Bella blushed thinking she should not have said anything.

'*Of course*, good point.'

Bella had hoped to engage the woman further in conversation; but with the ease of a professional who was well seasoned in working at social engagements, she had vanished without appearing rude.

Bella turned to Ava, and pulled a joking anxious face.

'*Wow* these sort of staff take life a bit too seriously don't they? I was only making a joke, but she seems to be horrified at the thought of any familiarity between her and her boss. Guess that's how it is in this world; I am glad I'm not part of it.'

Ava and Bella were about to continue talking further when Evelyn de Varley appeared in front of them.

'Mrs Stone?'

Bella and Ava turned to meet him.

'My name is Evo. I was your husband's employer. I am deeply sorry for your loss; he was a good man.'

'*Thank you.*'

Evo continued, 'I would like an opportunity to talk to you properly if that is OK, in private? Shall we go to my study *now*? Would that be OK?'

As Bella's brain was working out how best to handle this offer and what answer to give, her mouth opened, and she heard her voice saying, 'Yes of course.'

Evo smiled, 'Great, come this way.' He took Bella's arm in such a way that she realised she was now committed to the move, but she did not in any way feel threatened.

Evo turned to Ava, 'Please excuse us.'

They passed from the window, through the middle of the room to the door, and out into the hall. Just before leaving the room they passed Matt who was talking to Ollie.

Without showing any concern outwardly at all Matt turned to Bella.

'Everything alright Bella, are you feeling OK?'

'Yes thanks Matt; I just want a word with Mr de Varley – sorry Evo about Pete. We will be back in a moment.'

Bella and Evo crossed the hall and went deeper into the house. Finally, they reached another set of doors. He pressed his thumb into a small dark panel on the door which lit up blue; there was a motorised click, and he turned the knob and pushed the door open. Evo then beckoned Bella to head inside; this she did.

Bella reckoned they were on the other side of the house. This room was a smaller version of the drawing room they had just come from. This time though, there was an enormous partner's desk in the expansive bay window area.

Befitting for a man with a hedge fund I guess, thought Bella. She was surprised to see how clear the desk was. There was a pot to hold some pens, a closed leather-bound folder in the centre of the area right in front of the big leather arm-chair, and a large business phone to one side with a stretched curly cord that spoke of much use. There was a bronze of a man on a horse with some dogs and two antique lamps, one on either side of the desk. Just like the rest of the hall and the drawing room, there was a heavy smell of highly polished Oak.

'Please Bella, come and take a seat.' Bella did as she was requested.

'I am glad to have finally met you. I wanted to apologise and explain why I had not made contact, as well as explain all the secrecy around Pete's employment.'

Bella's eyes widened, she wanted to know for herself so much, but also, she felt part of the team, and did not want to let Max, Matt and the others down. She tried to subtly reach into her clutch bag and swipe her phone's voice recording app into life. It was proving to be a struggle to get it to work.

Her odd movements caught Evo's eye.

'Is everything alright?'

'Oh yes thanks, *sorry*, I was looking for a hanky, I don't want to cry but I might.'

'Of course, I understand.' With that he passed her a box of tissues from a side table.

'Thank you.'

For some reason, a generalised panic was building up in Bella's mind. She felt she had to say something neutral to cancel it.

'Your housekeeper seems nice?' As soon as she heard the words come out of her mouth, she realised it sounded odder than a silence would have. Calm down, Bella told herself.

Evo looked at her quizzically, but that soon changed to a smile.

'*Yes* she is.'

The smile vanished as quickly as it had arrived.

The enormous partner's desk that currently separated them made it truly clear who was in charge, and reminded Bella to keep her wits about her. Unlike Evo's momentary candour about mundane domestic life, that desk was definitely in keeping with the style and trappings of a billionaire.

Bella realised she was just going to have to commit everything she was about to hear to memory. She tried to remain calm and control her breathing.

'Right Bella, where do I begin...'

CHAPTER 21

In the drawing room, Ava moved over to join Max and Matt.

'Is everything going to be alright do you think? – Does one of us need to make an excuse and go and find them?'

Max shook his head.

'No need, Bella will be fine.'

'You are right Max, of course. I was just worried.'

'Bella would be *delighted* that you care Ava. I think she will be fine though. Another drink anyone?'

They all nodded. Max subtly moved his empty glass into wider view of the room whilst talking to Ava and Matt. The butler noticed, and soon their glasses were refilled.

Bruno had made an excuse to head to the loo, and had annoyingly been directed where to go by the butler. He had hoped to be able to have a snoop on his own. Having finished and washed up, he headed back. Entering the hall, he noticed there was no one around. He could hear the voices coming from the drawing room. On his way back he tried various doors, but they were all locked.

That's a bit odd is it not, he thought to himself.

Heading back to the drawing room he passed the open doors to the dining room. It was all set for the evening and the candles were already lit. There was one more set of doors to try; Bruno decided to risk it. He got to the large set of veneered double doors and tried the handle. It opened. He pushed the door open, closing his eyes a little in case the doors emitted a squeak or worse, triggered an alarm. Neither seemed to happen. When the door was open wide enough, Bruno stepped into the room, it was in total darkness. He reached for the wall and to his delight instantly made contact with the light switch panel. He let out a small chuckle to himself; he couldn't even manage that at home when he knew where the light switches were.

The room was warm and had the same oak panelling smell as the rest of the house. Bruno flicked a couple of switches and the room revealed itself. It was almost as large as the drawing room, but instead of sofas and chairs taking up the majority of the space, there in the centre of the room was a full-sized billiard table. The balls were all laid out waiting for a new frame to be played.

Bruno quickly cast his eye around the room before turning to leave. That was his intention anyway. However he was stopped in his tracks. On the wall to his left was the most stunning oil painting; it was a landscape. Even from where he stood, Bruno could tell it was old. He didn't know how old; he was not an art expert, but he had seen enough great works in his time in art galleries to recognise something when it was this special.

He wanted to go closer and get a better look, but knew he had better not. There may well be some sort of proximity alarm. With that Bruno took a step back, turned off the lights, quietly closed the door, and headed back to join the others hoping that his extended absence had not been noticed.

Across the hall, Bella had made herself comfortable and got herself as calm as she could be. In recent months, she had spent her every waking moment pushing and pushing for a truth she was convinced was being kept from her. Now that there was a chance to get to this truth, she was not about to blow it by panicking.

Evo sat himself down behind his desk, and lowered his chair so his eye level matched Bella's; a polite gesture that she appreciated.

'As I say, *where to begin…*'

Bella looked him straight in the eye and smiled in order to put him at his ease.

'Anywhere you choose Evo.'

'Alright then. Before I begin, I need to ask you to agree to total confidentiality in respect of what I am about to tell you. Not from your friends here tonight – I understand that would be too big of an ask, but from everyone outside this house; please don't discuss what I am about to tell you with another living soul, ever.'

Bella gave an earnest look.

'Of course Evo, *of course.*'

'Well, I am not sure if you are aware, but I manage a hedge fund based in London.'

'Chantmarle Capital – Yes I have heard of it; I have certainly read about it.'

'That's correct. Well, I am not sure how much you know about the financial world, but currently it is becoming increasingly difficult for hedge funds like ours to keep a competitive advantage. We still have our methods, but some of my people noticed that one of our competitors was always acting on the same information we had gathered. They were always just ahead of us over several different sectors and industries; after a detailed investigation we found – well – we found nothing at all. That told me one thing.'

Bella didn't mean to, but she had interrupted before she could stop herself.

'It told you that you had a leak somewhere inside the business, and you needed someone from the outside to investigate.'

Evo sat still for a moment, his mouth slightly open before he composed himself.

'I could not have put it better myself. What *did* you say you did for a living?'

Bella laughed, 'I didn't.'

Evo continued.

'Well that is where your husband came in. I used a security consultancy to identify someone to lead the charge so to speak, and after an exhaustive search, I chose your husband.'

Now it was Bella's turn to sit in silence for a moment. She was learning something new about her beloved husband, and hopefully moving things slowly towards finding out how he really died. Nothing the team had uncovered did anything to persuade Bella that she might be wrong. Her gut had been right all along. There was way more to her husband's death than misadventure. Bella brought herself back into the room realising Evo was waiting for her to speak. She had missed what he had said, so went with the safe guess of, 'OK.'

That seemed to work.

'Because of not knowing who I could trust at the office, Pete was to be based here at Nalebury, but we had a cover story that he ran security for a house I own near Reading.'

'So that is why Pete was out this way then, he worked from this building.'

Evo looked around the room and nodded, 'Yes, he was based here. I should mention he did ask if he could tell you the truth once you were married, but I said no. He did want to though.'

'And – the disused quarry where his body was found, that is yours too?'

'I am afraid not. I have *nothing* to do with that.'

'Oh, so you can't shed any light on why he was found dead there?'

'I am really sorry Bella, *I cannot*. Pete was not

even supposed to be here that day. As far as I was aware, he was in London following up a lead.'

Not being able to think of what to ask next, Bella began to panic; silence crept into the room like an asphyxiating gas. Her worry that she was missing a key question to ask grew with every moment, as did the tightening in her chest. She worried that with every second of silence, her chance to interrogate this secretive man was slipping away. In the end Evo spoke first.

'Look, I am so sorry there is nothing more I can tell you. Pete was my lead investigation on this, helping me orchestrate the best approach to catching the culprits. He was superb at his job. I wish I had more to offer but I don't. The rest of the details are specific to the hunt for the mole. If I thought for one second any of it was relevant, I would share it with the police, and with you guys. Thing is though, what I am dealing with here is white collar crime. It will most likely turn out to be someone taking some financial kick-back for passing on information. That is quite different to murdering someone, not to mention I don't think it would be worth anyone's while.'

Bella thought for a moment.

'Well excuse me for being so blunt Evo, but are you not a billionaire. Are the sums of money involved not at the level where someone might be prepared to kill?'

Evo looked a little taken aback.

'On paper – *yes* – I am a billionaire, but the

fraudulent transactions I am talking about are in the hundreds of thousands and maybe single millions, not more than that. Those sums are standard for a hedge fund to deal in, they are not exceptional, so I don't think the risk ratio is up there for murder.'

Evo stood up.

'If you don't have any other questions shall we return to the others?'

Bella also stood up.

'Of course. I really do appreciate you telling me all this. I know you were under no obligation to do so, and I do thank you very much.'

Evo came close.

'It is my pleasure, and if there is ever anything I can do for you – *please*, you only have to ask.'

Bella looked directly into Evo's eyes. They were kind eyes; there was a good soul in there somewhere, she thought. She gently put her hand on his, '*Thank you Evo.*'

They headed back to the drawing room. Evo walking with Bella, her arm through his like she had seen on so many romantic films. She appreciated the support; she was not used to high heels and the variation of solid, highly polished wooden floors and rugs that were not fixed down.

They stopped in the doorway and everyone swung round to face them.

'I am sorry everyone for keeping you so long. Shall we go and eat? Please – follow us.' Evo waved a hand gesture to back-up his sentence.

They entered the dining room and Bella thought it very definitely a room decorated to a man's taste. The panelling on the wall was very dark, matching the floor. Large tapestries hung on two of the walls. One wall housed the two windows, and only a quartet of small oil paintings of hunting scenes. On the other wall with the fireplace hung three much larger portraits in oil of various smart looking gentlemen. The butler made sure Ava found her seat, whilst Evo showed Bella to her seat on his right at the head of the table. Opposite her, on Evo's left, was Matt. With everyone being seated, the butler left and closed the doors.

Bella placed her clutch bag on the floor after she had sat down. She noticed Evo, who was now also seated pressing a silver button in the floor with his foot. After a minute, the doors opened and the butler walked back in first, followed by three smartly dressed younger men all carrying various dinner related silver trays. Drinks were poured, and the commencement of the meal followed.

The party dined on Gravadlax followed by Rib of Beef and then some insanely delicious cream and fruit pudding. As the two designated drivers for the night, Matt and Max felt they had drawn the short straws when they saw the special New Zealand white wine served with the fish and the red 2005 Pomerol that was served with the beef.

The meal passed quickly and was as enjoyable as any meal where you were on your guard and working could be.

They adjourned back to the drawing room afterwards for coffee to finish off the night. Jonathan and the other couple made their good nights and retired for the evening. Ava took her seat as a natural lull in conversations fell across the room. Norton took this opportunity to follow a hunch. Deciding directness might be the best approach, he looked straight at their host who was sitting on the club fender by the fire and began.

'We were out and about the other day and came across this old, abandoned tunnel which one of the locals said you own; *is that correct*? And – if so – what are you going to do with it?'

The instant Matt realised what Norton was doing, his mind went into overdrive, and it felt like his heart rate and blood pressure headed far north of what was normal and safe. Norton, what are you playing at? The question rang out loudly in Matt's head, though to the rest of the room his face registered no change in mood.

As soon as he heard the word tunnel, Matt closely watched Evelyn – who by now had insisted everyone call him Evo, to see any tell-tale signs of being caught out.

'Nothing… not even a flinch.'

He is either well prepared or has nothing to hide, thought Matt.

Evo looked very relaxed and turned more central to the room, rather than solely towards Ollie, with whom he had been talking.

'Well, I was hoping to keep my ownership of the tunnel quiet, and I have gone to some considerable lengths to do so, but obviously my big secret is out. *Yes* – I do indeed own The Nalebury Portal. What do you think of it?'

Bruno who had not said much that evening chipped in.

'Unbelievable is the word I would choose, perhaps remarkable also if I was pushed to choose two words.'

Evo grinned like a child with a new toy to show off to his mates.

'*Yes*, it is a very strange place isn't it. Pretty remarkable feat of engineering by the looks of things.'

'What's with all those stone theatrics on the façade?' It was Joe's turn to join the conversation.

'Truth be told, I'm not sure. All I do know is that it wasn't always forgotten and abandoned. It was once a major tourist attraction; even Royalty visited. I guess it was to make more of an occasion for those who had travelled so far to see the place. After all, there is nothing to see inside, especially back then when there was no electricity and only lamps to light your way.'

Joe continued, 'Have you ventured inside?'

'I have, a little way in. There is a roof collapse, so I have not been further than that. It's not safe.

You guys didn't go in did you?' Evo looked around the room.

Matt spoke up before anyone else, 'No, we didn't, we just admired the façade and then left.'

Evo gave a short nod.

'Good, *please be careful*, it's an *extremely dangerous* place, I would rather you stayed away from it to be honest. *I don't want anyone getting hurt.*'

Matt decided it was his turn to push a bit more. He wasn't happy that Norton had started this, but it had provided some information so he thought they might as well keep going.

'Dangerous – do you mean these *Shadow Tides*?' Matt was watching Evo even more closely now; mind you so was everyone else except for Ollie.

Evo's face straightened a little.

'*No I do not*, that is just an old wives' tale dreamt up by bored villagers and the local press to dramatize some accidental drownings; there is no such thing as a Shadow Tide.'

Ava looked puzzled.

'But they are referenced in relation to real deaths around The Portal are they not?'

'They are by locals and the media. In reality all of those deaths were due to drowning, not anything supernatural. That tunnel is just a large hole in the ground that is two miles long and lined with brickwork. There is nothing else to it. It was a crazy thing to attempt when it was built, that is why so many people died. It was humans just pushing boundaries beyond what was possible, and as a result people died. Of course, that doesn't make a good story in the pub does it, so it has to grow arms and legs.'

By now Evo was losing some of his sheen.

'I am sorry, I know you were just asking, but all that sort of talk annoys me. I want to turn it into a tourist attraction, re-open it and run boat trips from this end all the way through to the other side and on for a few miles. It is already going to be a risky venture; I don't need local gossip putting the project in jeopardy.'

Evo paused to take a drink from his large whisky.

'*Who* put you on to this Shadow Tide nonsense anyway?'

'We met some strange man. He approached us back at the car when we finished our walk back from your tunnel. He started ranting about the Shadow Tide and how the place was possessed and haunted etcetera,' said Matt.

Evo took another drink from his glass and muttered.

'For goodness sake – Did *this idiot* have a name?'

'Yes, he called himself Alastor.'

Evo gave a single jolted laugh.

'*Oh* him... he is a pain in the backside, enough said.'

After that Evo's mood lifted and they all spent the next twenty minutes making small talk. Matt led the conversation into thanking Evo very much for all his hospitality, but that they should probably be leaving. They said goodbye to Ollie in the drawing room, and then all said thank you and goodnight to Evo on the doorstep. The evening had turned cold, and everyone's breath was visible, the car windows had condensation on the outside. They walked across to the cars. Halfway, Bella turned back, returned to Evo and gave him a light kiss on the cheek.

'*Thank you.*' She whispered before returning to the cars.

Ava lent forward from the back seat, 'So is Ollie staying there the night then? I didn't know he knew Evo that well?'

Matt glanced at her in the rear-view mirror, 'No – neither did I to be honest.'

Before long they were all back in the hotel room. Bella and Ava both kicked off their high heels and flopped on the sofa. Max and Joe got everyone a drink. Everyone had plumped for a tall glass of cold water.

Joe looked at Matt, 'Didn't you guys recognise Evo's house keeper?'

Matt gave a pensive look, 'No, should we?'

'It's the woman we met in The Wellspring pub with Old Fred. She was the one that served us, and drove him back to Nalebury.'

'So she probably tipped Evo off then, that's probably how he knew we were here. What's up Max, something troubling you?'

'No, not really, just unimpressed with Evo; he clearly doesn't pay his house keeper well if she has to work in his pub kitchen as well. I can't say I like the guy.'

'Indeed.' Matt pulled the whiteboard around to face everyone.

'So, what did we think of this evening then?' Matt cleared a space on the board, 'Anything we need to be writing down?'

In truth there were only two areas to examine. They waited to be updated on what Bella and Evo had talked about and to go over any plans as a result.

Bella recounted step by step what happened in Evo's study. Matt made a few notes on the board, and then asked Bella what overall feeling she got from Evo.

'At first, I thought he was genuine and we were barking up the wrong tree; but then he did something that made me think he *is* somehow involved, or at least he has something to hide, however minimal his involvement may be.'

'Why do you say that?'

'Because, when I said I was grateful for everything he could tell me about my husband's work life, as I knew very little, I would swear that Evo physically relaxed. His shoulders dropped at least half an inch. I notice these things.'

'It's OK Bella, we believe you. *Good job*, well done.'

Bella blushed, 'Thanks guys.'

Matt wrote The Portal on the whiteboard.

'Right, The Portal, do we believe what Evo said

about it? He was very convincing I'll give him that.' The team discussed the merits of what each of them thought for a while, but it was clear they could not draw any absolute conclusions.

It was Max who put forward the plan for the next day.

'I think we are going to have to go and have a proper look at The Portal before Evo gets a chance to put more security in place. I think we need to go and have a proper explore, and I think we need to do that tomorrow.'

After a few minutes it was agreed that they would. For now though, it was 2 a.m. and everyone needed to get some shuteye. They would meet back in the Operations Room tomorrow at 11.30 a.m. giving everyone a chance to catch up on some sleep. Tomorrow they would need their wits about them.

CHAPTER 22

Despite it being work, the evening out in different surroundings together with the good food and wine had helped relax the team enough that they all got a good night's sleep. By the time 11.30 a.m. the next morning came around, they were all refreshed and rested enough to cope with an explore of the portal.

The cars had been sorted, the correct kit placed closest to hand. A couple of inflatable dinghies with small electric motors had been purchased at 9.00 a.m., much to the delight of the lakeside shop's owner.

Max and Matt had had a meeting with Bella who had taken the day off to stay and be involved. She had agreed to a further two days funding. Bella had pushed very strongly to come with them to the portal, but Matt was equally forceful. Bella accepted that the team could not be totally free to devote all their attention to their investigation if they had to keep an eye out for her.

Before long the two cars parked in the same spot as they had before. They had looked on the map and did not fancy parking anywhere else. Matt had texted with Ollie that morning to find out if he had stayed overnight. He had. Matt asked Ollie if he would distract Evo for the morning. Ollie had said he and Jonathan had some stuff to discuss with Evo so it should not be too difficult, and would do his best. Hopefully that would just buy the team enough time to have one quick look around inside the portal.

If Alastor re-appeared and started to have a go, they would cross that bridge – so to speak – when they came to it. Everyone put on the lightweight body suits they had been given. Attached the non-slip soles to their boots, and began carrying the boxes containing the dinghies and the motors down the path towards the bridge, then back along the towpath.

Once at the entrance, Ava ran through the instructions for inflating the dinghies. It's pretty simple apparently. You just open the top of the box, fold the top right back so it is not in the way and then pull the orange ripcord. The dinghy will instantly inflate itself, popping out of the box. Just make sure the ground all around the box is free of anything very sharp.

This they did, and before them, where moments ago there was only two large boxes, now sat two brand new bright red four-man inflatable dinghies. A few moments later, the two small electric outboard motors had been fitted, and the dinghies carried to the entrance of the portal. The strange concrete ramp sloping down into the water meant that they had to carefully carry the boats for the first few feet into the canal.

Once they had done so, they carefully climbed aboard the dinghies; taking care to place their boots on the floor mats that Ava had the sense to bring from both the cars. She was pretty sure the studs in their boots would burst the floor of the dinghies without too much problem. They adjusted the depth of the outboard motor's propellers to the shallowest settings that would still allow good steering and propulsion.

Matt in one boat and Joe in the other were in charge of the super bright LED lights they had brought with them. They powered them up, and suddenly the thick curtain of darkness was instantly pulled back with a super bright and very clinical light. Ava looked as far forward as her eyes would let her see. She was wrong – the curtain had not been pulled back, it had simply retreated much further into the portal. It was still there, only much further back now, and served to give some indication of just how long this tunnel was.

Matt whispered, 'Right is everyone ready?'

Despite his whispering, everyone heard him as if they were standing right next to him – such were the acoustics in this weird place.

Everyone quietly spoke, '*Yes.*'

Matt signalled forward to Norton who was operating the forward boat, and with a gentle hum and a gurgle of water, they slowly moved deeper into the bowels of the portal; with no idea what they were about to encounter. Norton had managed to find an app that would tell them how far they had travelled with or without phone service, which oddly seemed to be stronger in the portal than out.

The journey was uneventful and took a while. There was just row upon row of the same painted brickwork whenever they cast the beam from one of the torches over the walls.

It seemed like quite some time before Matt finally spoke.

'Ah the back wall. Slow down guys. How far have we come Norton?'

Norton looked at the data his app was providing, '2958 meters and it has taken us about half an hour.'

Matt swung round to face the middle of the boat, 'What's that in old money?'

Norton did some quick mental calculations before choosing the conversion on the app to see how close he was.

'About 1.833 miles. Is that the end, I see brickwork; it looks a different colour though.

The torch Matt was holding nodded slightly with Matt's movement.

'Yes we are at the end. It's not a wall though, it looks like the roof.'

Ava and Bruno chorused together, 'The roof?'

'Yes,' Matt whispered, 'It looks like the roof has fallen in, and not recently.'

He shone the torch up to the ceiling. It was there, but with a different type of brick to the ones blocking their way, 'I guess the roof is unstable and the old brickwork not up to it anymore. I think someone has repaired the roof with a more modern and durable brick, and not bothered to haul all the old bricks back out yet. I guess Evo wants it kept blocked to stop people playing in here. I guess no one has come through here in a long time.'

Both dinghies were side by side now, and it was Joe who replied to Matt.

'You're wrong boss; at least I think you are.'

'What makes you say that?'

'What have we not encountered on our way along here, that if the place was abandoned, we definitely should have?'

Max answered his brother instantly; his brain had picked up exactly the same missing element.

'Ah yes, what's in every spooky story you read, and what have we not encountered in here. We certainly should have but we haven't.'

'*Cobwebs*,' said Norton in quite a loud voice, 'Not a single cobweb in the place. I have more cobwebs in my house than there are in this portal. That's not right – *that's not right at all*.'

They all agreed. Matt thought for a moment.

'Who has the selfie-stick?'

It was handed to him. He placed his phone on it, attached the gizmo that allowed him to remotely take photos, activated the flash, and hoisted the phone up towards the portal roof, where the new brickwork was. When it was at the right level, he took several photos before lowering the phone back down into the dinghy. He examined the photos closely.

'Yes, that looks new. I guess this is a recent repair. How far does it come down the wall, can anyone reach any of it?'

Max realised he could.

'Yes I can Matt, what do you want me to do.'

'I know we shouldn't, but any chance you can just scrape off a small amount of the mortar, and the surface of one of the bricks, then place them in two separate bags?'

'Sure thing boss.'

'Great, then we can compare it and see if it matches the sample for Pete. I just wonder if he was in here for some reason supervising things, and he was hurt in the fall. Maybe Evo moved the body simply because he didn't want the attention and rubberneckers down here ruining his tourism project.'

'That would make sense,' said Norton.

'Well, I don't think there is anything else to see, what sort of depth do we have Ava?'

Ava reached into her bag and pulled out her mini sonar, and dipped the sensor into the water. 'Six feet five inches to the bottom.'

'Thanks.'

Matt cautiously lent over the side of the dinghy and shone the bright light into the water, 'Well that's equally odd, look at that. I can see The Portal floor below us, and it is as clean as a swimming pool in here.'

Cautiously the team took it in turns to look. It did indeed look like a swimming pool.

'This cleanliness doesn't match with a long disused collapsing tunnel any more than the lack of cobwebs does.'

A couple of agreements came from the darkness. Matt didn't catch who it was.

Norton's voice was the first to break through the darkness after a moment's silence.

'Whatever is going on here – unless these repairs are very recent, I think we have a link to Pete's death with this place. That said, I fear for Bella that we are going to just end up with more questions than answers.'

Matt turned his light back on.

'I think we can turn around and head out of here; there is nothing else to see. We can go back to the hotel, look up what we can on disused tunnels, and go from there whilst we wait for these samples to be analysed.'

They turned the dinghies around one at a time, and slowly made their way back to the mouth of the portal. All in all, they were back on dry land in just over an hour. Packing up and heading back down the towpath to the cars took another half an hour given the effort required to pack up the dinghies.

Once back at the hotel they ordered some sandwiches and drinks, and discussed what they all thought was going on with the portal. The consensus was that Evo probably just didn't want people in there whilst he tried to restore it, and conjecture was pointing to how people like Evo massively protect their privacy. Had there been an accident with Pete, they could all very easily see that Evo would have the body moved. It was what they had talked about in the billionaire world; how money and power could turn down the volume on morality.

A bike courier turned up to collect the samples and whisk them off to Dr Brett. Matt had already arranged for a comparison to be rushed through between the concrete sample in Pete's head and the one they had just collected. If there was a match as everyone expected, then they would need to call Inspector Stimpson and share their findings with him. He would be the one to decide if any official action was required.

Matt flicked shut the laptop, 'I can't find anything online about tunnels and tunnel floors that are clean. Not clean like the one we saw. I am not really sure what that tells us though.'

'Either it's a result of the recent repair works, or someone's pool man got lost.'

Everyone laughed at Norton's comment. It took an edge off the evening that no one had noticed was there until it was gone.

'Shall we all head down and have something to eat. Dr Brett said it would be after ten pm before he would get a chance to look.' Matt then walked towards the door.

Everyone headed down to the restaurant. The weather had taken a turn for the worse. It was raining, and there was a cool breeze blowing, so they ate inside. After the previous night's feast, no one was that hungry and the evening passed quite quickly.

They were back in the Operations Room hanging on for Dr Brett's call. Matt had just poured everyone a coffee as his phone rang. It was 10.05 p.m.

'Hello Matt speaking.'

Matt wandered towards the balcony doors, which for the first evening were closed. In lieu of being able to walk up and down the balcony, Matt paced at the far end of the room.

'Oh really? OK, what can you tell me... anything?'

The gaps between Matt talking were fairly decent, so everyone in the room took this to mean Dr Brett was imparting some detailed information. In fact he wasn't, and Matt looked a little down-hearted when he had finished the call.

'Well I have to say I am definitely surprised. The samples we took from The Portal wall today certainly *do not* match the sample from Pete's wound.'

The length of the silence that followed spoke of everyone in the rooms surprise at this revelation. Bella got up from her chair with some purpose. Matt assumed she was leaving to head back to her room. He started to get up also when Bella began to speak.

'You have been kind enough to update me with all your findings, or more accurately your lack of findings today at The Portal. So, I am just going to come straight out with this; tomorrow morning – *I want to visit The Portal for myself*. I mean to go with *or* without you. I would not dream of asking you to trespass with me, but if any of you are happy to come, I would be delighted. I intend to head there about eleven thirty, *Good night*.'

With that she promptly left the room.

Matt got up and went after her. They could hear his voice out in the corridor.

'Bella… *Bella… wait please*.'

CHAPTER 23

It was 11.30 a.m. and everyone was gathered in the hotel car park by the cars. Max and Matt had – for the first time in their working career had a heated conversation the night before. Both wanted the other to persuade their headstrong client not to visit the portal; even though they both knew it was not their place, or their right to tell Bella what to do. After all, they worked for her; but both cared for her, and didn't want to see her come to any harm. It was not that either was spooked by the portal, despite its sinister reputation. It was simply a case of being concerned by what the portal represented in the real world; namely, a large body of deep, cold, dark water and that inevitably posed a real danger to any human being who was ill prepared.

'OK let's load up and go.' Matt's face had not lightened much since he and Max had talked. He did not want to be accompanying a client on a planned illegal trespass into a dangerous building; but he equally would not dream of letting her go in there alone. Bella had put him in an awkward position.

Before long they were back again on the side of the road close to the portal. Matt took Bella to one side. He had not been sure how to play this, but his anxiety was rising rapidly. Bella had shown how strong minded she was, so for both their sakes, he was willing to insist on a couple of ground rules whilst she was with them. After all, he was responsible for everyone here but her.

'Bella a quick word please before we go up there, *I'm not happy about this*; The Portal is a dangerous place with deep, cold water, darkness and nothing on the sides to hold onto if you end up overboard. We are all going to wear life jackets, you need to also. *More importantly*, you need to do *exactly* as I say whilst we are in there and not question me. You can question me later when we are all safely back outside; but *I can't have you endangering my team's lives*. Does that work for you?'

'Yes Matt, that works for me, and for the record I *do* appreciate you accompanying me here.'

Matt's anxiety lifted a little.

'Good. Sorry if I seem a little heavy handed, but the reality is we should not be here, and neither should you.'

'Totally understood.'

'Shall we then?'

'Yes Matt, we shall. Did I see you had a selfie-stick?'

'Yes we do, why?'

'I have a plan, but nothing that will cause any problems I assure you.'

'Right everyone ready, let's gather up and go.'

'*Err* boss, just a quick word if you don't mind?'

'Sure Norton.'

Matt and Norton wandered off a distance from the rest of the group.

'Look I know Bella is insisting she do this and all, but I want to register my protest. I think this is a *very bad idea*. I don't think we should be doing anything that puts a client in potential danger. If she goes on her own, well fair enough; we can't stop her doing that, but we should not have anything to do with this. What if she ends up in the water? This is a very arrogant way to behave.'

'*Arrogant*? How do you get to that? It has absolutely nothing to do with arrogance. I have tried to talk her out of it – and for the record I *do not* think this is a good idea. I have also had a word with Max, and he assures me she will absolutely come down here on her own. I have taken advice, considered the pros and cons and decided this is the best option. *OK*?'

Norton shook his head.

'*No – not really, not at all* in fact, but you're the boss.'

Matt turned to head back to the others without saying a word. Norton had been out of sorts from the start of this case, Matt made a mental note to have a talk with him back in London, when the case was closed. He had never thought Norton would behave like this; something must be troubling him. Matt would try and help Norton when this was all over. For now though, they would join the others.

Bella was very much undergoing the same experience they had all had when they first saw it.

'Wow, even the detail you guys provided in your reports can't prepare you for this place. I don't think there is anything else quite like it in the world. I would not actually have liked to come here alone to be honest.'

Before long everyone was kitted out again, and aboard the re-inflated dinghies that sat just inside the mouth of the portal.

'I am sorry Bella, this is going to be very boring for you; there really is nothing to see.'

'No I get that, but I just wonder.'

'Wonder – wonder what?'

'Well I was going through one of the cupboards in our flat, and I found a small plastic box with a solitary white plastic card in it. What really caught my attention was that the card had absolutely no markings on it at all. I thought that was odd, and wondered why Pete would keep a blank plastic card in a box. I took the card out and examined it. That's when I noticed something peculiar.'

Bella paused for a moment. She was not sure how the team were going to take the fact she had kept something potentially important from them. Looking at them, none of the faces registered anything Bella took as anger, so she tentatively continued.

'Well it didn't make sense until a couple of days

ago – but I had looked closer at the card, and it was not totally blank. It had a hologram on it. A very faint one, but it's there none the less.'

Bella reached into her pocket and took out the card and handed to Joe who was nearest to her. He examined it.

'Oh yes. It's a logo; it looks like it is a small bird in flight coming into land. Is it a Blackbird?'

'Yes, I think it is.'

By now the card had made its way around everyone, and was with Matt. He twisted it in the light and sure enough the logo appeared.

'So what do you think this is then?'

'I guess it is some sort of key card like hotels have, though this feels a lot more substantial than those, and...'

Matt made firm eye contact with Bella, he didn't want anything being held back that might adversely affect Bella or his team's safety.

'And *what*?'

'Well, the first couple of nights I left it by my bed at home. I was wondering whether it had any significance and whether I should tell you about it. My point is I looked at it a lot, and it never did anything odd.'

'But *it is* doing something odd now?'

'Yes Joe, ever since I took it in my purse to dinner with Evo.'

'And…. What has it being doing?'

'It has started flashing red. Once every hour.'

Everyone's eyes widened a little.

'*The whole thing flashes red, and it has been doing that since you were at Nalebury for dinner*?'

'Yes Max. Sorry, I probably should have said something, I don't know why or what it is doing.'

'I hope Evo didn't spot it flashing.'

'No, I'm sure he didn't, it was deep in my purse.'

Matt began to hand the card back to Bella.

'I have seen something like that before. You are right, it is a key card; they have a similar looking thing for the labs at Refract Speech. I have seen Ollie with one. There is a chip inside there, and it has a small rechargeable battery. The card flashing red means it's asking to be recharged. You holding it must have woken it up; or it sensed a compatible charging station in Evo's office. With no identifier on it, we have no way of knowing where it's for. I am guessing you thought it was for here?'

Bella nodded.

'Well…I wondered.'

Max came forward and looked in Bella's direction.

'And you brought it here to see if it did anything?'

Bella nodded again.

'*Well* it can't harm, though we saw nothing that even remotely resembled an access panel or slot when we were here last.'

Matt gave a knowing smile.

'Well, we wouldn't. The whole point of these card systems is invisibility. The card readers are hidden in the wall, so that any potential thieves or intruders have no idea where to look in order to try and override the system. I guess having something on the wall that is very clearly a card reader or lock gives intruders something to target. This way, they have no idea where it is. Ollie did mention that's the reason the cards are a bit more substantial. They have to carry a battery because they have to be strong enough to transmit a signal through a wall. That allows the reader not to give off any strong signals, which means intruders can't scan for it either. I think whoever owns this card has the same system the Refract Speech Labs do.'

Max picked up the thought process the others were all following.

'So – I am guessing these systems are far from cheap, and you don't put them on cleaning cupboards to protect the mops and the vacuum cleaners.'

'No indeed Max, you only have one of these systems if you have something you are determined to protect from prying eyes.' On finishing his sentence, Matt dropped the card back into Bella's hand.

'So, what's your plan, you want to swipe it as we go through The Portal? I guess we could.'

'I thought we could somehow hold it close to the wall, and maybe at some point something will happen.'

'OK Bella, good plan,' said Max, 'In fact we can

lock the card into the selfie-stick and hold it close to one wall on the way in, and then the other on the way out. It might take us a bit longer as we probably need to go slower. Are you alright with that Matt?'

'Yeah sure, can't harm to try.'

Bella had been handed the selfie-stick with the card attached. Bella tried to stand up in the dinghy and lost her footing. As she slipped, her left hand which held the selfie-stick instinctively jabbed out and struck the wall. At this moment Max caught Bella, and in one move managed to rescue her from her fall.

'Are you OK?' asked Max.

'Yes thanks – wow look at that.'

Max followed Bella's stare, and his eyes came to rest on the key card at the end of the stick. The whole card was glowing green. Bella passed Max the selfie-stick, and he swiped it slowly across the area of wall nearest to him. Suddenly there was a large humming sound, and something seemed to be running towards them along the top of the roof; it was coming at speed.

'*What – the – hell* ...?' Norton looked around in different directions in an almost comical manner.

'*Lights*, they are lights, coming on one at a time from the deepest part of The Portal outwards. Some of these fake bricks in the roof are actually lights. That *is* cool.'

Once on, each light seemed to grow rapidly

in brightness, until the entire portal was now bathed in a modern white LED style light. Instead of some old haunted abandoned building full of exciting possibilities and adventures, the whole place took on the character of some modern clinical establishment. Whatever these smooth fake bricks that lined the portal were coated in, it acted as some sort of reflecting material that seemed to brighten up in the light.

Bella shivered. For a moment she was back in the characterless hospital corridor where she waited to see Pete's body. There was something reminiscent of that place here, now these lights had removed any romantic notions Bella may have had about the portal. It was revealed to be exactly what they all really knew it to be. A very large-scale feet of human engineering, clinical in nature and purpose; not some secret gateway to another dimension. Whatever the façade and the path up to the portal entrance conjured up in anyone's imagination, at the end of the day this was just an enormous pile of stone; how much damage could it really inflict on anyone?

Whilst everyone's eyes were adjusting to this increasing bright light, Max took the selfie-stick and ran it around other sections of the wall. They all watched Max's actions. Close to the portal's mouth, about twelve feet from the hidden light switch they had found, the card glowed green again. Suddenly, Max felt a vibration through his feet and heard a large humming sound apparently coming from behind the wall. He looked down into the water and saw some small whirlpools forming as if a plug had just been pulled out below them.

Max's voice was powerful and clear, in the same way a doctor dealing with an emergency might bark orders at those around him.

'Bella, *get out of the dinghy now. Now. Out and get out of The Portal now. Everyone, out now.*'

There was a mass exodus, as people tried to balance the slippery floor and the water with not hanging around. All the movement in the water caused even greater disturbance, and meant that Max could no longer determine what was caused by the team, and what was caused by the strange phenomenon. He was still looking when he felt a hand around his collar.

'Out means you too Max, *come on.*'

It was his twin Joe. He followed the direction his brother was gently pulling him in, and in a matter of moments they were out of the portal, and standing on the bank in the sunlight. Everyone listened intently. There was no sound. A couple of moments later, the two dinghies silently drifted out of the portal and rested on the lip. After a couple of minutes Max looked at everyone, and then slowly began to head back towards the portal entrance.

Everyone else stayed on the bank, though Joe was beginning to head towards Max when he heard Max call out.

'What *is* this place?'

Joe carefully entered the water, as he didn't want to rip his waterproof suit, and headed towards where his brother was standing. Where the wall on the left had been, there was now a gaping hole, and it revealed a massive room. This room also had water to the same depth as the portal, but there tethered up to a floating pontoon, were three large boats with enormous fans on the back of them, and three two-seater jet bikes. There was also a large store of fuel. Behind them up on a large metal shelf was two dirt bikes and two ATVs; together with hydraulic handling arms that were bolted to the wall.

'Wow *indeed*, what is this place Max? I think it's someone's toy box. What exactly is going on here?'

'Hey guys, *come* and look at this.'

Everyone gathered round, peering into the room.

Max scratched his head.

'I guess that sound was the hydraulics for this enormous door. I can't think what else it would be.'

'Why don't you wave the card back at the same place? See if it closes again,' Bella said.

Max did as Bella suggested. Again, there was a swirl of water and the noise returned. This time everyone stood still. Within one minute, where the entrance had been, once again there was a solid stone wall that gave no hint to being a door.

Matt gave a little shake of his head.

'Well that snazzy entrance is in stark contrast to those old rotting oak doors a few feet behind us.'

Ava looked round to remind herself exactly what they looked like.

'You're *not* wrong.'

Matt looked around at the group.

'Right shall we try again; I really don't want us spending all day here. Whatever Evo is up to, this place is clearly being used, so let's not hang around any longer than we need to. We don't need his kind of legal power being directed at us for trespass. We might survive any fine, but wouldn't survive paying his legal fees if we lost.'

As they headed deeper into the portal for the second time, the new lights shining down on them meant that anxiety in relation to any imminent danger was gone.

Bruno looked up at the portal roof, and then around the area there were in.

'I also hope he doesn't forward us his electricity bill since we turned all these lights on.'

They had gone slower as agreed, and Max had held the selfie-stick against the wall the whole way, but the card had not changed colour again, and no more sections of wall had moved to reveal any other caverns of delight. They had passed a couple of bricks with a single letter marked on them throughout the journey. No one was sure exactly what they were, but it was mutually agreed it was probably some sort of old marking system for distance into the tunnel, or depth of water from the early days when the portal was used for its original intention.

Matt spoke rhetorically.

'I guess we missed these lettered bricks last time as we only had torches to flash about, we were mostly pointing them forwards.'

'Perhaps the letters told something to the boys who used to walk the barges through the portal back in the day.' said Norton.

'I can't make sense of them.' said Bella, 'I think I must have missed a few. I have seen a large S and a T and a Y but that's all.'

Ava pointed slightly ahead, 'There's another one, I think that is an X. Maybe X marks the spot.'

They were all distracted as the mound of bricks in the middle of the tunnel slowly hove into view. Both dinghy captains throttled off the small electric outboard motors, and let the dinghies come to rest in their own time.

'*Blackbirds.*'

Ava's outburst caught everyone off guard a little.

'I'm sorry, what?' Matt carefully repositioned himself in his dinghy to look at her.

'In here? Did you see a blackbird in here? I wouldn't have thought so. Not this far in anyway.'

'No no... Blackbirds *generically* speaking, not *specifically.*'

Matt looked confused, as did the rest of the team.

'What have blackbirds *generically* speaking got to do with us here, now?'

'Sorry Matt.' Ava gave a short laugh, 'I should have explained myself rather than just shouting that out, but it just suddenly popped into my head. It was simply that ever since we saw the hologram on that key card, something has been nagging at me.'

'And now it has come to you?'

'It has… Chantmarle Capital the name of Evo's hedge fund.'

'*Yes?*'

'Well I have just remembered that I read somewhere, or it was in a crossword, that Chantmarle means song of a blackbird. I think it was Norman French or something like that.'

'Interesting. Well it's certainly another link to Evo. Seems odd that he has put the logo on a card that otherwise is meant to keep things anonymous. But if it's the same system that he uses for his security at the office, then maybe they just use the same cards to save money. If that's the clue that breaks the case, it won't be the first time a rich person has been undone by their penny pinching.'

'Yes, as I say, it just popped into my head.'

'Definitely worth having more confirmation though Ava, good memory skills.'

Now the dinghies had come to rest against

the mound of bricks blocking the portal. The rubber noses of the dinghies bounced gently off the bricks at water level. Matt gave a few moments silence, he watched Bella looking around. He would give her some time before suggesting they head back. Max passed the key card back to Bella, and collapsed the selfie-stick, placing it in the floor of the dinghy.

About five more minutes passed before Matt spoke.

'OK Bella? Are you happy if we head back now? There is nothing down here, that card hasn't opened any more secret doors. I really think we should leave.'

Matt was expecting some resistance from his client. As it turned out, he need not have.

'Yes thanks. I can see there is nothing here. I did have to be sure though. If I exhaust everything in my mind so that I can have no doubts, then I will slowly be able to get on with my life. That's why I need to do this, or the doubts will continue to win, and I will be stuck in limbo forever.'

'Of course Bella, *I* ... *we* understand totally, that's why we are here with you. Now this is all done though, let's leave. Captains turn your vessels round please; let's go back towards the sunshine.'

The second Matt said the word sunshine; all the lights went out at once, plunging the portal back into darkness. Everyone kept calm, but seven pulses quickened in that moment. Two of the team reached for the bright torches they had brought with them and turned them on.

Bella took the key card and zipped it up safely in one of her pockets; then shivered and rubbed her hands up and down her arms. Not wishing to reference the lack of light or appear scared, she carried on with the previous conversation.

'That would be great, I am suddenly feeling the goose bumps. I guess it's all linked to the emotions of coming here.'

Ava gave an almost imperceptible shake of the head.

'*No*, I don't think it's *just that*. I feel it too. It's *more* than goose bumps, suddenly there's a cold wind in here; *I don't like it...* there wasn't one a moment ago.'

Ava studied the water and listened to the outboard motors.

'The dinghies are needing more throttle in order to maintain speed, it's as if... *well* as if we are suddenly in tidal waters. It's almost imperceptible, but look at the water. Now it has a direction of flow. It *didn't* have that before.'

Everyone carefully looked to where the water met the walls. Ava was right, the water was showing clear signs of movement and directional flow.

Matt had not noticed the wind, given his collar was raised over his neck.

'Could just be that the wind is blowing outside,

and that it does somehow make its way in here.'

Ava tried not to look too concerned.

'That's the problem Matt. The direction of the wind; *it's coming from inside The Portal, it's behind us.*'

One word fell out of Matt's mouth before he had even noticed. *'Inside…'*

CHAPTER 24

Matt sat for a moment, trying to process what was happening and to come up with the practical, calm solution that would explain what was going on.

'So you are saying the wind is blowing one way, and the water is moving in the *opposite direction*?'

Ava gave a solemn nod, 'Yes.'

In Max's head alarm bells were beginning to sound loudly. He had good sea legs and these dinghies were not even rocking, yet deep in the pit of his stomach he began to feel sick. Properly sick. As he tuned into his body he also noticed his heart was racing. He rubbed his hand along the side of the dinghy, it left a sweat mark. He was sweating and he had not even noticed. His anxiety had built very subtly.

Ava spoke again, 'So from still air and still water, we now have a breeze and a tidal flow. *Since when do tunnels contain their own weather systems?*'

Joe, Max and Bruno chorused together in the same slightly stilted voices, '*They don't.*'

Matt was experiencing the same physiological symptoms Max and the rest of the team were. He had to regain his composure, he had to function properly, he had to ensure their client and his team were OK. From his seated angle, Matt was able to subtly clock Bella's face and posture without making it obvious. For now, she was either doing a tremendous job of pretending to be calm, or she was oblivious to the impending dilemmas Matt felt sure were on their way. Breathe Holland... breathe, slow small breaths in and out; one, two, one, two... good. Matt could feel his body relax a little. He consciously focused his mind; he wanted the next sentence out of his mouth to be authoritative without being alarmist.

'*Everybody*, make sure you are well positioned in your spots, and that you can secure yourself from slipping. Have you all done that?'

He could hear the word yes in six different voices. Good.

'Captains, more speed *now* please.'

Two voices came back, both with the same word.

'*Affirmative.*'

'Good.'

Matt turned to look at Bella with purpose. Despite the poor light, she clocked him doing this out of the corner of her eye, and turned to face him as best she could. He had decided to tell a small white lie in an attempt to keep things calm.

'Bella, I don't want you to be alarmed, the reason I want us to get out of here quickly, is that I think The Portal floor may have collapsed somewhere behind this roof fall. I think that is why the water is now pouring in that direction. These dinghies are only really for light inland water use, and I don't want to risk us getting pulled against the bricks at any speed; and then having to swim nearly two miles out of here.' Matt managed a convincing and reassuring smile.

'Understood, yes I wouldn't mind giving a two-mile swim a miss today thanks.'

Her answer seemed to contain enough of a relaxed tone, that Matt took it that, for now anyway, Bella was oblivious to their potential danger.

Matt's inner monologue was getting more anxious. This bloody Portal, nothing is as it seems. It's abandoned and yet it's immaculately maintained, its solid old walls are actually doors; and now we have water pouring towards what should be a solid blockage of brick and mortar. On top of all that, the place now seems to be demonstrating it has its own weather system.

Ava's choice of one word had triggered Matt's PTSD and anxiety. Tidal, as in a Shadow Tide? Before he could control his stomach muscles and calm his body, a small amount of sick headed up his throat. Turning away towards the wall, and slowly bending over the edge of the dinghy, Matt got rid of it into the water. Luckily due to the shadows being cast by the beam of the torches, no one had caught sight of what had happened.

Bella had her eyes fixed firmly forward. Good.

Matt was just composing himself, when a loud and relatively high pitched beeping sound started echoing around the portal walls right beside them. It was coming from the other dinghy. Matt could see a red flashing light on its outboard motor's control panel. He was just computing what that might be, when a second almost identical sound started to emit from the dinghy he was in.

'What does that noise *mean*?'

'It's a low battery indicator, we are both below ten percent and it's dropping fast. I am not sure we are going to make it all the way on battery power.' Ava spoke in a manner that didn't overly hide her concern.

'*Damn.*' Matt thought for a moment.

'How deep is it here Norton?'

Norton brought out his app, 'The water level here is six foot and two inches.'

'OK well we have no option, just keep going for now and let's think. Ava, anything in your research we can use."

'I am afraid not. When The Portal was originally in use, it seemed to be that the bargemen would lie on their backs and walk the barges through, but we can't do that in these rubber dinghies. That was why this tunnel only operated specially designed tall barges, because of the extra roof height in here.'

Matt rubbed his hair whilst thinking.

'No worries, sure we will be out of here in ten percent or less.'

Matt's inner monologue was on a different thought process. Plan B Holland, we are going to need a plan B.

'...What was that?'

Everyone looked around. Suddenly there was dust in everyone's hair, and the eyes of those who looked up.

'What was that enormous thumping sound guys? That sounded like a giant's footstep. And look at the water; it's full of vibration waves.'

The torch lights had shown Bruno was now as white as a sheet.

'I don't know. Matt, I think we need to leave a *little bit quicker* if we can.'

Suddenly the water level rose by what felt like several feet in height. Matt had looked to make sure everyone was wearing their lifejackets. He was about to shout to jump for it and swim when he had a falling sensation. He panicked. Had he just blanked out and fallen out of the dinghy? Before he had time to answer, he landed hard on his backside and a jarring pain ran up his back. His brain was now full of confusion. Why did that hurt? Why were his nose and mouth not full of water? He came to quickly. They were all lying in various positions on the portal floor which was totally dry. There was no water anywhere. It had all vanished at once, all of it. Matt leapt to his feet and shouted to check everyone was alright, they were.

Bruno got to his feet.

'*What happened there?*'

He was still in his dinghy. He climbed out, the dinghy malformed briefly as his weight was all concentrated in one place, and then popped back into shape as soon as he was out. It looked rather stupid sitting on a stone floor with no water around.

Both outboard motors were higher pitched than they had been, their propellers were just spinning in the fresh air. The noise was adding to the sense of alarm, so they were both instantly shut off.

Joe was already on his feet, brushing himself off having checked Bella was OK first.

'I don't know; this place is like some fairground ride from *hell*. Has it sprung a leak? *Where the hell did all that water go, and so quickly*? That has to be some kind of record.'

Max knelt down and put his hand on the floor.

'Can you feel that vibration? I thought I might just have pins and needles but it's real. Look at this, the mortar between the tiles on the floor. It isn't mortar. It's a grey coloured metal surface with loads of small circular holes. The whole floor is porous.'

Matt's eyes widened as his brain put the last pieces of guesswork together for what was going on. Alastor's story about the Shadow Tide didn't reference a sudden water loss. Perhaps... perhaps there is just a massive collapse somewhere in the portal floor and it has simply drained. Then again...

'How far does anyone reckon we are from the exit?'

Bruno was looking at his phone, swiping and typing. He had no idea how it was working in here but he wasn't about to look this particular gift horse in the mouth.

'About five minutes, if we move *now* and we move *fast*.'

Matt looked around, 'OK everyone, you heard the man. *Let's move now*. OK Bella?'

'Yes I have started training for the London Marathon so yeah.'

'After you then. *Let's go*. Get anything essential you need from the dinghies and let's go.'

They began to run, their pace mimicked by the flashlight beams dancing off the walls; Matt offered various motivations to keep the pace up. We might just make it out alive. Matt thought. As he was finishing that thought, an extremely strong, cold and damp wind blew in from behind them, working its damp sensation down their necks. Then it overtook them. It was also heading for the exit.

'*That can't be good*.' shouted Ava.

No one replied, full agreement was a given. They all kept quiet, conserving energy and concentrating. There was a very real chance one or all of them were not going to make it out alive;

especially given what had been released to come and hunt them down. In Matt's mind he scrambled to remember the name Alastor had given to this wind. It flashed straight into his mind, The Harbinger Breath. The next thing over the top of us is going to be a huge wall of water that has just displaced all that air.

His next thought was even more unsettling. Well at least you got to the bottom of all the previous cases, this is the first fail, but it's also likely to be the last. Despite building up a sweat with all this running in waterproof suits and lifejackets, Matt shivered at that last thought.

He forced himself to look around to everyone whilst they continued to run for the exit. He clocked Norton moving to take his life jacket off.

Matt's voice bellowed around the cavernous chamber.

'Lifejacket's stay on, that includes you Norton. There is every chance we are going to need them shortly. *Leave – it – on.'*

Meanwhile, Bella found herself nursing a surprisingly calm thought. At least I am about to be with my husband once again. The thought gave her an inner calm, but it also troubled her a little. Was she really done with life to that degree? Was she really that accepting of what she was quite sure was her impending death?

CHAPTER 25

Matt's voice pitch altered as people's voices do when they are running.

'Everyone *OK*?'

By now the exit was in clear view.

'We have about two hundred yards to go, and we are out of here.'

Matt was a bit puzzled. Why didn't my voice echo? Carefully he looked round. In that instant, every millilitre of his blood ran ice cold. As his eyes turned, he caught sight of the wall. He could see the long shadow that had been described to them by Alastor racing along the wall, swallowing it up in the darkness; a gigantic black liquid wave was closing in on them fast. Jolts of electricity shot down both of Matt's hands then lingered in his fingertips.

His training kicked in. Better to prepare for the impact, try and protect themselves as much as possible against the inevitable. Matt gave the speech as authoritative and non-alarmist as possible.

'Try to keep calm, you need your chest to be as relaxed and unrestricted as possible. We are going to get picked up by a wave of water in the moment. When I say 'now' slow to a walk and catch your breath as much as possible. When I say '*brace*' stand still, take in as big a breath as possible and curl yourself up into a ball. Protect your head with your arms and hands as best as you can. Try and not go rigid.'

'Now.'

Matt looked across to the others, to his delight everyone had instantly done what he suggested.

'*Great I…*'

As Matt began to congratulate everyone and try and instil any calm that he might be able to, he was knocked off his feet; managing to resist the urge to open his mouth as the shock of the ice-cold water hit him. He hoped the others had equally managed to resist. He felt himself being carried along at high speed. Something that momentarily felt like a boot struck Matt in the head. His last feelings were of a stabbing pain to the back of his head followed by his body going limp. Then – nothing.

CHAPTER 26

Bella became aware of a pain radiating all over her face. She slowly came to. As she opened her eyes, she could see she was lying on the ground, it was some sort of path. As her vision restored itself, she could see a pair of feet coming towards her. They were clad in some sort of dark coloured work boots. She lifted her gaze. Connected to the boots were a pair of jeans.

She recognised them; she certainly recognised the shape of the thighs in them.

'*Pete*... oh *thank God*.'

Bella forced herself to wake up, and to finally accept this had all been one monstrous dream.

'Boy have I just had the most *bizarre* nightmare.'

Bella started to recount to her husband the key points of her ordeal. How she had never been totally sure he was dead given his body was not recognisable, her tracking down her old flame, and how he and his people were helping her solve the mystery surrounding Pete's clearly now mistaken death. Pete smiled and told her to stay still. He continued to walk towards her. It looked like he was coming from the direction of the portal, but the lights all seemed to be back on. He must have turned them on when looking for her. So he did work here.

Pete told her not to move until a doctor could get to help her. She must conserve her energy. It would all be alright. Bella smiled and nodded very gently; her head was pounding.

'Promise me Bella, *you will not move* until help comes.'

'I promise. I'm just so pleased you're OK, and that *horrendous* dream is over.'

Bella started to feel a warm fuzzy feeling flow through her body. It felt like it started in her core and radiated out in all directions. This warm feeling was much stronger than the cosy feeling she often got when being with Pete. Her eyes were closing. She would do as Pete said; it was just great to be back with him alive. She would get well, and put all of this nonsense behind her. If she ever had such a vivid nightmare again, she would seek help for her mental health.

'*Bella...*' She could hear Pete calling her. Bella opened her eyes as much as she could.

'Yes Pete, I'm doing as you say. I'm staying still. It's very bright, I have never seen such bright sunshine, I'm sorry I'm squinting.'

'Bella... wake up. Stay *there*.'

This time Bella instantly opened her eyes, squinting as she needed to.

'Stay there, you mean *stay here... with you.* You're frightening me *Pete*, I don't want to go back to that nightmare, *not* for another second, please don't make me; *hold my hand.*'

Bella relaxed a little as Pete lent forward to take her hand. That would be enough for her, she would close her eyes. She waited a moment, but where there should be a feeling of warmth from another human being, she only felt intense cold. She yelled, then closed and opened her eyes again. This time, there was no bright light, there was no Pete. Everything was still. Bella recognised where she was. She was on the canal towpath, the pain in her face was caused by the beech tree nut husks as they pressed into her skin; there in the distance was the road bridge.

The last thing she wanted to do was yell for help, but something told her she had to. Inhaling as deeply as possible, and focusing on making her voice as loud and carrying as she could; Bella prepared herself to shout as loud as she ever had.

One…two…three… Bella had hoped to count to four, but as she reached three, she felt a blow to the back of her head.

CHAPTER 27

The next thing Bella was aware of was a familiar smell. One she knew held only negative connotations, though at present she could not place it. The smell grew stronger, it was odd to smell it out here in the fresh air though. A different sensation began to wash over her. What is this feeling? The sensation surged a bit more, then she knew; she was coming round. She would prepare to shout again for help, hopefully someone was going to hear.

Just as Bella was about to attempt her first shout; panic began to set in. Bella was able to work out the panic was being triggered by that smell, but what was it? It was not a smell she was regularly familiar with throughout her life, but still it was extraordinarily strong, and the associations extremely negative.

Oh no, thought Bella, I remember that smell, seeing Pete for the last time, it's the smell of the morgue. I am dead. I didn't make it. What happens next? Slowly a light began to filter in, brightening in intensity. A few moments later and Bella's eyes were opening and she was rapidly becoming aware of her surroundings. First she was aware of the roof, it looked like a generic non-descript roof in a commercial building.

It had commercial light fittings recessed into the roof, and there were a couple of smoke detectors, the type you only really see in hotels and office buildings. Well I can't be dead yet then. Unless... surely the afterlife doesn't come with the same fixtures and fittings as normal life on earth?

She felt her left hand tighten.

'Bella? *Nurse*, I think she is coming round.'

Bella recognised the voice instantly, '*Max* – is that you?'

'Yes Bella, I'm here, you're going to be OK, you're in hospital.'

Bella opened her eyes.

'Max – oh thank God you are OK. What *happened*?'

'Shhh Bella, just rest, the nurse is coming, but you need to lie still.'

Bella wanted to make sure she was OK for herself. She wiggled her toes and could feel them all; she could wiggle her fingers also. She took from that she was not paralysed, so that would do for now. She totally relaxed. Her brain was now awash with activity as she slowly came back to being properly awake. Pete was dead – she had employed Max – the portal – the Shadow Tide...

Bella felt her energy draining again.

Through her partially open eyes, she could see a white figure moving about, it was a nurse. She was telling Bella to rest and assuring her all was OK.

Bella wanted to ask how the others were doing

and were they OK; but everything went dark and she fell into a deep sleep.

Bella slowly woke up again, she had no idea how long she had been asleep for, but this time she felt much more rested. The room came into view much quicker, and she didn't feel as groggy.

She looked around; all the beds were full, but there was no one visiting any of them. From the angle she was lying at, Bella could not see who was in the beds. She assumed it was the rest of the team. Turning her head to look in the other direction, she realised she was on a small ward. On her right was the wall containing the windows. It was dark outside. Various machines hummed and clicked, but there was no talking. Opposite the doors to her ward was a small reception desk with a nurse. Bella raised her hand and waved. The nurse noticed and came over.

'Hey there, how are you doing?'

'I am OK thanks, what's wrong with me?'

'I am pleased to say nothing is wrong. You were unconscious when you were discovered, and you looked like you had been thrown a long way, so we took you for a CT scan and other tests to make sure you didn't have any internal injuries. I am pleased to say you don't have anything seriously wrong; you are fairly battered and bruised though. – What you need is plenty of rest.'

'Is everyone OK?'

'As far as I am aware, everyone is doing fine.'

'And we all made it out alive?'

'As far as I am aware, *yes*.'

'Where is everyone?'

'Mostly they are in the ward next to yours. We just could not get everyone in the same ward.'

Bella sank back into her bed and let the pillow embrace her, 'Ah, OK'

'What time is it?'

'It's five-thirty in the morning.'

'Ah, that's why it is so quiet. Has Max the man that was sitting with me gone home.'

'No, he's next door, he's in one of the guest rooms, catching some much needed rest. He sat with you for a long time waiting for you to wake up. Try and get some sleep for the next few hours. When he is awake he will be in to see you straight away. I know that much.'

Bella felt her energy levels draining again. She did not seem to be holding her charge for long. A sign she needed to do as the nurse advised.

The nurse turned to leave.

'Thank you,' it was all Bella could manage. The nurse turned back towards Bella and smiled.

CHAPTER 28

'Are you OK?' Evo was asking the question as a battered, wet and dazed Norton climbed into the front seat of the small car.

'Of course I am, but no thanks to you, *you idiot*. What were you thinking? You realise what you've done?'

'No, what have I done?'

'By releasing a Shadow Tide onto the team, if any of them have survived, they will never in a month of Sundays let this drop – you have basically just attacked a hornet's nest – *well done* mate.'

Evo began driving, heading back to the manor.

'Calm down, they are all fine. We checked. A couple are unconscious, the rest are dazed. I think Mrs Stone was coming round, so I had to whack her on the head with a stick to ensure she didn't see me, or any of the team rescue you.'

'And I *strongly* urge you to remember Norton, I have not done anything, not really. Now stop being so melodramatic; let's get you back to the manor, dried off, and hidden whilst we come up with a plan to get you back into the fold.'

Norton put his seatbelt on slowly, the movements of which were exasperating the pain in his shoulder.

'Oh I have a plan to keep them occupied and

distracted mate, don't you worry about that. Can you drive faster, I am in serious need of some of your stupidly expensive whisky.'

CHAPTER 29

The speed with which Bella felt herself waking up this time told her quite how knackered she had been before. She came to, sat up in bed and stared out of the window; she was desperate to speak to the others and to get back to the hotel. Obviously, Bella was extremely grateful for what the hospital had done for her; but she did have an extremely comfortable hotel room down the road waiting for her that was paid for.

The morning procedures of the hospital came and went, as did various members of the team, everyone was being discharged this morning. By some complete miracle no one had sustained even a broken bone. The nurse that had joined in the conversation with Bella, Max, Joe, Ava and Bruno commented that she thought it was a combination of Matt's instructions in how to best protect themselves when the wave hit, the life jackets, and as she put it, the luck of the devil.

As they were all being escorted to the hospital exit in their respective wheelchairs; Matt came towards them. Bella wanted to get up, but knew she should not.

'How great to see you, you survived also.'

'Morning Bella, you too, yes I did.' His smile seemed forced.

I wonder what's up? Thought Bella. We are all here – oh wait, no we're not.

Matt was talking to Ava and Bruno in a hushed tone. Without waiting for him to finish talking, Bella blurted out, 'Where's Norton? Where is he, is he alright?'

No one spoke. Bella felt herself begin to panic. Matt turned directly to face her.

'Now Bella, I really – we really do not want you to panic, Norton is missing; but let me quickly stress he isn't dead. I have helped the police and emergency crews search the whole area, and his body is not there. We have also been back into The Portal and he is not there either.'

Bella's mood began to darken.

'This is all my fault. I should never have pushed things so that you all came with me into that bloody portal.'

Against instruction, Ava got out of her wheelchair and wandered over to be with Bella. She rested her hand on Bella's shoulder.

'This is not on you Bella. It was either just an accident or a wilful act of violence, but either way it isn't on you, OK?'

Bella nodded, 'OK. I understand.' But inside, the guilt still lingered.

Matt spoke before Bella had time to add anything else.

'What we think happened is he may have been washed further down the canal than the rest of us. There is a door-to-door search going on at all

the properties nearby, barns and farm outbuild-
ings, and other hospitals in Cheltenham and
Gloucester are being checked.'

Bella nodded, 'Where are we then?'

'Swindon.'

Bella nodded again.

A man walked into the reception area where
they were all waiting and walked over to them.

'Are you the Holland party?'

'We are.'

'*Good*, then your taxis are ready.'

In a very short matter of time they were heading North West along the A419 back to their
hotel.

Until now, the hotel had been great, but at no
point had it felt like home, now it did though.
Everyone was looking forward to a rest and a decent meal once they knew that Norton was safe.
Matt went off to call DCI Stimpson for an update.

The others all gathered in the Operations
Room. It was beginning to feel very familiar.
The hotel staff, as efficient as ever had brought
a tray of sandwiches and fresh dispensing flasks
of tea and coffee. Everyone took a hot drink, and
waited for Matt to return from his phone call,
hopefully with some good news.

He did indeed return, but with no news. He was
able to share that an extensive search had been
made of the vicinity, but that Norton was nowhere to be found. They had even used thermal
imaging from a helicopter. The police had called

a halt to the search for now, but were running requests for help on TV, papers and local radio. That was all they could do for now.

'Right everyone, we need to make a plan. I know everyone is worried about Norton as am I, but I think the best thing we can do for him, and ourselves is rest and re-charge our batteries for the rest of today and tonight. Then – hopefully tomorrow we will be in a better place to help find him. It is eleven am now. Let's all grab a couple of hours of sleep then we can begin with at least some...'

Matt's sentence was interrupted with a crash as the door to the Operations Room burst open. Everyone swung their heads round to see what the commotion was; the commotion was Norton, standing in the doorway looking exhausted.

Everyone got up and made their way over to see him, asking him how he was, and encouraging him to come and sit down. Matt followed up at the rear, having first closed the door.

Matt let Norton and the rest of the team settle down, and the questions die down a little before he spoke.

'I am glad to see you back with us in one piece. We have been looking for you everywhere, as have the emergency services. Have you talked to anyone in the emergency services?'

Norton pursed his lips and sat back into the sofa, 'I have actually. DCI Stimpson and two of his lackeys are downstairs. They are just having some breakfast before they come up and speak to us all.'

Matt took himself a seat on the opposite sofa.

'So, what happened to you? Where have you been?'

Norton rubbed his hand across his chin left and right, tilting his head on one side looking across at everyone.

'Bristol.'

'*Bristol*? How did you end up there?'

'After that fairground ride from hell, thanks to our friendly hedge fund manager; I literally did end up in a hedge by the way, I stumbled up the steps towards the road. I think I blanked out a couple of times. I finally made it to the top of the stairs and fell into the road. The next thing I knew I was in the back of a car with this kindly couple arguing about where the nearest hospital was. The driver – a man I think was talking about asking a local, but the woman with him said they should take me back to a major hospital, one they knew how to get to quickly. They took me back to their hometown, Bristol.'

Matt rubbed his head, 'That was really kind of them. I don't think it dawned on any of us to look that far afield. We were going to rest then re-focus on this area, especially the lower sections of the canal.'

Norton spent the next twenty minutes providing any small details he could remember, not that any of it was relevant or revealing; and in turn the rest of the team filled him in on what their experience had consisted of. The hotel concierge brought in two large, fresh jars of rice, so that Matt could finish drying out both the car keys and various mobile devices. Matt thanked him again for arranging the safe return of the cars to the hotel car park.

Matt gathered them all around.

'Look, I want a quick word before Stimpson arrives. Something is seriously off with that guy. We were nearly killed, and he hasn't done a damn thing about looking into who is behind these Shadow Tides; he doesn't seem the least bit interested, other than making sure we were all found. When I told him about Evo, and that this was essentially attempted murder, he told me "Not to be so hasty and to calm down." Let's just keep him out of things for now, at least until we have had a chance to review things ourselves, OK?'

A few moments later, there was a firm triple knock at the door. Matt got up to answer it. It was who they were all expecting, DCI Stimpson and two colleagues. His manner was a little less relaxed this time, not that it had been overly welcoming the first time they had all met. He asked if everyone was well and recovered. As he did so, he glanced at the whiteboard that had been pushed back to the wall with a bed sheet covering it.

'Much as I am glad you are all OK and no one was badly hurt, I am afraid I am not here just to check up on you. Mr de Varley has expressed concern that he specifically asked you *not* to go into the portal as it is unstable and unsafe. He is...'

Bruno interrupted, '*That portal is indeed unsafe*, but that has nothing whatsoever to do with it being unstable. In fact, it's been a while since I have seen such an old building in such superb condition. It's dangerous because *he* wants it to be. He has something to hide.' Bruno's voice got louder the more he spoke.

DCI Stimpson waited quietly for him to finish. He appreciated they were all still suffering from shock, so he would permit this emotional release without countering it, and stamping his authority.

'That is as maybe sir, but at the end of the day, it is private property, and you were specifically asked not to go in there by the owner. Trespass is mostly a civil matter, but that is what the law will initially focus on. Unless you are saying that someone deliberately tried to hurt or kill you, in which case that is obviously a criminal and therefore police matter. Is that what you are saying?' DCI Stimpson stared unblinkingly at Bruno, then after a moment he slowly looked at the rest of the team, inviting them to comment.

'No – that's *not* what we are saying, though if we were, is it something you would give credence to?' said Matt.

DCI Stimpson shook his head, 'No, not on the face of it. If you were making an allegation of that nature, would you have anything to back it up with?'

'Not in theory or in fact *yet*,' retorted Matt.

DCI Stimpson gave a sharp nod of the head, 'Good.'

'So, are you all still investigating the death of Mr Stone? Is that why you were down at the Nalebury Portal?'

'It is,' Matt tilted his head in the direction of the DCI.

'And have you found anything concrete yet?'

Matt was about to speak but Bruno chipped in first.

'Concrete, that's an odd choice of word isn't it?'

DCI Stimpson gave an almost imperceptible shake of the head, 'No, not really.'

He continued, 'So can you give me an idea of how much longer you are going to be here?'

Matt was becoming irritated. His thought was that DCI Stimpson was extending himself beyond his powers.

'No, we can't. Partly because we are not sure and partly because, *to be honest*, it's none of your business.' Matt wanted to provoke the DCI and see if he could rattle him.

For his part DCI Stimpson just smiled and spoke in a more friendly tone.

'God no, of course it's not, I just don't want to see you guys hurt. If you are going to stay here poking about, please refrain from trespassing anywhere from now on. Mr de Varley is a powerful man around here. If he phones my boss and gives him grief, then I get a call and get the grief and I do not need more grief. Am I clear?'

Stimpson took the stony silence to mean everyone understood.

'OK then, well enjoy your stay and remember; if you find anything that warrants further investigation, then please get hold of me. Like I said before, my door is open to anything like that. I am not a stupidly proud man. If you find evidence that shows I got it wrong, I hope you will bring it to me first.'

Matt felt it would be in the team's interest to show some willing. He changed his persona to also be more open and friendly.

'Of course we will, that has always been our intention. If we find anything – concrete as you put it – we will be sure to let you know straight away. Do you have a business card?'

DCI Stimpson reached into his pocket and handed Matt a card with his contact details.

Matt took it, 'Thank you, you have our details?'

'*Oh yes.*'

DCI Stimpson turned and walked towards the door, his two colleagues in front of him led the way, one of them opening the door. Just as he was about to pass through the door, he stopped and turned back to face the team.

'I really do request that you *leave Mr de Varley alone*, and *stay off his land*. It's going to make my life a lot easier, and I think he may well press charges next time. Please don't take advantage of his hospitality.'

Matt furrowed his brow and looked directly at the DCI.

'*His hospitality*?'

'Yes, he had you all to dinner.'

'You know about that?'

DCI Stimpson continued to walk out of the room, the male colleague still holding the door.

'Yes I do, down to the menu, the wine list, and the guest list. You name it, I know about it. Goodbye for now.'

With that DCI Stimpson was gone and the door was closed very gently with a quiet click.

CHAPTER 30

Ava was the first to speak after Stimpson left.

'You're right Matt, something is off with him. How can he be more interested in trespass than attempted murder?'

Matt put a finger up to his lips whilst he crossed the room and put his hand out to grab the door handle. As he fully extended his arm, to his great annoyance and an instant internal flash of rage, he noticed his hand was shaking badly. The PTSD that he had spent the last few weeks conquering was back. Channelling his instant seething anger into the effort of ripping the door wide open; Matt stepped out into the corridor. He had expected to find Stimpson eavesdropping, but there was no one there. At the end of the corridor, the slow closing fire door that could not be rushed was also closed, so no one had lingered.

Walking back into the room, Matt closed the door remarkably gently; a demonstration to himself and his PTSD that he was still in charge, and ultimately calm. He was refusing to succumb to the hyper-vigilance that his condition was trying to initiate. The others all remained quiet, waiting for him to speak. Matt paced the room a few times, rubbing his hand up and down the base of his neck.

Walking up to the window, he looked out across the lake. He was trying to get his PTSD back under control and trying to make a plan. He reminded himself he was in charge of these people, he was ultimately responsible for their wellbeing at work, and he nearly got them all killed; not to mention their client. What the hell had he been thinking.

'I am sorry to have put you all in such danger, it's a miracle we are even alive. I made a bad judgement call and I am *sorry*.'

The others all began to protest verbally that of course it was not his fault, but he raised a hand to stop them. The room fell quiet again.

'I appreciate your support guys, *I really do*, but this is on me.'

Matt walked over to get himself a drink of water, he managed the heavy jug without issue; but on lifting the cup, his tremor caused it to spill.

'*Damn it.*'

Leaving the cup, Matt walked out onto the balcony. He breathed in slowly and did some breathing exercises to help calm himself back down. It took more doing this time than before, but he was still back in control soon enough. Once he felt calmer, Matt lent over the balcony and gazed over the lake. He wished to God they had never taken on this case.

They do say no good deed goes unpunished, he thought to himself. In truth they should never have taken this case, there was a clear verdict from a well investigated death. It was obvious the police and the other official bodies had all done a thorough job. They should have gently refused. Still, there was no use crying over spilt milk; they had taken the case, and it had been a perfect storm of situations that had got them where they were. A well-meaning, decent man in Max, a decent bunch of supportive friends in Matt and the rest of the team, and a very strong-minded determined wife and widow in Bella; who was understandably consumed with grief and paranoia.

Matt had let Bella push them too far with this; way more than he would ever have allowed any other client to get away with. No one was specifically in the wrong, it had come from a well-meaning place, but it had to stop now. They could all have been killed. There and then Matt resolved to get the case back on an official footing, and bring it to a close one way or another. As he came to this decision, Max approached him and rested his hand on Matt's shoulder.

'You OK boss?'

'*No.*'

Matt took a couple of breaths of fresh air in whilst working out how to best phrase the following few sentences to Max.

'I'm sorry, but we need to bring this case to a close. I...*we* have allowed Bella too much involvement in this, and too much control. It's come from a good place, but it nearly got us killed. Because of this personal connection, we have dropped our professional checks and balances; we have to correct that now.'

'*But…*' Max began to talk; Matt stopped him.

'That's just it, *no more buts*. Do you understand how close to death we all came in that portal?

'Of course I do, but we are so close to getting somewhere.'

'But we're not though are we, not *remotely*. My head is spinning, I can't even remember how many days we have been on this case, and we don't have one single shred of substantial evidence to show for our efforts. Yes we have found plenty of circumstantial evidence, but that's all. I hate to say it, but sometimes the truth stays hidden and there is nothing we can do about it. It's totally crap, but there it is; it's certainly not worth dying for.'

'I know but what about Bella?'

'We tell her as gently as we can, that despite what we've found, there is nothing more to be done. We will refund her all her money; the business can afford to take the hit. When she wakes up and comes to join us, I will tell her it's over.'

'*Two more days* boss, that's all we are asking. We have a slightly different plan. Come and hear it.'

Matt followed Max into the Operations Room, all the while displaying a less than happy look on his face. They waited a moment for Norton to come back into the room before the meeting commenced. The team explained to Matt that they thought instead of looking into historic events from over a year ago, they should change things up a little, and try and get some fresh information from one of Evo's trusted members of staff. The whole team agreed, Evo was the most likely candidate to ultimately be behind Pete's death, though if it had been intentional, whether he would have been directly responsible was debateable.

Matt listened to their plan to work on a key member of Evo's staff, and to try and get them to somehow incriminate him. The plan was that once the team had enough solid information to incriminate Evo; they would hand it all over to a trustworthy police officer other than Stimpson. As the team elaborated on their plan, Matt relaxed. It was never going to work, at best it was a long shot, so he went along with it. They would feel he had let them win. Once they found no one was going to dare to talk to them, he would then find it easier to bring the final curtain down on this dangerous farce, and head home. First though, he knew he would have to play-act a bit. Not something he wanted to do; but he would on this occasion and live with the guilt if it got them all safely home.

The lives of his colleagues... his friends were far more important to him than finding out who killed a man who was already a long time dead. The living were more important.

Bella appeared and joined them for the second half of the meeting, she was well rested and despite her close brush with death seemed surprisingly buoyant.

Norton continued leading the explanation; this plan appeared to be his idea. Matt interrupted. 'Who in Evo's employ do you think you are going to be able to trick into sharing any damning information?'

Norton suddenly looked serious, 'Eva.'

Matt looked appalled, '*His housekeeper...you're mad.*'

Norton shook his head, 'No, I think it will work.'

'But she knows us all, she met us all at dinner that night at Nalebury, she will know what we are up to; there isn't a hope in hell's chance she is suddenly going to share any damning information she may have about her boss's involvement with Pete's death. If she hasn't told the police anything, she won't tell us.'

'No you're right,' said Norton, that's why I *don't* propose that it be one of us. In fact, I think there is only one person on this planet who might be able to lean on her sense of duty and decency. The dead man's widow.'

Matt looked horrified, '*Bella...* Are you seriously suggesting we send Bella in, after what has just happened; *seriously*, what is wrong with you these days? You've been odd this whole case, get your act together pronto, or you and I are *properly going to fall out.* I'm not even sure why we are having this conversation.'

Norton didn't seem to be phased – that in itself seemed odd to Matt.

'I'm just getting things done, it's the only option; you know it makes sense.'

Matt's whole face instantly flashed red, 'No fucking way, *absolutely not.*'

No one spoke for a moment, Matt had never been unprofessional before, and never with a client present, now he was calling Norton out in front of their client. Matt for his part was desperately trying to keep control. He decided to keep totally quiet for a moment or two.

After a while, it was Bella that spoke, 'Matt could you and I have a word outside, just us?'

Matt got up and walked slowly outside on to the balcony with Bella. He turned to close the glass doors, as he did so he glared at Norton, before turning round and walking towards the edge of the balcony.

The warm wind blew across Bella's face and the smell of cut grass filled the air. Somewhere below she could hear the lawn mowers cutting the hotel lawns. Walking along the balcony, she reached the spot where Matt was leaning over the railings. Taking the same position next to him and admiring the view of the lake, she waited a moment before speaking. She did not want Matt to feel pressured.

For his part, Matt had managed to calm himself

in the few moments he had had alone. He decided he would speak first.

'I'm sorry Bella. I'm sorry if that sounded rude or was unprofessional, but we are a business, and I need to take responsibility for everyone's welfare. Norton had absolutely no right to suggest putting you up for that role. You are a client, *not* an employee; if you come out into the field with us, you are ultimately my responsibility; you do understand that?'

Bella turned to face him.

'I do Matt, of course I do. You have all showed me nothing but kindness and support. Not to mention that in the few days you have been investigating the case, you have moved things on more than the police managed to do throughout their whole investigation.'

'I get how much you want to get to the bottom of this, I honestly do, but do you really want to put your life at risk? Because that is potentially what you would be doing. If someone did murder Pete, and we keep poking about, they may try to kill any or all of us; not to mention the fact, *I think they just did.*'

'I understand that, and I have given it a lot of thought. I tried to investigate this on my own long before I came to you guys, and that thought did cross my mind. I decided it was worth the risk, I know Pete would do the same for me, I just know he would. I want to do the same for him. If there was another way, then yes sure, I would consider that first. It's not like I have a death wish, but we both know there is no other option. Time is fast running out given how long ago Pete died, and we both know the person the housekeeper is most likely to open up to is me.'

Matt pursed his lips and shook his head very slowly.

'Are you not happy to just let sleeping dogs lie, and just live with the official verdict? *You're adamant you can't do that*?'

'If there is one thing I can be sure of in life at this current time Matthew Holland, it's that I can't leave this particular sleeping dog alone.'

'If you are sure then Mrs Stone.'

'I am *very sure* Mr Holland.'

'Right then, we had better go and join the others, and formulate a plan; *but you absolutely will have to agree to some failsafe measures. No excuses and no arguments.*'

Bella stopped Matt, turned to face him and gave him a very reassuring look.

'I promise I will agree to them. I have no desire to die.'

'No, *me neither.*'

They wandered back into the room.

Matt convinced himself that it was best to let them try and get the housekeeper to betray Evo; there was no chance of that. Then everyone would accept they have done their best, and Matt would meet much less resistance when he closed things down.

'OK, so I have agreed that provided Bella concedes to some terms, that reluctantly I can see that this is our only hope. There is a chance that the housekeeper might open up to Bella; but if at any point things look dangerous, I will pull the plug and we will call it a day, and that will absolutely be the end of it.'

'Norton, let's develop your plan. But first a recap. Do we really think Evo is behind this?'

'It has to be him,' Joe said, 'Based simply on the fact he was Pete's boss, and he owns The Portal. If we are still assuming that is where Pete died, then Evo must be majorly involved. Who else would be so affected by a death there? He is clearly up to something at The Portal that he doesn't want anyone finding out about. Tourist attraction; utter nonsense. That's just a front for whatever is really going on there.'

Matt sat back into the sofa and played along.

'OK, yes good point. Let's have a couple of avenues of investigation here. Let's get a couple of people looking into Evo in more detail; what is in his life that matches to The Portal, what is he really up to with it? Then let's have another couple of you looking into more background on this whole Shadow Tide phenomenon. Hopefully, anything we find out will be of some use or leverage. The last two of us will be close at hand as a protection detail should Bella need us.

Matt wrote the three categories on the whiteboard.

'OK, investigation of the Shadow Tide; Joe & Max, why don't you take that one.'

'Then investigate Evo; Ava and Bruno, you guys take that one.'

Bella interrupted, 'Sorry, I forgot to give you this earlier. I can't see how it will be of any use, but I thought it would be better here than at home in a drawer.' Ava was closest so Bella handed the item to her. It was a second security access card that looked just like the last one. 'I didn't know it existed until I found it when I was cleaning the other night. It had fallen down the back of the chair Pete sat in most evenings. It hasn't glowed or anything, I have no idea if its active.'

Matt gave Bella a gentle nod and a smile, 'Thanks Bella that might come in useful.' Matt then turned to look at Norton.

'That leaves you and me as security detail for Bella at all times, to make sure she comes to no harm, OK?'

'OK boss, yes, happy with that.'

'Good,' said Matt, 'Let's get to it then.'

CHAPTER 31

Joe and Max were both grabbing a coffee.

'OK bro,' said Joe, 'Any thoughts on how we do this?'

'I *do* actually; fancy a quick trip into Cirencester?'

Joe took a drink before answering.

'Sure, what are we going to be doing there?'

Max pulled out his phone whilst talking.

'I want to find a DIY store and put a theory to the test.'

Joe continued to drink his coffee. His brother had always been intuitive and a quick thinker. During their childhood, Joe had learned it was always worthwhile to go with his brother's ideas.

They finished their coffee, then headed out in the car to Cirencester. At the DIY store, they picked up some length of large rigid plastic pipe, foam, glue and a bucket, and then headed back to the Operations Room. They carried the stuff out onto the balcony and Max began to set things up.

After some considerable time, Max had constructed a rudimentary model of the inside of the portal, complete with the roof collapse. However they tried it; they could not get a large, fast moving volume of water to come out of the end of the model portal, the flow was always drastically reduced; the roof collapse acted like a gigantic baffle.

'There we go then.' Max put the bucket down and put all the parts used in his experiment back up against the wall.

'Was that all about the roof fall? You're proving it's fake, and that there is no way the volume of water that struck us could come from behind that pile of bricks. What are you thinking? That it is fake and retracts into the floor?'

'Yes,' said Max, 'I'm thinking something like that, or… at least a variation on that theme.'

'Do we need to prove this; does that mean you want to go back into The Portal?'

The colour drained from Joe's cheeks. Going back into that portal was not something that was high on his to do list.

'Not at the moment,' said Max, 'I think we should first get our ducks in a row. Do some research, then present our findings to Matt. There's no way he is going to sanction another visit to The Portal for safety or legal reasons.'

'No – not a hope in hell.'

They both wandered back into the Operations Room. They were alone, everyone else was out.

'So Max what's the plan, if there is one?'

'When we met him, Alastor told us to read our history books. I think we should head to the local library in Cirencester and see what we can find on the Shadow Tide phenomenon. It will be a good place to start. I would certainly expect to see some reference to it in books, as well as in copies of local newspapers.'

Joe grabbed the keys to the Audi.

'Sounds like a plan, let's go.'

About thirty minutes later they were standing outside the library. They paused outside for a moment. Joe motioned to his twin to take the lead.

'After you guv.'

Max pulled open the door, and they went inside. It was like many local libraries. Clean and warm, but the carpet was not in its first flush of youth. Posters adorned the walls encouraging young people to read; and a notice board contained information about various classes available. The smell of paper and books was lightly present in the air.

They headed over to the reception area.

'Hi, we have come to do some research on a local mystery if that is possible, though we are not members. Is that OK?'

The librarian assured them it was.

'What sort of mystery are you interested in? I might be able to point you in the right direction.'

Joe and Max looked at each other for a moment. This would be the first test into the wider local knowledge of the Shadow Tide. A blank expression now would almost answer their question without the need to do any more research. They watched the librarian closely as Max asked his question.

'We were wanting to look up what you have on the Shadow Tide that occurs at that old disused canal tunnel on the outskirts of the town. Do you have anything?'

Without so much as a flinch the librarian said she would lead them to the local history section. They followed her.

She stopped beside a wall of books. Next to it was a computer terminal, and at the far end was a microfiche machine.

'This is all our local history section here. We have newspaper records on this computer, and the older stuff is over there on the microfiche machine. Do you need me to show you how that works?'

'Thank you,' Max said, 'No, that's fine thanks, we are both used to using them.'

The librarian smiled, 'Well I will leave you to it, and if you need anything else, I will be over at my desk.' She then left them to it.

Joe leant in to whisper to his brother, 'Well she didn't look totally surprised by your request did she.'

Max shook his head, 'No, it didn't look like the first time she had heard that name. I would have expected her to ask what it was.'

'Yeah, me too.'

Joe moved over to the computer terminal, glanced at the laminated instruction sheet beside it for searching the library catalogue, and then proceeded to type Shadow Tide into the search box.

'Here goes nothing.'

He hit the enter button. An hourglass appeared whilst the computer gave some thought to his request.

A moment or two passed, and the screen went blank. Then some green text began to cascade onto the screen in the style of an online simple catalogue. When complete, it provided two entries.

Joe and Max looked at the titles. Two books were listed as clearly referencing the Shadow Tide.

Max noted the book's location numbers.

'Well I was genuinely not expecting one result, never mind two. Perhaps there is something in this after all.'

They both headed to the book shelves, and worked from either end. Max came to them first. He took them both down.

'Found them.'

Joe wandered over. Max handed him one of the books.

Joe looked at the title, Things to see in and around Cirencester.

'Looks like an in-depth guide of what to see around here for the visitor. Let's have a look see.'

Max watched on as Joe lifted the book up to his face and flipped through the pages, breathing in the smell.

'What are you doing?'

Joe lowered the book once all the pages had come to rest.

'I wanted to see if this book smelt new or not.'

'And does it?'

'No, it doesn't smell new. I'll have a scan through it. What have you got there?'

Max replicated his brother's process, and breathed in the resulting draught.

'This doesn't smell new.' Max flicked through the pages, 'It also looks like it has been read a fair bit.'

Max turned the book over to look at the front.

'A History of the Canals of the Cotswolds. Another Catchy title.'

They both took a seat, and began searching through their books for Shadow Tide references. Some time passed before they spoke further.

Joe spoke first.

'What is the general gist of your book then in reference to the Shadow Tide?'

Max looked up from what he was reading.

'Very much a warning to stay away. I was almost sold on them being genuine when I saw there were books referencing the Shadow Tide, but it is only mentioned in one section, and the tone is slightly different to the rest of the book. I am not so sure this is legit. I have an idea.'

Max surreptitiously took out his phone and held the book under the desk; he took a photo of the cover, the information pages containing the ISBN number, and then the first and last pages together with some pages of the index.

He then put the book down on the table, 'What about yours Joe?'

Joe put his book down also, 'Well I think it's closely related to yours?'

'What do you mean?'

'Just that it is the same setup. There is only one section referencing the Shadow Tide and it advises caution, and not to bother with The Portal. I think both these books have been planted here. Joe took the lead from his brother, and also took some photos, making sure not to be caught.'

Max took the books and put them back on the shelf.

'I don't think we need anyone who might be following us to see what we looked at, are you happy to put a few fake searches in that computer to throw them off.'

Joe put in some searches he thought anyone following them might buy, and they left the library. Once outside, the warm air from the library was replaced with a cooler, but fresher breeze. To their left further down the street a man lit up a cigarette; the strong fresh smell of the smoke blew in their direction.

'Can I borrow your phone?'

Joe handed his phone over, 'Sure, why.'

'Well, it dawned on me that if someone has planted a copy of these books here, then they have probably been able to doctor search results, and put copies in online bookshops. Looking all that up will not help us, but I can think of one place where I doubt even Mr de Varley has thought to doctor copies of the books. One call should answer all this for us.'

Max typed and swiped on Joe's phone for a few moments before bringing the phone up to his ear. A few moments passed, Max took the phone away from his ear and typed a number, then put the phone back to his ear. A few more moments passed.

'Hello? Ah hello, I wondered if you might be able to help me; I wanted to ask if you had a certain book in your library. I have the ISBN number and the title...You can, that would be great thanks.'

A brief conversation ensued, lasting only a few moments.

'Well, thank you for your time.'

Max cupped his hand over the phone's mouthpiece.

'I'm speaking to someone at the British Library, they pretty much have a copy of every single book ever officially published, I was hoping they did not have a copy of the book, but they do.'

Max took his hand off the phone's mouthpiece.

'Sorry, thank you for your time.'

Max took the phone away from his face and was about to hang up. As he did so, his eyes lit up and he quickly put the phone back to his ear.

'Hello, *hello*? Are you still there?... Ah good, sorry I don't suppose you are able to access your copy of the book easily are you? It is important, I promise. You would, oh that would be great. Yes, I wondered, would you be able to let me know the page number on the last page?'

Joe began to follow his brother's logic.

Max began talking again.

'Yes, that's right, if you are able to call back on this number that would be great, thank you. I look forward to hearing from you.'

Max hung up and handed the phone back to his brother.

'I like your thinking. You're thinking it is much easier to doctor a book that already exists, than create a whole new one.'

'I am; and in thirty minutes we should know the answer. The lady on the other end of the phone has kindly agreed to go and look it up, and call us straight back. If Evo has doctored this copy here, then it would not be beyond them to muck about with online results; but I don't think they will have gone as far as messing with the copy in the National library. If the page numbers on the last page match the book we have just seen, then I'm wrong, and the books are genuine; but if it doesn't…'

Joe was nodding.

'If it doesn't and the number is noticeably different then…'

'Then we would have ourselves the first piece in this particular puzzle.'

'We would indeed.'

They turned and walked back to the car.

'You fancy a coffee in town whilst we wait.'

'I do, thanks.'

The two of them wandered through the alley-way that brought them into the centre of town. Although the temperature was not as high as it had been over the last few days, it was still pleasant. They found a coffee shop where they could sit out on the street and ordered something to drink. They sat in comfortable silence for a while. The voices of other customers blew in and out on the breeze along with the smell of fresh brewed coffee and hot toasted sandwiches. The strongest smell was warm tomatoes and warm basil. The brothers had finished their coffees and were just debating whether to order another when Joe's phone rang. He handed it straight to Max.

'Hello, yes I did, sorry yes my name is Max, I should have given that to you before. Yeah... exactly.'

A moment's silence prevailed whilst the person on the other end of the line was talking. Joe could hear a voice, but not what was being said.

'Ah OK, well I am very grateful. What was the number on your last page?' Max made a note of the number on one of the paper napkins.

'Thank you again for all your help, I really do appreciate. Good bye.'

Max handed Joe his phone back and pulled out his own phone and interrogated it for a moment, before looking at the number on the paper napkin. He began to smile.

'It's too early to say Got You Evo, but – I think we are on the right path. Look at the page number difference between the book we saw today, and the one in the National library.' Max paused a moment whilst he checked through the photos he had taken on the phone, 'Yes according to the index, the number of pages in the chapter about the Shadow Tide match exactly to the difference in pages between the two books.'

'Well, *isn't that* interesting,' said Joe. 'That can't be a coincidence.'

'*No, it can't.*'

'I also don't think there is any need to look into the second book. The fact someone has gone to serious lengths to doctor even one book is all we needed. So, whenever these Shadow Tide's first came into existence, it tells us someone is going to considerable lengths and expense to try and make them older than they are by altering books.'

'And furthermore,' said Joe, 'Someone is also paying people off to imply the same thing verbally.'

'Yeah you're right of course; Alastor is clearly involved in all this at some level.'

'Yes, unless he was fed the same line and genuinely believes it.'

'Hmmm.'

Max looked up at his brother as they began

walking back to the car.

'I don't think it can be that, he said he had known it since he was a child. I think he must be more involved in this than that.'

A short car journey found the brothers back at the hotel, they wandered to the Operations Room expecting to find some of the others there, but it was empty. They sat opposite each other at the table having got themselves some water. Max flipped a fresh A4 pad and pen towards Joe from the pile and took a pad and pen for himself.

'I don't think we are going to find who altered those books in the library, so it's probably not worth looking. Like everything else with this case, it all happened so long ago that the trail has gone cold. Probably not a good use of resources.'

Joe agreed.

'We think Evo is behind this anyway, so I am not sure we need to.'

'The problem for me,' said Joe, 'Is that for the life of me, I can't see the benefit in creating these Shadow Tides; what does Evo get from them? I mean how much does it even cost to shift that much water, that quickly with no obvious cash benefit. Either we are missing some financial angle or it is just utter madness and Evo is losing his mind.'

'That's a seriously good point. How do you move that much water that quickly? Maybe investigating the how will give us the who. We should make up a list, and then do some research.'

'Good plan.'

Four hours had passed before either of them spoke again. Max was the first to speak.

'So, I have searched for any reports in relation to local water-table problems, or anything that could point to water going missing on some large scale, but there is nothing online anywhere. So it is not being diverted from anywhere obvious or public as far as I can see.'

'OK.' said Joe. 'I have looked into professional wave systems for pools and for laboratory testing and there is nothing I can see that will create what we witnessed. They all need the water in place already; so that doesn't fit with what a Shadow Tide is. That's all a bust. From all I can see though, anything involved in large volumes of water is extremely expensive. The cost is way above just trying to create some drama around something you want to develop as a small tourist destination. It doesn't add up. There has to be something else going on here. What I can be sure of is there is nothing out there listed anywhere on the internet that is a Shadow Tide machine. Damn it!'

Max beamed a smile, 'Joe, you legend, *that's it*. You've just given us the break we need. Brilliant.'

'I have?'

'You're saying damn made me suddenly think dam, as in construction of. That suddenly brought back a memory of our meeting with

Alastor by the cars that first time, and him mentioning explosives.'

'I don't remember him saying explosives.'

'He didn't; he referenced a specific type of explosive.'

'And you are thinking a layman would have said explosive or dynamite, not listed a specific type...which means.'

'Which means Alastor is not a layman, but well versed in explosives; so perhaps an engineer in dam construction.'

'Exactly. Mark mentioned something about dam construction, didn't he? And of seeing Pete with someone who had worked with him on a dam project? I think our first job tomorrow is to find Mark, describe Alastor, and see if he can give us any pointers as to his real name. That might lead us closer to what is going on at The Portal, and with these Shadow Tides. I guess for now its meeting time.'

CHAPTER 32

Ava and Bruno were sitting in the far corner of the hotel's outdoor bar area. Ava looked up from her tablet.

'I have done a pretty in-depth search on Evo and on Chantmarle Capital, there is nothing negative coming up. There are a few vanity articles, but nothing much; though I guess that doesn't mean anything on its own.'

'No,' said Bruno, 'It only means they haven't reported any wrongdoing, not that there isn't any. That said, maybe there isn't anything to write about; it could be exactly what it appears to be; a well performing hedge fund.'

A pause ensued before Bruno continued with his verbal thought process.

'Of course – it could also be that the Chantmarle Capital legal team are using all their clout to keep journalists in line, and that there is a story; it's just not been exposed properly yet. My gut tells me something is up with that man.'

Ava looked up at Bruno, 'I agree.'

Bruno put his tablet down on the table and looked across at Ava.

'Well maybe there is a way we could test out whether there is in fact a known story, but for whatever reason no journalist will run with it.

They might not be willing or able to publicly say anything but, in private – well, that could be an entirely different matter. It might be worth giving Ollie a call and asking him if he can put us in touch with any financial journalists that he thinks might have looked into Evo.'

Ava picked her phone up from the table. It was warm to the touch from lying in the sun.

'Good plan, I will give him a call now and see if he can help.'

An hour or so passed whilst Ava waited for Ollie to return her call. She and Bruno had just ordered lunch and were handing the menus back to the waitress when Ava's mobile rang. For the next ten minutes she talked with Ollie about what she and Bruno were proposing. Periodically Bruno looked across at her, and could tell the call was a positive one. Ava finished her call as their lunch arrived. The prevailing breeze made sure the smell of two freshly cooked burgers arrived just ahead of the waitress who was bringing them. Ava waited until the waitress had withdrawn from their table before divulging what she had discussed.

'Ollie is going to send over the name of one of the journalists that have interviewed Evo a few times now. He knows the journalist better than he knows Evo, so he says he is fine with asking for a favour. He says it will be worth our while and we are in luck, the journalist lives nearby so hopefully he will be prepared to meet with us. I'll give him a call after we've eaten.'

A short time later, Ava called the journalist. He lived near Stow on the Wold which with summer traffic was about an hour away. Although wary at first, Ava had worked her charm on him, and he had agreed to meet them in a café in the town in an hour and a half.

'I guess him being cagey means there is something to all this. If there was nothing to say, I guess he would have said so.'

Bruno agreed with Ava's assessment. They grabbed the keys to Bess from the Operations Room; there was no one there. As they crossed the car park to the Range Rover, they noticed the Audi was gone. Bruno looked at Ava as he wandered round to the passenger side of the car.

'I am guessing Joe and Max are out exploring too.'

'Yes, I guess they are, I know that Matt, Bella and Norton all hired bikes from the hotel to cycle over to the pub. They still plan to ambush Eva. Hopefully it will work.'

About fifty minutes later, Ava and Bruno pulled into the centre of Stow on the Wold. Finding a parking space took some doing, but eventually they parked on the outskirts of the small town beside a rural Estate Agent's shop; they then wandered up the hill to the café that was to be their rendezvous location.

As they walked in through the open door, the smell of baking and coffee greeted them. The

café was packed and the atmosphere was conviv-
ial and loud. It was the perfect cover for a clan-
destine meeting. The diners were all involved in
their own conversations, and no one gave the
couple who had just walked in through the door
a first glance, never mind a second. Ollie had
called them back before they set off and warned
them that the journalist had called him back in
a panic, saying he regretted agreeing to meet
them, but after some pressuring from Ollie; he
had agreed again, but had been reluctant to; so
that they should expect it to be a waste of their
time. They weren't hopeful, but had decided to
come all the same.

Ava looked around the café. All the tables had
more than one person seated at them except
one. In the far-left corner near a window that
looked out on to a garden, sat a dishevelled man
hunched over his computer. Ava glanced across
to Bruno. He signalled they should go over.

'Mr James?'

The man looked up, slamming the laptop shut
as he did so.

'Yes, sit down… *sit down.*'

They did as directed.

Bruno lent forward so he was able to talk
quietly and still be heard over the high noise
level.

'Thank you for seeing us.'

The man did not make eye contact.

'I said to Ollie, I have nothing much that will

help you.'

'No,' Bruno said, 'I get that, but we could use anything that might help us. Just something that might point us in the right direction. We're only private investigators, so we have no clout. Nothing you say to us will go in any official reports, or get back to Mr de Varley.'

Mr James was not convinced. Ava was about to talk when a waitress came over and took an order from them. The conversation turned to general chitchat whilst they waited for the tea to arrive. Once it had, and the waitress had retreated, Mr James's manner and tone changed to a more serious and conspiratorial one.

'*OK*,' he said, 'I'll tell you what I know. I have no proof I'm afraid; you will have to take what I tell you at face value. It's nothing revolutionary; just something, that on the surface doesn't make sense.'

'We would be grateful for whatever you have to share.' said Ava.

'OK, as far as the hedge fund goes, that is legitimate. It's exactly what it appears to be. We were able to look into them well enough to satisfy ourselves that there is nothing shady there. They do appear to have made the odd random investment here and there over time, but then so do many hedge funds. The thing is, without knowing what their end goal is, what appears to us as a slightly odd play, could actually make a lot of sense if we understood their entire play book.'

Ava put her cup down on the table.

'So, if not the hedge fund, then what?'

Mr James took a moment. Ava could not work out whether he was still hesitant to share his findings, or whether he was enjoying the theatrics.

'Simply put,' said Mr James, *'It's Mr de Varley himself.'*

Bruno found himself getting a little impatient. He felt at any moment, Mr James would decide against telling them; but he felt if they could just get him started it would be fine.

'Evo? *What about him?'*

The journalist recoiled in horror at Bruno's question. Ava and Bruno gave each other a confused look. What had caused such alarm?

'You called him Evo. You know him personally. Why are you here, *what is this?* 'Mr James slid his laptop towards him and began to get up.

Ava reached out and put a reassuring arm on his. Making clear eye contact with him, she explained in re-assuring tones that they did not know Evo. Just that they had met him once for dinner in relation to the investigation, he said "Call me Evo." and that neither of them talked to him much during that evening. She explained that for what it was worth, they felt he was up to something, and somehow involved in a murder.

Mr James settled down.

'Oh I wouldn't know anything about that, but OK, sorry, I'll continue. It is just that men like Mr de Varley; they can cause serious trouble if they see you coming for them. *I have to be very careful.* Truth be told, I am working on my last big exposé. My wife has convinced me to retire; this job is not doing my health any good. Billionaires like de Varley can ruin your life in ways you can *barely imagine.'*

A moment of silence ensued whilst Mr James regained his composure. This time Bruno kept quiet and waited. Mr James took a further moment to compose himself before continuing. Then he dropped his bombshell.

'The *problem* with Evelyn de Varley is that *he is a fake – He is someone else's construct.'*

It was Ava's turn to look surprised; she had not seen that coming.

'Someone else's construct?' she repeated, 'What do you mean *exactly*?'

'Just that, he is a front man and a fake as far as being the guy who is genuinely running Chantmarle Capital.'

This time it was Bruno and Ava that let the silence fall whilst they processed this revelation.

'*Whose construct is he*?' Bruno asked.

Mr James gave a shake of his head.

'*That* I don't know.'

'But you know he is one,' said Ava. 'How, if you don't mind my asking?'

'Well I am actually an economist first and a journalist second. My parents are both economists also, so I have grown up around the complex economic theories that someone in Mr de Varley's position would be aware of. I got to interview him at length once, and when we got beyond a certain level of understanding, he clearly was out of his depth, and didn't know what I was talking about. I changed tack and went down another route, and again he got lost beyond the basic principles.'

Mr James paused to take a drink from his cup.

'It was then that I noticed he had placed his hand in an open bowl of individual sweets by his chair. I swear I saw him look like he was squashing one of the sweets, I wondered if he was just nervous. Anyway, a moment later and a PA appeared in the room, apologised and said something vital needed his attention, and he was ushered out. That was it, interview over. Once he had left the room, the woman returned and very politely, said I would need to leave, and thanked me for my understanding.'

Mr James paused again for a moment before continuing.

'It was then that I had a lucky break. As I got up to leave, I noticed my car keys had slipped out of my pocket, they were lying on the sofa, quite far back; I knew the PA couldn't see them. I left the room doing my best to chat to her, and make her feel important. Then, as we got to the elevator, I patted my trouser pockets, saying my keys must have dropped out. I headed back to the room. With the PA close by my side, I spotted a water cooler across the office, and began to cough as subtly as I could, and asked if I could have a glass of water. She kindly obliged. The logistics meant I would have about thirty seconds at the most to check out my theory. I moved quickly into the room and grabbed my keys, then I thrust my hand into the bowl of sweets; there was something in there, fixed to the bottom. I looked up and could see the PA heading back towards the room. Quickly, I brushed the sweets aside and there it was. A silver button with the word call engraved into it. *Well*, that was it, once I saw that, *I knew*.'

Ava and Bruno looked at each other again. A level of slight disbelief showing on both of their faces.

'You assumed that button was there so that should he get into difficulty; he could call for a PA to come and get him out of trouble,' said Bruno.

'*Exactly*,' said Mr James with an air of triumph. 'That is all though I'm afraid. Other than what I have told you, I have no proof. When I called back to follow up for the rest of the interview, they were cooperative, but I could only ever get to see one of their senior analysts; and I am sure I was followed for a while, though that is just a gut feeling. Again, I have no proof.'

'That's alright Mr James, no proof is a concept we have got very used to on this case.' Ava and Bruno gave each other a knowing smile.

Mr James began to pack his things away.

'Well I hope that has been of some help, I guess the drink is on you guys?'

Bruno nodded.

'Thank you for your time Mr James, I think you've helped us a lot. It certainly gives us a new lens to look at our investigation through.'

Ava and Mr James walked out into the street, waiting for Bruno, whilst he paid the bill. Ava thought that Mr James seemed keen to be on his way. Once Bruno appeared, they both thanked Mr James and he headed off in the opposite direction. Bruno stopped dead in his tracks, turned and jogged after Mr James.

'Sorry, one last question if that's OK?'

'OK.' Mr James seemed even more keen to be on his way.

'You mentioned that the hedge fund had made some odd investments. Can you remember what any of them were?'

'Yes. There was really only one that stood out. They bought into a company that was involved with the construction of hydroelectric dams somewhere in Europe; Germany *I think* it was. The only thing that was odd was that they paid way over the odds for it. None of my team or anyone I spoke to about it said they could see how they would ever turn a profit on the investment.'

'*Thank you*,' said Bruno.

Mr James gave a nod and in no time had rounded the corner of the narrow street, and was gone. Bruno walked back to join Ava and they wandered back to the car.

'What did you ask him?'

'I wanted to know what the odd investments were.'

'And what where they?'

'Just one apparently,' said Bruno. 'An unprofitable investment in a company that specialises in hydroelectric dam construction in Europe; Germany he thinks, but he can't remember for sure.'

Before long they were heading back down the Fosse Way in traffic that was just as heavy as on the way up. They sat in silence for most of the journey, digesting and analysing what they had learned.

'So the dam aspect is most interesting isn't it? I mean it's all about large volumes of water being moved around,' said Bruno.

Ava kept her eyes forward and took a moment to answer; she was considering what Bruno had just said.

'Yes, it is possibly a connection to The Portal. Do you think he is developing some sort of power station there? Some sort of clean tech energy he doesn't want anyone to know about? Perhaps the Shadow Tides are a bi-product of the process, or occur when something goes wrong?'

Bruno scratched his chin.

'Yes, I think so. That would make more sense. If they were after the tech from that dam company, then if it helps them develop some new clean tech that will be worth billions; it suddenly becomes a sensible play.'

'And where better to hide the development of such tech than in an old tunnel. Create a whole back story of folklore to explain away the strange phenomena until you are ready to unearth the tech to the world; making sure you keep a serious advantage over your competitors.'

Bruno nodded and then looked across at Ava, 'What do you reckon to the story about Evo being fake?'

Ava contorted her face a little.

'To be honest, it wouldn't be the first time the CEO of a company didn't understand fully what the geniuses below him were doing in his name. It could be his ego stops him admitting as much, especially if he was looking for a puff piece in the paper.

Bruno agreed.

'Fair point. So how do you reckon Bella is getting on with her crazy project?'

'To be honest I am worried for her. We still don't really know what we are dealing with here. I don't trust Evo. If Eva tells him that Bella has been trying to get her to talk, there is no telling what he might do. Hopefully they will have some news for us when we get back to the Operations Room.'

CHAPTER 33

It had taken Bella, Norton and Matt a good couple of hours to get to the pub where some of the team had met Old Fred, and where Eva sometimes worked. Matt and Norton had both suggested that they took a car or a taxi, but Bella said she wanted to look like she was genuinely out for a cycle. She felt that would be more believable for getting Eva to perhaps consider talking to her, and she felt part of that was having a legitimate reason for passing; like being out on a bike ride.

Just short of the pub, Matt and Norton had hidden their bikes and themselves in a nearby field, just on the other side of the A433. They made sure they had phone signal, and told Bella she was not to hesitate to call them if things even remotely looked like they might go wrong. Matt had further told Bella that if he did not hear from her with a test call within the next ten minutes, they would come over to the pub; because he would take it to mean there was no phone signal there, and she was not safe.

They watched Bella cycle up to the junction, turn right along the main road and then left into the car park. Matt activated his stopwatch.

'You really are taking this seriously,' Norton said to Matt.

'Yes, I really *am*.'

'But Eva is no match for Bella physically, I don't think there is anything to really worry about?'

'No, but we don't know who else is there. We don't know what we are dealing with yet. We have already been caught out once with the Shadow Tide, I am not risking things again. Do you not get that someone tried to kill us, and Stimpson and his men don't seem in the least bit concerned? They didn't even pretend to do their job properly and interview any of us about what happened. We are clearly on our own out here, so we need to make sure we leave nothing to chance.'

Norton wasn't actually looking for an argument, but he knew when to leave things alone. On balance it was a good idea. Matt had pulled himself up into the squatting position. Norton could tell he was getting ready to go in. The enforced ten minutes were nearly up.

Matt's phone rang, he answered it and said 'Fine.' He then put it back in his pocket and laid down on the ground again.

'She has enough signal then?'

'She does for now.' Matt's tone conveyed he was not at all confident about this particular part of the investigation.

Now inside the pub, Bella got herself a drink and a menu. She made her way to the small table where the door from the kitchen entered into the eating area. It would be a good vantage point from which to watch Eva at work before making a move. She just hoped Eva would be here today. What Bella had not told Matt and Norton was that she had come here without checking whether or not Eva was working today. Bella had not wanted to show her hand by enquiring, especially as she did not know who she could trust in the pub.

As luck would have it, Bella was still looking at the menu when the diminutive, hunched figure that was Eva came through a door at the back of the pub. Eva was looking in another direction and it gave Bella a chance to lower her gaze to the menu, and not make eye contact. That would help her with the surprised look she would need to demonstrate when Eva came over.

After a few moments Eva began to walk towards the kitchen door; Bella panicked and looked awkwardly down at the menu. She mentally kicked herself. Get a grip Bella. She told herself aggressively. You have one chance at this. Luckily Eva seemed preoccupied with something and wandered passed without even noticing Bella's presence. This is your one chance. Bella told herself.

Another five or so minutes passed, and Eva came out of the kitchen, again passing by without so much as even a glance in Bella's direction. Bella's confidence grew.

Choosing something from the menu, she got out a tourist cycle guide and spread it out on the table. When Eva came back this time it was make or break; she would lift her head and make positive eye contact with her, and say hello. Remember to look pleasantly surprised, she told herself.

About five minutes on, she clocked Eva heading back to the kitchens with an order from another couple on the other side of the bar.

'Hello Eva.'

Eva stopped in her tracks and looked across at Bella.

'*Mrs Stone* – hello, how are you?'

Bella could not see any sign of suspicion or concern on Eva's face. Just genuine surprise.

'I'm OK thanks. I decided to stay on and cycle around the area before I am due back at work. I'm not sure it was a good idea, but the exercise has done me good I think.'

Eva smiled, 'Are you looking for something to eat?'

'I am, yes please. The bike ride has left me very hungry.'

'What can I get you to eat?' Eva pulled out her pad.

'I think I will just go for Scampi and chips thank you.'

As Eva was writing down Bella's order and table number, Bella had a sudden inspiration as to how to try and get Eva to engage with her.

'I think,' said Bella standing up, 'I will actually sit on that side of the table; then I can look out towards the fields, rather than into the room, what with it being such a great day weather-wise.'

'Right you are Mrs Stone.' And with that Eva was gone into the kitchen.

Bella positioned herself on the kitchen door side of the table. Laid out her map, placed her phone near her glass, took out her keys for her flat, and positioned her debit card in just the right spot. It was to play an important part in her upcoming masterpiece, and should do more than just pay for lunch. The scene was set.

Bella felt good about her plan, especially as fate seemed to have intervened. On the wall to Bella's left was a mirror that from where she sat, allowed her to see through the small glass window in the kitchen door, and therefore see when Eva was coming. She tried to watch the mirror as carefully as she could; without making the angle of her head too obvious to anyone who may be watching her. The pub had lots of nooks and crannies, and it was perfectly possible someone could be watching her every move without her knowing.

She saw Eva coming, and could tell she was carrying food. Eva came out of the swing door and Bella could see she was carrying one plate of Scampi and chips. As Eva circled around Bella to set the plate down, Bella managed to accidently on purpose knock the table with her knee just at the right moment, so that her drink spilled all over the plate of food, her map, her purse, her phone and her debit card. The look of surprise on

Eva's face at the instant and unexpected carnage told Bella she had pulled it off to look genuine.

'*Oh I am so sorry Eva*. That is totally my fault.'

The drink had started to run towards Bella, giving her the perfect cue to add more drama to the scene by standing up quickly. Now the pint glass that she had picked back up fell and smashed onto the plate, covering the food in shards of glass.

'I am really having a bad day.'

Eva was standing looking on, taking a moment to register what best to do. She thought first she should just allow Bella to sort herself out before beginning the clear-up operation.

Bella had a short window in which to execute the main part of her plan. She scooped up her things including her phone and debit card. Before giving Eva a chance to respond, Bella dropped these items into Eva's hands. 'Please would you hold on to these for me for a few minutes and put them somewhere safe. I need to go and wash my hands. I want to make sure I didn't get any shards of glass on them. These items are my whole world. I don't want to risk leaving them here unattended, though I'm sure your pub is very safe.'

Eva found herself taking the items without really consenting to the move; and with that, Bella found her way to the ladies in order to clean up. In reality her plan was to wait for several minutes, and hide in one of the cubicles if necessary. She had watched something somewhere on TV or online, that had explained if you want to get someone to trust you, you first let them to see you trust them.

Bella was not sure if there was anything to it, but it had sounded plausible when she had watched the video, and it was all she could think to try. Like most things in this investigation, there was little to go on, so she winged it with the only thing that came to mind.

After what she felt was long enough without beginning to annoy Eva, Bella washed up, made sure her hands smelt of the bathroom soap, and then headed back out to the restaurant. By the time she had got back out, the table had been cleaned up, and Eva was nowhere to be seen. Bella headed towards the bar.

The barman looked concerned.

'Are you alright Miss? Is there anything I can get you?'

'Just the bill, thank you.'

She wanted to convey upset, but not overdo it.

'There is no bill to pay.'

Bella looked at him quizzically.

'No bill?'

The barman gave a slight shake of the head.

'No Miss, there is no charge, the manager has said so. He is sorry about the accident.'

Bella looked spooked for a moment. The last thing she wanted was for Eva to get into trouble over this, that would not help the mission.

'*Oh no*,' Bella spoke quickly. '*It was not Eva's fault*; it was totally my clumsy move. I don't want her to get into trouble.'

Now it was the barman's turn to look slightly quizzical.

'No Miss. I know it was not Eva's doing, it was just felt that it was an unfortunate accident; and as a token of thanks for coming to dine with us today, there is no charge.'

Bella looked awkwardly at the barman.

'Well that is kind. *Thank you*.' Then she stuttered again, a second quieter 'Thank you.'

'Eva will be out with your things in a moment, she is just drying them off in the kitchen for you.'

'Great, can you tell her I will be waiting outside if that's OK?'

'Of course, not a problem.'

Matt and Norton had seen Bella re-emerge from the pub. Norton whispered that now she was out and safe, he needed a pee; so he crawled off on all fours to reach some cover where he could stand up without being seen from the pub. Something glinted on the ground, it caught Matt's attention. It was Norton's phone. Matt picked it up to place it on the grass incline they were watching from, so Norton didn't lay on it when he returned. Matt looked at it for a moment. It wasn't Norton's phone, it was a different one. But it had to be his, he had been lying on it.

Without thinking Matt swiped it open. He couldn't believe what he was seeing. It was open with the text message app showing. A text had been composed, but not sent. It had just one sentence.

They are on to you; they are trying to
get your housekeeper to talk.

Matt's head was spinning. He couldn't think straight. He closed the phone, and decided he needed to get a grip and think about this calmly when back at the hotel. He replaced the phone where he found it; but buried it slightly deeper in the grass, and made sure he wasn't looking when Norton returned. Norton said nothing on his return, and out of the corner of his eye, Matt could see him stick it back in his pocket.

Bella headed further across the car park, breathing in the bright summer's afternoon; the warm smell of beer and hot cooked food was replaced with fresh air. She crossed the car park to sit on one of the benches and wait. Forcing herself to think of Pete, and how much she missed him soon brought things flooding back. The last few days of drama had acted as a mild distraction, but that was all they were. Soon tears were in her eyes. She felt she needed them if her second stage with Eva was to work.

A couple of moments later and Eva appeared at the table. Bella's plan worked better than she hoped. Eva instantly sat down.

'Oh my goodness Mrs Stone, are you *OK*?'

Bella dried her eyes as best she could, and before speaking, she reminded herself these tears were legitimate; and that this woman might be her only chance at finding out what happened to her husband. Furthermore, if during what Bella hoped was going to be a lot of conversations it was revealed that Evo had a hand in Pete's death, then all was fair.

'I am, thank you,' said Bella. 'I just have these moments I'm afraid. I just miss him so *so* much.'

Eva sat in silence, she wasn't really sure what to say, and thought it best to give Bella a moment.

Bella continued, 'Tell me, did you ever meet my husband; *did you like him*?'

Eva's face remained blank, expressionless. Bella began to worry that she had played that card too soon in the game and blown things. She was half expecting Eva to get up, make her excuses and walk away. As it happened she need not have worried. Eva's face broke into a smile. Bella noticed through the slats in the table, that although most of Eva's body was facing Bella straight on, her feet were pointing away. Somewhere she had read that was a sign that someone was still ready to try and get away. Play it cool, she told herself.

Waiting for a few moments to see if Eva would say anything, Bella kept quiet; Eva would have to say something.

'I did meet your husband a few times Mrs

Stone. I am only Mr de Varley's housekeeper, and some of his office staff can barely manage to say hello when they visit Nalebury, especially the ones up from London; but your husband always made time to say hello, and ask how I was. I remember one day he was at the manor for a meeting and it was snowing. Mr de Varley was late getting back from Cirencester, and Mr Stone saw me carrying the shopping in from the car. He came out of the office straight away, and insisted I go inside and sit down. He brought all the shopping in for me, and then he made me a cup of tea in my own kitchen; there's not many that would have done that, a real gent of a man if I may say so.'

Bella didn't have to play act the smile that was radiating across her face right now. She was taking genuine great pleasure in hearing about her husband, and being reminded of the qualities that led to her falling in love with him so quickly.

Appreciating that no amount of acting was going to allow Bella to show such a genuine expression of enjoyment, she seized on the moment.

'Please Eva, I know you will be terribly busy, and you probably get little time off, but would you meet with me and have some lunch. I would love to hear about your encounters with my husband. I am not sure if you are aware we were only married for three months before he died, so I don't have an awful lot to remember him by.

In place of the memories we would have built in time, I am hoping to build up a store of other people's memories of him to help me. Would you be prepared to do that, at your convenience of course?'

Bella's stomach was in her mouth whilst she waited for the response. She had placed her bet, and the wheel had been spun; it was just a matter of waiting for the result. It felt like an age.

'Yes Mrs Stone, I will. Your husband showed me great kindness, it is the least I can do for him in return. I have a day off tomorrow, where would you like to meet?'

Bella worked very hard to keep her expression and her voice calm.

'Where do you live Eva?'

'Not far, just in the next village over.'

'Great. Is there a pub or a tea room there?'

'There is indeed. There is a pub called The Tame Swan.'

'Great,' said Bella, 'Perhaps you would allow me to buy you lunch. I will be going home the following morning, so it is the last chance I have.'

Bella was hoping that added white lie would get Eva thinking that if she did this, then Bella would be gone.

'That would be very kind indeed Mrs Stone, thank you.'

'Great. Is twelve thirty OK for you?'

'That will be fine.' Eva smiled. 'Now I had better get back to work, or I will be in trouble with the landlord.' As she got up to leave Eva slid Bella's items she had dried off back across the table to her.

'Of course Eva, thank you. I will see you tomorrow.'

With that Eva wandered back across the car park, taking an order from another table before she vanished inside the pub. Bella for her part went over to her bicycle, and headed off back the way she had come. As per Matt's instructions, she did not stop by the field he and Norton were in; but cycled on further, passed the parked up black and empty car, on under the railway bridge, and waited around the corner for her colleagues to catch up.

They appeared in due course, and having pulled off the road so that they could not be seen, Bella updated them. She had explained that she had got her card wet, so hopefully it would not work, giving her an excuse to come back with payment, but that in the end, that ploy was not needed. Matt had been a little cautious that the meeting had been so easy to arrange. A couple of hours later and they were back at the hotel and had returned the hire bikes.

CHAPTER 34

Everyone was now in the Operations Room; they each gave a verbal summary report on their findings. Once that was done Matt stood up at the white board.

'So, what do we have in summary. Evo suspected to be a front, but on balance probably just can't follow his brightest employees; and that he has made an odd investment in hydro technology. We can't see how at the moment, but perhaps Evo's involvement with hydro technology is linked to his ownership of The Portal.'

Matt was quiet for a moment whilst he wrote the notes on the board.

'Then we have the Shadow Tide. Someone has gone to a great length to give this some sort of fake background; we think to hide the fact they are a relatively new event. We agree it is most likely an overzealous attempt to keep people away from The Portal, or they are a bi-product of whatever process Evo's people are developing there.

The white board pen gave the occasional squeak as Matt wrote. The familiar smell from it caught in Matt's nostrils from time to time.

'And then finally,' he said, 'We get to Bella's efforts to get Eva to open up, which she should have some more information on tomorrow. Well where does that leave us then?'

The team talked openly for a few moments, the result of which was their most likely thesis.

'We are all agreed then,' said Matt, 'That the most likely scenario is that Pete accidently died in The Portal, where Evo is developing some sort of new clean energy technology; and with Evo's desire for secrecy, and his I'm a billionaire and the normal laws of the land don't apply to me routine, he had the body moved, without any thought to anyone but himself.'

In their own way, everyone signalled they agreed.

'OK, so everyone is happy to continue with their research in their own areas until we either disprove or prove this theory we have developed, or we run out of time.'

Again, everyone agreed.

'I think all there is to do is to add a massive well done, and I think we should have an enjoyable evening; does everyone want to eat together? Max, can you hold back, I just want a quick word.'

As they wandered out, Bella joined Joe, 'As I will be at lunch with Eva tomorrow, do you guys want this... just in case?' Bella handed Joe the other key card.

'Thanks, I hope we won't be using this.'

'No, I know, but Ava has the other one, so it makes sense.'

CHAPTER 35

Matt motioned to Max to join him out on the balcony. As Matt went to open the door he seemed to be struggling with the lock mechanism, despite having had no problem the numerous times before.

'Everything alright boss?'

'*No*, not really. Max do you trust me, *I mean properly trust me*?'

'I do, one hundred percent; why what's up?'

'I need to ask you something very random. Then I need you not to ask me why I asked you, *can you do that*?'

'Of course, this is work; whatever you need.'

Matt leant against the balcony for a moment.

'OK. Do you trust Norton? I mean like you trust the rest of us?'

Max's answer was not what Matt had been expecting.

'No boss, *I don't*.'

'Thanks, I appreciate your candour.'

'*Always*.' Max gave Matt a reassuring smile.

Being good to his word, Max began to walk towards the door. It was obvious his boss needed space to process whatever was going through his head. For his own part, Max was surprised at how easy the answer had come to him. He hadn't realised until he had been asked.

Max held the door open. 'I'm starving... shall we?'

CHAPTER 36

Having passed a pleasant evening at the hotel, everyone was ready to go again the next morning; pleased that they were making progress.

After breakfast Ava and Bruno were sitting out on the balcony, planning their next move.

'I'm not getting anywhere further with research on Evo. There just isn't that much out there about him. He must have a team of people managing online stuff about him. Is it worth trying to get a copy of a birth certificate, or trying to trace his earliest years?'

Bruno looked at Ava for inspiration.

'Could do I guess. That takes time to get hold of though; perhaps we should focus on trying to find more recent stuff about the hedge fund, but try and do things differently.'

'What if we try some facial recognition analysis with Evo's photo rather than a text search, and see what that shows up, if anything?'

'That is an inspired idea. We can get a photo of him, send it to the Refract Speech labs, and ask them to run it against any online photos that they find. That might throw up a visual pattern we aren't seeing yet. I'll send one now.'

They were both surprised when the phone rang an hour later. It was one of the lab techs.

They would send over their findings. A few moments later, Ava and Bruno were each reading through a copy of the report. It made interesting reading; nothing they had investigated had led them to see this, but an analysis of photos had picked up a trend.

'So,' said Ava, 'Evo has been buying up an amazing amount of art. I guess that's not in itself odd. He does run a hedge fund after all. Perhaps you hedge the risky investments with more sensible long term secure investments like old masters and fine art. I guess that's the point of a hedge fund?'

'Yeah.' Bruno slid a photo across the table that he had printed out. 'Do you recognise anything odd about this photo though?'

Ava took her time looking at it. Try as she might, she could not see anything particularly odd about it. There was a photo of Evo and some other people drinking champagne at what looked to be an office reception. In the middle of the group was a large, stunning landscape painting, painted in oil, and sitting on a large easel. On the wall behind was the Chantmarle Capital hedge fund logo.

'No, I can't say that I see anything particularly odd with this picture. Just looks like Evo and some of his work colleagues sharing a drink, and celebrating the purchase of that painting.' Ava flicked through the accompanying report. Her mouth dropped open.

'*Fifteen million pounds… For one painting.*'

Bruno nodded very slowly, 'Yup and that seems to be one of the cheaper ones. There is another one listed in the report he bought in the last six months that he paid thirty million pounds for.'

Ava gave a disbelieving shake of the head.

'Even for a hedge fund, surely they are large sums of money for something so losable. I mean so much value in something so small.'

'Yes,' Bruno continued to flick back and forth through the report, 'I wonder if that is not exactly the point. Maybe Evo is looking to get his money out of the business. What if there is something wrong with it, and he is trying to get the money out of it, without spooking investors. Would that not be the perfect way to do it?'

Ava gave a moment's thought to Bruno's proposal.

'Yes, I guess so, but what makes you say that?'

Bruno lent across the table and tapped the painting in the photo a couple of times with his finger.

'*That's* what makes me say that.' He tapped the photo of the fifteen million pound painting.

'Really – why?'

'Because *I've seen* that painting *before*.'

'*You have*?' Ava sat up in her chair, '*Where*?'

'Not far from here actually. It is hanging in Evo's billiard room at Nalebury. I… *err*… well I noticed it when I had a little snoop after going to the loo when we were there for dinner. I will swear it's there, hanging on the wall.'

'Is that allowed? I guess if he owns the business it is. Him having it at home I mean; rather than locked in a bank vault, or at the office.'

'I don't know,' replied Bruno. 'I'm not sure how these things work; like you say, if he owns the business, then I guess so. What I do think is that we should probably see if there is anything else art world-wise about Evo, as that seems to be a focus; though how that would connect to The Portal, I can't imagine. No one would be mad enough to keep fine works of art worth millions of pounds in a damp tunnel in the middle of the countryside, would they?'

'No, I guess not.'

They both hoped the next couple of hours of research would tell them more.

Twenty minutes into the research session Ava's phone rang, it moved about on the smooth surface of the table as it vibrated. Ava leant in and picked the phone up.

'I don't normally answer blocked ID calls; it's usually to ask if I was involved in an accident recently, and if so, I'm due a pay-out.'

Ava answered the call, and putting the phone on loudspeaker, she placed it on the table.

'Yes?' she said in an abrupt manner, 'What do you want? I'm not interested in whatever it is you are selling.'

A well-spoken voice replied.

'I am not selling anything Miss Scott, and on

the contrary – *I think you will be interested in what I have to say.*'

For a few moments none of the parties spoke.

'I'm listening,' said Ava. She was keen to get this joker, whoever they were off the phone, so the line was clear for the call they actually wanted.

The voice spoke again.

'I gather you have been looking into Evelyn de Varley and Chantmarle Capital?'

'*How the hell do you know that?*'

Again, silence, before the voice continued, 'Nothing sinister, I assure you. Mr James told me about your cosy café chat. He and I have worked together in the past. He told me of your encounter, and that you seemed to be genuinely keen to get to the bottom of what is really going on with Mr de Varley. He thought that my observations of Mr de Varley would perhaps benefit your investigation. What I am not prepared to do is provide my name, or contact details, but I will tell you what I can on this one phone call.'

Ava moderated her tone to a more conciliatory one now that she knew she was not about to be told she could claim on her imagined accident, or that she had won a cruise.

'Well in that case, we would be very grateful to hear what it is you are prepared to share with us. I should explain you are on loudspeaker with my colleague.'

'I guessed as much,' said the voice, 'Good afternoon Mr Moss.'

Bruno sat up in his chair. '*Hello.*'

The disembodied voice continued, 'I know you are busy, as am I, so I will get to the point quickly. It is just that I work – I should say I worked for the UK government in a minor role. It doesn't matter what I did, I was a small cog in a big wheel; but my work did bring me into contact with Mr de Varley for a period of about six months a few years back.'

Bruno had grabbed his tablet and was setting it to record the conversation in case it would be of use later.

'You certainly have our interest, please continue.'

The voice obliged.

'Well suffice it to say, I am one of the Whitehall types that people get to meet when they are making a lot of effort to lobby the UK government.'

Ava interrupted.

'And just to be clear, it's in this capacity that you met Evo – I mean Mr de Varley?'

'*It is,*' responded the voice. 'Are you familiar with the concept of Freeports?'

Ava and Bruno looked at each other blankly. 'No.' they both answered.

'Well in principle, Freeports are buildings, or a series of buildings in which people can bring items of value into a country; and as long as the items don't then leave these buildings and travel further into the country, then there is no tax to pay on the item in question. They can stay in the Freeport or leave the country again, and no tax is due.'

'Sounds like a tax dodging exercise to me,' Bruno said dismissively.

'It can be *yes*, and there have been some incidents that would appear to follow in that vein, but to be honest there are also plenty of legitimate reasons for them to exist where it is not about evading or avoiding tax.'

'And we have these Freeports here in the UK?' asked Ava.

'No,' replied the voice, 'Not *yet*, but it is only a matter of time before we do. Generally speaking, the UK government does see them as a positive thing.'

'I see.'

'Good,' said the voice. 'Anyway, to get to my point, Mr de Varley's team approached us early on before Freeports were a priority for the UK government; but they made a good, robust argument for the creation of a couple of Freeports in the UK. To that end, we said we would consult further with them, and that is when Mr de Varley became more personally involved. He started attending all the meetings. Not something I have ever seen someone of his standing do at such an early stage. He was polite, focused, open and direct, but something was off; I could not put my finger on it at first.'

'Oh,' said Ava. She wanted to ask a whole load

of questions, but did not want to lead this person in any direction. Rather she just wanted to hear his story in his own words; though now they were onto this topic, she could not see that it was going to be relevant. Torn between being polite and hearing this out, or shortening the call, she decided to just let the voice continue. It would be a while before they would be getting the call they were really waiting for.

'*Well*,' continued the voice, 'In the end it turned out that what Mr de Varley was actually proposing was totally out of the question. He wanted the government to contract out the customs roles to his own employees, and allow him and his people to run the whole operation. He suggested there would be plenty of checks and balances in place. Well, there was just no way in the world the UK government was going to run with a proposal like that, not in this day and age. The potential for fraudulent activity was too great. So that was it. The project was dead in the water. De Varley and his cronies pulled out... almost stormed out in fact, and the government has ploughed on with its own plans in respect of the creation of Freeports in the UK. I have to be clear, there was no suggestion that the de Varley team and Chantmarle Capital were up to no good; it was just the principle that allowing a private company to do all that they were proposing was a nonstarter.'

'Yes.' said Ava, 'I can see that. There is no way

that makes sense.'

'No quite. Well that is not the main point. From what I got from Mr James, I cannot see the remotest connection between the Freeport business and what you are investigating. I just gave you that background so you could understand the context of what I am about to tell you.'

Ava and Bruno raised an eyebrow at each other.

'It is simply this,' continued the voice, 'That in all my years of service and government employment, I have never seen anything as odd. It's nothing remarkable in and of itself, but at the same time it really must point to something.'

Bruno was getting impatient, he wanted to hear the punch line.

'Well, it was just that in all my dealings with him, his body language just did not match his chat.'

'I am sorry,' said Ava, 'I am not sure I follow.'

'No indeed, I am not making myself clear. Sorry. From his spoken words and communications, Mr de Varley was very driven about his Freeport project, massively so in the way many Billionaires we deal with are. Often acting like spoilt children who are not getting their way for the first time when they meet an obstacle. He would be threatening things like, he would leave the UK and take his business and his money with him; then in the next breath, he would be offering things he could do for the UK, which to be honest is what I would expect from someone like him. *But his body language didn't match, not even remotely*. His body language was that of someone who actually was not really bothered either way. He just did not appear to have any real cares or concerns. As I say, I have never witnessed that before. When you meet someone and they say they are angry, the body language matches. The same when happy. With Mr de Varley, his moods changed, *but his body language didn't*. It was as if he was some third-rate actor. His odd behaviour has stuck with me all this time, so I guess it's relevant somehow. I just can't be sure *why*. When Mr James mentioned his conversation with you guys, something in my gut just told me I should tell you. I hope it is of some small help.'

Ava spoke, 'Well I am sure it will be. Both Bruno and I very much appreciate you taking the time and the risk to share this with us. We will give this a lot of thought, and see how it fits with what we know. Thank you again.' She did not have the heart to tell whoever this was that they were already aware of this sort of thing with Evo.

'*My pleasure*,' said the voice before hanging up, and with the sound of a click he was gone.

Bruno leant forward and stopped the recording app on his tablet.

'Not legal I know, but I wasn't sure what we were going to learn there.'

'No indeed. I didn't have the heart to tell him we already know about Evo living off his staff. and not quite grasping the true nature of what is going on at the small detail level. The problem with this case has been the same right from the very start. It all happened so long ago we have nothing concrete to go on from any angle. No witnesses, no fresh crime scene, in fact no crime scene at all...'

Ava stopped mid-sentence when she saw Bruno's expression. It looked like he was having a light bulb moment. Ava quickly scanned back through what she had said. She alighted on one word. Concrete.

Ava blushed, '*Oh*, that wasn't the greatest choice of word was it. A bit inconsiderate given how Pete died. I *didn't* mean anything by it though.'

Bruno gave Ava a smile that told her he knew she would never make such an unpleasant remark.

'*I know you didn't.* Your right about the word though. I think it might be the key to the whole mystery. We were on the right track with the specialist concrete before, but we went down a blind alley that's all.'

'Go on.'

'Well the problem with this case is nothing really makes sense. It all seems a bit farfetched and stupid to be honest, and that is what has been holding us back. No indisputable solid leads and all we do come up with seems pretty unlikely. I mean who sets up a secret lab to develop clean energy technology based around hydroelectric dams in a county that doesn't have the topography to support something like that?'

Ava said nothing in the moment Bruno stopped to breath and gain clarity on his thought process before carrying on.

'So, we keep searching for a different answer when we come up against a slightly odd theory; but what if that is exactly what is going on here. What if Evo is doing something very odd. Suddenly everything begins to make more sense. It's not like there are no eccentric billionaires in the world. He certainly wouldn't be the first by any means.'

Ava failed to conceal her surprise.

'So you think Evo really might be developing some new tech in The Portal, because no one would think anyone would do that in a county that they could never deploy it in?'

Bruno shook his head, 'No not quite. I think he is up to something in The Portal, but I don't think it involves developing some revolutionary technology. *If I'm right*, it is all to do with something that is as old as the human race itself.'

Ava looked incredulous, 'And what is that?'

'*Avarice.*'

'I don't think I follow.'

Bruno woke his tablet up and swung it around to face Ava.

'There.' He said pointing to the screen.

Ava read the article, speaking as she went.

'This is an article about some of the general

similarities between some of the existing European Freeports.'

Ava began to read out some of the listed similarities. 'Another common feature,' she said out loud, though not loud enough to be heard from any greater distance than where Bruno was sat opposite her, 'Is that these structures are all built to ensure they are resistant to earthquakes, a key component of which is specialist concrete.'

Ava folded the cover over the tablet and handed it back to Bruno.

'It's a Freeport. Evo has constructed an illegal Freeport right out in the middle of nowhere.'

Bruno put the tablet to one side, and then took a drink of water from his glass.

'Yes, I think he very likely has done exactly that. If we run with that crazy theory, everything suddenly makes sense.'

'You're right, it does. The reason why a business minded billionaire would buy a white elephant like that in the first place. The fact that if Pete accidently died there, or was killed there that Evo would not want anyone sniffing around, so he would move the body. It all begins to fit.'

Ava paused as she thought.

'Oh, but it still doesn't explain whether Pete was killed deliberately, or if it was an accident, and none of this explains the Shadow Tides.'

'Well,' said Bruno. 'I was thinking about that. I agree about it not helping us to get any further on the circumstances surrounding Pete's death, but I think the Shadow Tide can be explained, backed up by what Joe and Max found out in relation to the doctored books in the library.'

Ava was now sitting up straight, and both she and Bruno had instinctively leant forward across the table so that they were close.

'I think we were partially right about the hydro dam situation being relevant, but not to develop any new clean energy, I think it's probably a defence system. Think about it. If Evo has built a Freeport there, from a customs and excise point of view it can't offer any tax relief, so it has to be about storing items of high value for some other reason. If there is no tax benefit, then it surely has to be a secrecy benefit. And given the cost of building something like that and the sums Evo deals with, there has to be some seriously high value stuff down there. Even a state of the art alarm system on its own isn't going to be enough protection. Given the secrecy of the place, you also can't have high perimeter fences and armed guards walking about, or a large building that shouts go away; that would draw too much interest. But...'

'*But...*' repeated Eva.

Bruno moved in even closer.

'What if you developed a whole back story and a system that creates something that if you get caught up in it, there is a good chance you die. Then plant a few stories of people being killed. That's going to deter pretty much everyone but your most determined criminal, because firstly most people don't know it's there, and secondly there is a killer defence mechanism in place. Guard dogs bite. Shadow Tides kill. – Well, so it would appear.'

Ava sat upright, the sun was getting uncomfortably hot now, and she wanted the protection of the shade.

'What is wrong,' asked Bruno. *'You look horrified.'*

'I am Bruno. Don't you remember, the Shadow Tides taking lives, it's not a tale. People have died from them. *We nearly died from one.'*

Bruno looked a little ashen white despite the climbing lunch time temperature.

'That's what worries me Ava. Just what lengths will Evo go to to protect what he has down there.'

'Yes,' said Eva, 'And if he is willing to allow a death or two in order to lend credibility to his protection system, *then...'*

Bruno finished Ava's thought before she could, *'Then... it's perfectly possible he killed Pete, and that having shown us a wonderful evening's entertainment, he tried to kill all of us too.'*

They sat in silence for a few moments, the enormity of what they had just said sinking in. Not only that Pete may well have been murdered by his boss, but also it reminded them what a lucky escape they had all had from their encounter with the Shadow Tide.

Bruno finished the last of his glass of water and

gathered up his tablet.

'If you are up for it Ava, I would like to go to The Portal now. Park down by the road, and just carefully walk up the tree line with some binoculars, and see if we can see anything that would lend credence to our theory. Maybe a guard post or other high security device we have missed. It would be good to have something to back up our theory with when we tell the others.'

'Sure thing,' said Ava, as she too stood up and gathered her phone and tablet from the table. 'We should probably let Matt or someone else know where we are going.'

'Good plan,' agreed Bruno, 'We also need to grab some keys for one of the cars unless you have a set for either car on you already?'

'No I don't. Bruno?'

'Yeah?'

'You're not proposing that we go into The Portal are you? Not alone, or without backup because if we are correct...'

Bruno stopped and turned to look Ava straight in the eye, he wanted to reassure her.

'No Ava, there is no way I would consider putting our lives at risk by entering that portal until we have backup, or more idea for sure what is going on there.'

Ten minutes later, they were crossing the car park towards the cars. They had grabbed the keys to the Audi. There had been no joy contacting Matt, though they had left a handwritten note on the desk. As they got into the car Ava wondered if it had been a good idea to leave the note near an open window. The wind was picking up as the afternoon rolled on. She had tried to call Matt again, but his phone was still not responding, neither was Norton's.

CHAPTER 37

Bella had not long arrived at The Tame Swan. Again, she had insisted that she was going to cycle there, so Matt and Norton accompanied her. They hid two of the bikes out of sight, and again Matt insisted on setting up a vantage point, so he and Norton could keep an eye on what was going on and respond to any threat immediately.

Much to Matt's annoyance and concern, they discovered that there was no phone signal at the pub. Matt and Norton were with one service provider and Bella with a different one, yet all the phones registered no service. The venue was in a communications black spot, which did nothing for Matt's blood pressure and anxiety.

Matt had to take a moment to calm himself down. Whilst he was doing that, Norton had found a small side terrace that was further round the corner from the main terrace, and which was difficult to see. It was well hidden, and once Norton had moved a couple of the tables around, he assured Matt that they would have a good vantage point from which to watch Bella; furthermore, they would only be a matter of feet away. Rather than relying on technology, they would be able to rely on their eyesight. This clear and frank situation report allowed Matt to regain his inner composure.

Bella for her part had selected a table, and ordered a very expensive bottle of champagne. She had managed to talk to a few of the pub staff despite it being busy, and by luck, had managed to identify a member of staff that was only on their second week. They had been brought in to help with the extra summer customers. Bella had handed the waitress an enormous tip that had probably matched her entire week's wage, and requested that as soon as she saw an elderly lady join her, that she bring out the bottle of champagne already open. Bella then asked that when that bottle was down just below half, she was to bring out another bottle also already open without checking with Bella first. Bella assured the waitress this was vital as it was an old family reunion, and that they were trying to patch things up, so rather than check at the time, the waitress should do what was being asked of her without question. A further request from Bella was that the waitress was to wait at least forty-five minutes before bringing the lunch menu. This was something that the waitress was happy to do given how busy they were. That would allow them to get much of the lunch rush over before she had to worry about these two.

Matt and Norton positioned themselves in place, and Bella positioned herself so that she was in the shade, and that Eva would be in the sun; as much as Bella thought she could handle without asking to move.

Now it was just a case of waiting to see if Eva would indeed show up, or whether this operation had been a complete waste of time. Things seemed to slow down, and before long it was ten minutes past their agreed lunch date. Bella was beginning to get anxious. She began to question the moral aspects of what she was doing. She certainly felt guilty, and some shame that it was her intention to make an elderly woman, who clearly still worked long hours, who held down two jobs, probably for little pay, sit in the sun and get drunk. All in the name of hoping to loosen her tongue, and getting her to help get to the bottom of how Pete died for once and for all. It was her last chance, and if it worked; or even if it didn't and it was all for nothing, Bella would be sure to make amends. If she was unable to do that to Eva directly, then she would make sure to find some way to repent for what she was about to do. Perhaps a substantial donation of some of her remaining life insurance pay out to an age related charity.

'Hello Mrs Stone, I'm sorry I'm late, I was waiting inside. I didn't see you out here.'

Bella quickly composed herself.

'Not a problem, that's my fault. Sorry, I was just closing my eyes and enjoying the sun on this lovely day. Please take a seat.' Bella's stomach tightened. She felt bad already, but this had to be done. Her husband had not deserved to die, and the worst-case scenario for Eva was a blinding headache for a few hours.

Eva took her seat across from Bella.

'I think it might take a few moments to get served. I didn't think it would be this busy midweek, but of course it is summertime.'

'That is no problem,' said Bella, 'I hope you don't mind, but I have taken the liberty of ordering a bottle of Bollinger champagne. Just a small celebration of Pete's life. It would mean the world to me if you would be prepared to join me?'

Bella was worried that there were many reasons Eva might object to drinking champagne. She began to castigate herself for picking something like that, she should have waited to find out what Eva enjoyed as a tipple, if she even drank at all.

'That would be lovely,' said Eva, 'I do like champagne. Mr Evelyn gives us some very nice champagne at the Christmas staff party.

'Oh, that *is* great, *I am glad.*'

Not wanting to push her luck, or risk any early mistakes, Bella changed the topic to her cycle trips; how stunning this part of the world was, and how busy it seemed at this time of year.

Right at the allotted time, the waitress appeared with the champagne wrapped in a white cotton napkin and placed it in a cooler with two glasses. They really do things properly here, thought Bella.

As instructed previously, the waitress just set

the items down and left. Bella poured the champagne out. A third of a glass each. She didn't want to alarm Eva, and stop her drinking. She needed to do her best to get Eva to loosen her tongue and spill anything she knew. This was Bella's only chance and she knew it.

Bella handed Eva her glass, and picked up her own glass. She raised it.

'*To Pete.*'

Eva copied Bella's movement with the glass.

'*To Pete.*'

They both drank.

Eva was clearly savouring the taste. Bella was glad she had bought an expensive bottle. Eva can enjoy something she doesn't often get to drink, thought Bella.

'That is nice, a real treat, Bollinger is my favourite. Is this an R D?'

Bella had to actively ensure her face did not give away her surprise.

'Err – yes, it is the R D, 2004. Wow you really know about champagne.'

Eva looked down at the glass. Bella wondered if she was avoiding making eye contact. She guessed probably not when Eva then looked at her directly, though she did look a little flushed. Probably embarrassed, thought Bella.

'It is my one guilty pleasure. I have learned from my boss, and every now and again I treat myself to something special. I don't really drink, so it's a couple of times a year, but I have learned a little.'

'Oh, come on Eva,' Bella said, 'You just named the vintage from a single mouthful.'

Eva smiled, 'Yes, I get that looks impressive, but this is my local and once you said it was Bollinger; I know they only have two Bollinger options on their wine list, and this has that subtle hint of wood and nuts that I don't find in the non-R D version they sell here.'

This revelation had thrown Bella off track, but she wanted to relax Eva, so they talked further about champagne. Bella kept it on that light subject whilst they consumed the rest of the first bottle. Without Eva noticing, Bella had managed to make sure Eva had drunk the lion's share.

Once the second bottle had arrived, and they had eventually ordered lunch, Bella decided it was time to launch her enquiry.

'Thank you coming and meeting me like this. I hope you understand that I have to ask this; but do you know anything of what really happened to my husband?'

Eva's eyes widened, 'Would you excuse me a minute?' She then got up and left the table.

Bella started to panic, thinking she might have blown it. Had Eva just left? She would give it ten minutes and then accept she had just lost her one chance.

To her surprise, Eva returned after five minutes.

'Sorry about that, I needed to freshen up.'

'Of course.'

Eva lent forward so as to be able to lower her voice whilst ensuring Bella could still hear her.

'I have worked for Mr de Varley for a great many years, and he would never hurt anyone. Yes, he is a successful businessman, but he is a money man, a finance geek; he got rich by being clever, not using brute force. I will concede that his behaviour has been a little off in the last couple of years, but nothing at all to the level of having someone killed. Besides Mrs Stone, he was very fond of your husband.'

'I am sorry,' Bella said as genuinely as she could, 'I just had to ask. I hope you can understand?'

Eva nodded but said nothing. They sat in silence for a few moments. Silence was not something that Bella wanted. She didn't want this open chat to close over.

'He has been a little off you say?'

Bella modified her tone to be as gentle as she could make it. 'I hope he's OK, and it is nothing serious. Not money worries or problems with the business?'

'No, I think he is just stressed, he carries it all on his shoulders. He has a bright team working for him, but it is his name on the letterheads and his name if things go wrong.'

'And are things going wrong?'

Eva looked very awkward, Bella guessed she was not comfortable with talking about her boss like this, even if the champagne had loosened her tongue. Bella filled up their glasses again, and the food arrived. Eva looked relieved.

'Your Dover sole looks perfect,' added Eva as Bella's lunch was placed on the table.

'Thanks, I am getting food envy looking at yours though. That Pan-fried Red Snapper looks cooked to perfection.'

Bella was having mixed feelings. On the one hand, she was having heavy feelings of guilt at her moral wrongdoing, but on the other side of things, she felt things were going well. The previous near two years of relentless pushing for what really happened was proving an extraordinarily strong magnetic force in keeping Bella's moral compass from pointing true north; for now anyways. She had come this far. It's not like anyone is going to get properly hurt. That's what Bella told herself.

'Evo certainly seemed to be a very decent and kind man,' Bella said next. She had decided to go for the positive approach, and hope that her appearing to think highly of Eva's boss would help move things along.

Eva finished her mouthful of food.

'He is he really is; I have worked for him for as long as I can remember. *He is a truly good man.*'

Bella struck whilst the iron was hot.

'It must worry you considerably then if his behaviour is off.' Bella chose her next words with care, 'And it must be difficult for you carrying these worries on your own.'

Eva looked sideways and down at the ground. Bella wondered if she was having doubts about whether she should be speaking like this.

'To be honest Mrs Stone it is. It is a worry. I am not sure what to do, I am just keeping an eye on him, and I keep a little notebook detailing any incidents I think merit recording. Then I look back and watch for any dramatic increase in his odd behaviour. So far I haven't seen that, and I am not sure what to do if I do.'

'My mother was a nurse. If it would help, I might be able to shed some light on Evo's behaviour from what I have learned growing up in a house with a medical professional for a parent.'

Again, Eva waited until she had finished what she was eating.

'That is very kind Mrs Stone, it's not easy to pinpoint. It all seems to centre around that portal. Life was much simpler before that came on the scene. He has been obsessed with it ever since he first discovered it was potentially for sale.'

Bella went as slowly as she could so as not to cause Eva to back off.

'He wasn't bothered about the Shadow Tide stories?'

'He checked them out,' said Eva, 'He said it was all nonsense, just superstition.'

'*But it isn't,*' said Bella. 'Whatever it is, *it nearly killed us.*'

'*Oh*, there is something there right enough. I just keep out of all that, I have no idea what is going on. Evo sneaks down there at all hours of the day and night, and gets quite aggressive with me if I ask too many questions, so I have just stopped asking. It is easier not to and besides, I am his housekeeper, his business is none of my concern.'

'What can be down there that makes this so involving. I thought it was just to be a tourist attraction.'

'*That*,' said Eva finishing up her lunch, 'Is a good question, and one I do not have the answer to.'

Bella poured out the last of the second bottle, she was expecting Eva to protest, but she didn't.

'Would you like some desert Eva?'

'Oh no – thank you Mrs Stone I am very full; it has been a very spoiling lunch. I will need to walk home, and rest for the afternoon, before sorting Mr de Varley's evening meal out.'

Bella realised her window of opportunity was beginning to close. Correct timing or not, she would have to put her final strategy into play now. She began to speak quicker than normal, putting more purpose in her voice, in the same way a lawyer might do when cross examining a witness, though obviously she had to be careful not to overdo things and annoy Eva. She made sure to retain her genuine concern.

'Do you need a taxi home?'

'No, thank you Mrs Stone.'

'Will you be OK to get to Nalebury later?'

'I will be fine thank you.'

'Was my husband's job in the portal?'

'*Yes – I mean…*' Eva's face went bright red '*Well* that is to say, *I think he did*, I assume he did; though Mr de Varley would never talk business in front of me.'

'Does Evo have anything else around here, business wise?'

'Just the estate.'

'Yes, but my husband didn't know anything about agriculture.'

'*Oh right.*'

'Eva, *I need to know, did my husband die at the portal or in it*?'

'*No, of course he didn't.* He was found in a quarry, *you know that*, you were present at all the proceedings.'

Bella was beginning to get angry.

'*That is not what I asked Eva.* I asked you; *did my husband die outside the portal, or inside it*?'

Eva stood up.

'Look I am sorry, it has been a very pleasant lunch, I know you are grieving for your husband, but this has all been dealt with. My boss has quite enough to contend with, and he feels bad enough that Pete died whilst up here, but he is not to blame for what happened Mrs Stone; I am sorry, but there we are.'

Bella stood up also.

'I do appreciate you coming Eva, and all that you have shared with me, thank you. Let me walk you out.'

The pair of them wandered into the pub. Norton and Matt looked at each other, not sure whether to follow, or wait for a few moments. They decided on the latter. Then they would follow at a discreet distance, though looking at the way Eva had stumbled out of the courtyard, neither of them thought much harm could come to Bella just now. As they passed the table Matt noticed a large wet patch on the ground. Ah clever Bella, he thought. She must have been subtly pouring some of her champagne out on the floor to keep from getting too hammered.

Eva had politely waited while Bella settled up. With the tip included, Bella didn't think she had ever paid that much for lunch before in her life. If this led to resolving what happened to Pete, she would frame the receipt.

They wandered out into the car park.

'Well, Mrs Stone as I said, thank you very much for the pleasant lunch, it was most enjoyable.'

'*My pleasure*,' replied Bella. 'I really *do* appreciate you coming and thank you for all you shared. I am sorry if I got a bit pushy at the end there. My bad.'

'Really not a problem,' said Eva, 'Please don't give it another thought.'

Bella grabbed her hire bike and walked with Eva across the gravel until they got to the edge of the main road and the tarmac.

'Are you heading back to the hotel then? Please do ride safe if you do. You do know you can be done for riding a bicycle over the limit too. Maybe you should get a taxi?'

'That is kind, no I am fine,' replied Bella. 'I am going to cycle to the portal actually. I am going to have one last explore before I leave tomorrow.'

Eva looked horrified at the suggestion.

'*I really must insist you do not do that Mrs Stone*. Mr de Varley does not want people poking about there, especially until they can get to the bottom of the violent, sudden flooding issues. *Have you not learned your lesson?*'

Bella swung her head around sharply to look at Eva.

'*Is that a threat?*'

Eva for her part looked confused, 'A threat? Of course it is not a threat. I am concerned for your welfare, and I know my boss doesn't like people snooping around there. It's not safe. You already know that.'

Eva paused for a moment before speaking again.

'I really must implore you not to go anywhere near the portal Mrs Stone. *Stay away*.'

With that, Eva wandered off into the village, and in what Bella assumed was the direction of her home.

For some reason Bella was now adamant that she was going to cycle to the portal. Her blood was up, and her gut just told her that she finally had hold of the lead that was going to get her the truth about what happened to her husband. There was no way she was not going to the portal right now. She began to cycle forward when a strange force slowed the bike down and brought it to a halt. A familiar voice spoke. It was Matt, he had hold of the rear of the bike.

'*Where are you going Bella*? We agreed we would talk after the meal and plan together.'

Bella managed to quickly shake herself out of her weird mood.

'Sorry Matt. I have just managed to wind myself up, and also I am not a heavy drinker so I think I am fairly drunk.'

Matt was concerned things needed to cool off.

'Let's sit down and talk things through; you can fill Norton and me in with what was said. We couldn't hear anything.'

Slowly, Bella got off. Matt was relieved once she was separated from the bike.

'Come on, let's sit in the shade over there, and you can tell us both what you have learned.'

'I will do Matt,' Bella looked at him with a serious expression, 'But first there is one thing I need you to do, in fact the last thing I am going to ask you to do for me. Can you get us a taxi? I want to go to the portal and see if Eva or Evo turn up there. I am not talking about going in; just watching the road from a safe distance. Please do this for me.'

Matt could sense the earnest desire in Bella's voice, and he saw no harm in observing any comings and goings on the portal access road from a distance.

'Sure Bella, no worries. Firstly, how drunk are you?'

'Probably too much to ride safely. I didn't think about that.'

'Well that is fine.' Matt took out his phone. 'Let's get a taxi to take the three of us down and drop us off near The Portal, then you can tell us what was said whilst we wait for it to arrive.'

They sat in the shade and waited. Matt arranged for the hotel to come and collect the hire bikes, and Bella filled him and Norton in on what was said. When she explained she had got Eva to admit Pete died in the portal they were both amazed.

'*Well, you broke the case open then Bella. Fair play*. Your determination paid off. You got where I don't think anyone else was going to.'

Bella forced a smile, 'Yes but that might be as far as we get. *I still might never know if it was an accident or deliberate.*'

'Well,' said Matt, 'Why don't we wait and see, we still have some more time. I would not have thought we would have got this far, so *never* say never.'

'Indeed.' Bella's smile was more natural now. 'I do feel bad about using Eva like that, I will make amends to her once we are all complete.'

After about twenty-five minutes a taxi turned up and took them down to the portal. Matt got the taxi to stop short, and they walked in along the hedge line, and laid up on a vantage point waiting to see who, if anyone turned up. Bella reckoned that if Evo turned up in a panic, then she would be more inclined to murder than an accidental death, though what she would do with that supposition, she was not sure.

Matt, Norton and Bella settled into their vantage point, and Matt dug out his binoculars. He scanned up the access road, it all looked quiet. 'Of course he may have already arrived, or he may not come at all.'

Neither of the other two answered, they would just sit and wait. Matt was about to put his binoculars away when he realised he had not swung them to the left. He didn't expect to see anything, but he reckoned it was worth a glance; and indeed, it was.

'*Damn*. What is that doing there.'

The tone of Matt's voice made Norton sit up and take note.

'What?' he whispered.

'*Dougal*.' Matt hissed back.

'*Where*?'

'Here. He's here, parked up on the edge of the road, but there is no one inside. Do Joe and Max have him or Ava and Bruno?'

Norton gave a shake of his head.

'I have no idea.'

Matt took out his phone, '*Still no signal.* What is it about this part of the world; no phone signal in some places, and plenty in others?'

'*They will be fine boss.* They will be doing what we are, they will be watching. Maybe they have learnt something too. I doubt they have gone inside.'

'*I really hope they haven't.*'

Matt didn't sound convinced. In his mind, he was planning that this evening was definitely the time to bring the curtain down on this circus before anyone got hurt again, or worse. Bella be damned. He would not give into any more of her whimsical ideas or plans.

CHAPTER 38

Joe and Max continued from where they had left off yesterday afternoon; they went to look for Mark. It took them until well after lunchtime to find him, thanks to some well-meaning person sending them on a wild goose chase to Devizes. It turned out there were two Marks who worked in the hotel grounds; and the wrong Mark was equally surprised as Joe and Max, when he was hunted down by these two strangers at his sister's house on his day off.

When they finally found the right Mark, it didn't take more than a few moments for him to identify the tall man with the deeply blue eyes and the odd manner. Mark confirmed that Alastor was the man he had seen with Pete. He really was Jeff Pyke, and he was an engineer that specialised in hydro dam construction. Both Max and Joe had the same thought; it was probable that Alastor – Jeff Pyke also worked for Evo. The odd name Alastor or Jeff had used to describe explosives had come back to Max. Octogen; they had checked, it was indeed a specialist explosive your average person would not know about.

'We need to find Matt, he should be back by now, I can't get him on the phone. Let's head to the Tame Swan via The Portal, and make sure they haven't headed there. *I don't like this.*

They moved back to the main hotel car park.

'Bess is here we will take her. I will grab the keys from the Operations Room.'

Joe jogged off across the car park to the hotel, Max took out his phone and tried Matt. His phone went straight to voicemail. The same for Norton. He tried Ava and then Bruno, all with the same result.

A few minutes later Joe reappeared and unlocked the Range Rover. They hopped in.

'I can't get hold of anyone. Everyone's phones are off. There is no phone signal at The Portal is there?'

'No,' said Joe, 'Only deep inside it. I have a bad feeling about this.'

'*So do I*, let's get there fast.'

CHAPTER 39

Max and Joe sped down the country lane towards The Portal.

'Oh… *that can't* be good.'

Joe looked across at his brother, '*What?*'

'Dougal.'

'Where?' Joe scanned around.

'Over there. Parked up.'

'Oh… *indeed*,' replied Joe, 'Ava and Bruno must have headed into The Portal. We need to get there quickly, and warn them. They don't know what they are heading into. If we are right, and that's really a Freeport, there will be armed guards inside, and Evo has too much to lose. I have lost signal now on my phone. Why would they go in there alone?'

In that moment, Max experienced his first genuine panic attack. He wanted his friends safely out of The Portal at any cost. Rules be damned. Dam, that's it, he thought.

Coming to the bridge, instead of parking on the side of the road as normal, they turned off and drove down the small track that would bring them out on top of the portal roof. Half way along, Max did a three point turn and headed back out onto the main road, then to the access path that lead down to part of the canal below the dam. Max drove a little way down into the old canal floor. They both got out on foot and checked the floor was not too boggy. It was not. It would be fine to drive on without getting stuck, and should give them some much needed traction for their task. Getting back into the car, they quickly reversed towards the dam. They both hopped out, and between them, they fixed one end of the large chain from the back of the car to the dam supports, and the other to the car. They hopped in and Max rolled the car forward until it took up the strain, then he put more power down, the car's wheels dug into the ground, the engine note got louder, suddenly there was an almighty crack and in the rear-view mirrors they could see a wall of water coming straight for them. Max quickly drove the car up the bank and onto the towpath, whilst the water now flowing below them fanned out and flooded the area downstream.

Max backed the car along the towpath, and up onto the road, having unhooked the chain and put it back in the car.

'Are you going to tell me your plan Max? I have a nasty feeling I am not going to like this.'

'*You'll love it*; you are always one for adventure.'

'True but I like odds too. I like the odds of survival to be in our favour.'

Max moved the car off up the road; they sped up the dirt track following the bend to the left at the top. Joe realised they were now on top of the portal roof; the balustrade was just beside them.

Max spoke quickly and clearly.

'Bess are you listening?'

The car responded. A female voice spoke, and it seemed to come from deep within the dashboard.

'Yes Max I am listening, I can hear you clearly, what do you need?'

'I need you to mark this journey from when I say mark until I get out of the car, understood?'

The car responded, 'Understood.'

Max moved the car into the far corner of the parking area, away from the portal and the canal.

'Mark,' He barked clearly and loudly, having put the car in Park and taken his foot off the brake.

'Mark confirmed at this point.'

Joe's facial expression was one of incredulity.

Max clocked Joe's expression whilst he put the car into Reverse and carried out a fast J turn, resulting in the car's nose pointing towards a gap in the balustrade. The gap was the top of a very steep makeshift staircase that would eventually lead down to the canal water's edge.

'I know Joe, I know – I had meant to explain about the new upgrades to Bess and Dougal, but in all this carry-on I simply forgot. I will explain all the upgrades if we make it out alive.

Joe's facial expression changed quickly from incredulity to alarm.

'You mean *when* Max – *when… not if.*'

Max nodded, 'Sorry, yes, I mean *when*.'

With that, he put the car's gearbox into Drive and accelerated to the edge of the steep steps, before coming to a stop. Looking forward out of the car all they could both see was a large black bonnet, and ahead of that in the distance, nothing but trees and sky. Joe wiped his sweaty hands on his trousers and then placed them on the edge of either side of his seat for support, his hands sank into the soft leather upholstery.

'*Ready*?' Max looked across at Joe who was checking his seatbelt.

'*Ready*.'

Max moved the gear selector into Neutral, then moved it across to the left and waited for a moment. The car emitted three loud beeps. Max then moved the gear selector down to 1 and pressed the mode button on the gear selector casing; the word MANUAL now glowed red.

'Right, once I take my foot off this brake pedal there is no going back.'

Joe nodded and said nothing, Max took that as a complicit agreement to the manoeuvre.

Max lifted his foot off the brake pedal, the car began to creep forward, the bonnet began to tip downwards, and the occupant's view changed from the heavenly trees and sky to the dark canal and valley floor. Joe's stomach lurched. The car began to speed up. The car was sliding about slightly as it gained downward momentum, Max was making very gentle corrections to the steering wheel, being careful to keep his thumbs flat on the outside of it. Max's gentle inputs to the steering wheel had corrected the car's movements from side to side, and they were now on a very definite course, pointing them straight down into the canal water below.

They gained momentum as gravity pulled them towards their watery destination, and as they did so the rev counter began to rise substantially. The V8 engine was not complaining, but its normal muted wiffle sound had morphed into a loud howl as the mechanics of the engine fought the pull of gravity. Joe watched the rev counter climb its scale, 2 – 3 – 4 heading towards 5. Joe saw it only went to 8, and that they were still speeding up. He leant his right arm across and gave a gentle tug on Max's seatbelt buckle to make sure it was in securely. He then checked his own, they both were locked in place. If anything went wrong now, they were very likely to end upside down, in ice cold water. They would have to wait until the whole car filled with water before swimming out through the windscreen, or out through the tailgate, having smashed the glass first.

Joe was beginning to calculate how long that might take, and how much time they would need to hold their breath in icy cold water if they both had a chance to survive. The results of Joe's calculations were that their odds would not be great. Joe popped open the cubby box between the seats, and was delighted to see the glass hammer and seatbelt cutter was within easy reach. Please God be it that I don't need to be using that today, he thought.

As he was wondering whether to broach an escape plan with Max, their rate of descent began to slow. As Joe was relaxing, his heart once again jumped into his mouth as he saw Max aim the car straight for the canal, and drive over towards the edge of the water. He then swung the car to the left towards the façade and stopped for a moment.

Pressing a large button in the upper middle section of the dashboard, the car began to rise in height. One small circular orange light that was next to an image of a car sitting on a normal road extinguished, and the small circular orange light directly above it was now illuminated. Joe looked at the corresponding image for the newly lit setting, and in that moment he knew exactly what Max was about to do. The image was that of a car clearly in deep water. Within a couple of seconds of Max having pressed the button, the car had lifted itself up considerably. Once it was up to its full height, Max turned the car hard right, put it into Drive, hit the accelerator and drove at the water. The level was dropping fast as the water rushed out of the portal, and down towards the dam they had destroyed.

Joe's heart was in his dry mouth. What an irony, Joe thought again, given how wet they were about to become if Max didn't stop. He did stop though, and they were now sitting in some very long grass. Putting his foot on the brake, Max moved the gear stick to the right. Again the car made three loud beeps indicating the transmission was moving back to high range. Joe assumed they were parking up, and that Max was just going to move the gear stick into Park, and they would get a Jet Ski and go in.

Max didn't do that. He moved the gearstick into Drive and hit the accelerator. As the car tipped forward towards the water Joe instinctively lifted his feet out of the foot well against the incoming flood.

Max smiled at his brother's understandable reaction. Joe realised that rather than plummeting into the water they were just driving in. What Max had noticed on their previous trip to the portal that Joe had not, was there was an access ramp built into the side of the canal wall to allow gentle water entry, probably for boats and trailers etc. They drove down into the water and Max brought the car to a stop.

Joe looked out of the windows. The water was no longer that deep, the canal had drained much quicker than he had imagined. A couple of feet at most. As soon as the wheels hit the water, the escaping flow caused water to splash and foam up and onto the bonnet. It was still deep, and above the bottom of the doors, but not deep enough to be a problem. The car's engine would be able to breathe safely without inhaling water, and the car's electronics would be able to remain dry.

The car came to a halt and then started to slide.

'The combination of the slippery canal floor and the power of the water flow means it's trying to carry us in the wrong direction.' For a moment, Max looked mildly panicked. He managed to get the car to stop.

'Ah finally the penny drops. You want The Portal empty so we can drive in.' said Joe.

'Yes, fastest method I can think of doing two miles in.'

Max put the car in reverse, 'Now for the tricky bit.'

Joe looked across at him, '*Now for the tricky bit*?'

Max raised his eyebrows at Joe

'Bess?'

'Yes Max.'

'Are you still marking this journey?'

'Affirmative.'

'OK, now we are going into The Portal, I want you to keep us straight and stop us from bouncing off the walls. Understood?'

'Understood.'

Max slowly reversed the car towards the façade. As he did so the rear view mirrors dipped to show the black, wet journey ahead of them. The car came to a halt as its rear wheels rested against the concrete lip on the edge of the portal floor.

'OK that will work. Joe have you got Bella's

pass?'

'I do,' Joe reached into his pocket to grab the pass and handed it to Max.

'What are you going to do with that?'

Max reversed the car a bit further until he was in line with where he thought the control panel was to open the garage. He attached the pass to the selfie-stick lying on the back seat in order to get to the right height as if the water level was still normal. He held the pass to it and the door began to open.

'I want anyone coming behind us from our team to be able to get in there if they need to. You just never know, they may not be in here yet.'

Joe gave a slow nod indicating his understanding of his brother's plan.

'*Here we go.*'

With that Max accelerated and they moved up and over the concrete lip. The car's engine note climbed. The engine sound reverberated around the chamber, and together with the transmission and the water under the tyres, the noise was deafening. They kept the speed under 35mph, which was terrifying enough, and in a little under five minutes the reversing lights were beginning to light up the roof collapse brickwork.

Joe gave a positive nod to Max.

'Well that certainly cuts the commute time down.'

'Sure does.'

They both got out. Steam was wafting out from underneath the car. An aroma of hot dirty water hung in the air. There was a gentle hiss from this water evaporation, and rapid ticking from the car's engine cooling down.

Max grabbed the key card and the selfie-stick off the back seat again, so that he could reach up to the right area, and waved it around the walls. This time he was much slower, and tried to guesstimate again what height it would be done at from the boat or the jet skis that were stored back at the entrance. It worked. The key card flashed green, and with a rumbling and the sound of a hydraulic pump, the wall began to slide back to reveal another concrete staircase. Max went back to the car.

'Bess, you can save the mark to here OK?'

'OK Max done.'

'Good, so on your way out, if you have to go alone, you know what to do.'

'I do Max.'

'Is there anything else I need to tell you or do for that to work?'

'Nothing.'

'OK Bess thanks. You have your instructions.'

'I do.'

Max opened the tailgate of the car, and grabbed a rucksack and two lightweight jackets. He gave one to Joe.

'Here put this on.'

Joe did as he was told.

Max looked at Joe earnestly.

'I genuinely have no idea what we are walking into here. Do you have any ideas? Any thoughts on what we should do?'

Joe shook his head, 'No. Nothing, we could find absolutely nothing here; we could find a real horror. Ava and Bruno might not be in here Max, we might be over-reacting. I have never seen you like this before.'

Max pursed his lips.

'I know… I just have a real sense of foreboding. I don't want to take any chances.'

Joe swept his arm out forwards towards the staircase.

'In that case; *after you*.'

Once they had made their way up the first set of stairs, they were met with a small hallway with a second set. They were damp, and all the lights and fittings were clearly waterproof. Anxiety levels began to rise in both of them. The stairs ran around the outside of the wall, and in the centre at the bottom was a cage lift. On the wall there was a large metal box with two large yellow push buttons. Beside them one had the word Open, the other had the word Close. There was also a large red plunger that had STOP embossed into it in capital letters. Recessed into the same metal box was a small TV screen that was smashed. The word POWER was also written on the box next to a large green light that was glowing brightly.

'Someone has hit this in a temper by the looks of things,' said Joe.

Max came over to take a look, 'So they have.'

Joe ran his hand across the top left hand side of the metal control box. There was a word embossed into it.

'Must be the manufacturer for the control stuff I guess.'

Max squinted in the dim light.

'What does it say?'

Joe lit up the area with the torch on his phone.

'Just looks like it says CHARUN. Is that a make or brand you have ever heard of?'

'It is ringing a distant bell in my mind somewhere. Come on, let's climb the stairs and see what is at the top.'

As Max walked ahead, there was a loud clunking sound, and a momentary vibration rose through the floor.

'What the hell was that?'

'Err, might have been me. I pressed Open to see what would happen.'

'*Really*? Was that a good idea?'

They both looked above their heads, and around the room for a moment. They couldn't hear anything else.

'I guess it's all broken,' said Joe, 'Probably just as well.'

Guessing what Joe was thinking, Max whispered, 'I don't think this can be part of any flooding, not with the lift there, that doesn't somehow look like it has been designed to be submerged.'

Joe breathed out audibly, 'No, I was thinking that. We should be *OK*.'

They walked up the stairs, heading to the top, which led along a corridor. Metal cabinets were recessed into the wall with various pipes and wires coming out of them. Some had red digital displays showing various numbers. All the numbers were static, but there was no clue as to what any of them meant. The air was thick with moisture, both Joe and Max felt they were literally drinking in the atmosphere; they could feel it on the back of their throats. The end of the corridor came to yet another staircase which they climbed. At the top was a substantial looking metal door painted in dark grey. When they got to it, Joe put his hand on it. For some reason, the metal was cold and slippery to the touch.

Max ran his fingers around the door frame as best he could.

'I can't feel anything like a rubber seal or anything else that makes me think there is a tonne of water sitting behind this door. This looks like a service corridor, and all those panels we passed are not designed to get wet. You OK if I open this door?'

Joe looked directly at Max, his brow furrowed.

'You really think we should be doing this... I'm not sure any of the team are in here.'

'I think one way or the other we need to get to the bottom of what this place is before Matt pulls the plug on the investigation.'

Joe more or less agreed, 'We have come this far I guess.'

Joe knew neither of them should be here; they were beginning to do things that were very much out of character, this case seemed to have had that effect from the start. Max had just destroyed a dam and directly disobeyed Matt purely from a panic attack based on nothing more than a hunch that two of the team members had entered the portal against instructions. That was not normal Max. Up until this case, that would never have happened. Oh well, too late now, Joe thought.

Max rested his hand on the cold metal door handle, and pulled, then pushed it to see if there was any play in the door. There was. He pulled down on the handle. The door began to swing slowly inward and as it did so, no water appeared. Both men relaxed a little. This was definitely not a water-tight door. Whatever it was that lay in wait behind this door for them, it was certainly not an enormous wall of water. They could take a moment to breathe and calm down.

CHAPTER 40

Ava was trying to make sense of what she had just witnessed. She was giving it some thought as she crawled back from the edge of the canal; back to the rhododendron bush that Bruno was waiting and keeping watch in.

'Anything happening out there?'

'Yes you could *certainly* say stuff is happening. Anything happening here, still no one about?'

'Matt, Norton and Bella have arrived in a taxi. They have hidden themselves in that rhododendron bush further up towards The Portal. We should probably move up and join them. *Why*, what else did you see?'

'Oh it just looks like Max and Joe have destroyed the dam under the bridge, drained the canal and driven into The Portal in Bess. *Otherwise*, it's all quiet.'

Bruno's jaw slackened and his brow furrowed.

'*For real*? You're sure it was them, *not someone else*?'

'I know there are plenty of black Range Rovers in this part of the world; but I doubt any of the other ones would be driving into the canal and reversing into The Portal. Although I couldn't see the occupant's faces due to the angle, I was able to see the registration as the car drove down the steps – Y923JPP *it's definitely them.*

Bruno stood up and looked around before walking out of the rhododendron.

'What do you think they are up to?' He looked at his phone, it was still showing no signal. 'Do you reckon they think we are inside The Portal?'

'That or they are on to something major that couldn't wait. Either way, we should get in there and join them, give them some backup.'

Ava and Bruno joined up with Matt and the others. Matt had given a brief update on what had happened at the Tame Swan with Eva. Bruno thought Matt looked to be in danger of having a genuine heart attack when Ava had told the others what she had witnessed.

'*They have driven into The Portal? And they haven't come back out?* How long ago did they go in?'

'Just a few minutes ago, they are obviously onto something, or they think we might be trapped in there; guess that's the problem of having no signal for so long.'

Matt's imagination was running riot, he should have shut this nonsense down when he had the chance.

'Ava, did you say they have emptied the canal?'

'Yes, pretty much. It's certainly low enough to drive into.'

'Do you have Bella's key card on you?'

'I do.'

'Can you and Bruno head over to The Portal and

recce the site. Norton, Bella and I will go back to the road, find some signal and call the police. *I don't care what happens; I want this case shut down now, and everyone out of here and safe*. Sorry Bella enough is enough, we are definitely done.'

Bella nodded in agreement. She was suddenly worried for the others, and this was on her. For the first time since the start of this case, she was beginning to think of others wellbeing before vengeance for the dead. She would make do with what she had learned at the pub.

Matt realised he may have been a bit harsh with Bella. He pulled out his phone and swiped through some of his notes, until he found what he was looking for.

'Look Bella, it's not like you haven't got what you hoped for,' Matt paused for a moment to read from the phone. 'You can take what Eva admitted at the pub to the police; get a good lawyer, and then make a request to the Attorney General under section 13 of the UK Coroners Act 1988. They can then authorise that the inquest into Pete's death be started again. I looked it up before we first took the case; it was why I felt this was worthwhile. I didn't want to say anything until there was reason to. So in a way you have what you need, I hope that will be enough for you from us. I need my people safe.'

Bella gave Matt a quick hug.

'It is Matt, *thank you*.'

'Right Ava, Bruno, on your way; we will send

for help, then come and join you. Bella we will bring you back here and you will wait for the police – no arguments.'

'No arguments any more Matt, *I promise*. I want everyone safe too.'

With that, Ava and Bruno made their way towards the entrance of The Portal.

CHAPTER 41

Bruno and Ava had made it to the mouth of the portal. They had expected to find some sort of security given what Max and Joe had done; but the place was deserted. On finding the garage door open, and guessing it had been done by Max and Joe, Bruno only made one comment.

'Well done lads… good thinking.'

After what felt like twenty minutes, Ava and Bruno had worked out how to operate the hydraulic platform, and had the two all-terrain quads down with their engines running. All the water had drained out now, so it was not too long a ride into the portal before the lights of the quads lit up the reflectors in the Range Rover's headlights. They turned the quads round ready for escape and then shut off the engines.

They then spent the next few minutes interrogating Bess about what the other two were up to, and the car's AI had related what it had stored and processed. On the opposite side of the portal to where Joe and Max had gone, the wall was missing, much in the same fashion as the garage they had got the quads from. The opening was taken up with ramp that dropped down onto the tunnel floor.

'Bess, who opened this?'

'I am not aware, it opened a minute or two after Max and Joe went up those stairs. At the same time the rock fall behind sank into the floor.'

'Did it? No one appeared here though?'

'No one.'

Ava surveyed the entrance hall that had been concealed by the wall. It looked to be like an enormous loading bay complete with ramps and lifts.

Bruno had a thought.

'Ava, the lads will need Bess to escape if things go sideways, but if a Shadow Tide is released, it will destroy her and the quads, and cut the chances of an escape for any of us.'

'What are you thinking?'

'Bess do you think you could get yourself in here and up that ramp?'

'Yes.'

'Let us move the quads, then get yourself in there will you, it might keep you safe.'

Within very little time, the car and both the quads were safely inside the loading bay, and high and dry out of reach of any impending Shadow Tides. They could tell by the state of the floors and walls that no water level had been this high. Bess informed them that Max and Joe had taken a couple of warning beacons. There were no alarms, and vitals seemed fine, they didn't appear to be in any immediate danger.

'As there doesn't seem to be anyone about, is it worth us having a quick look on this side before joining the others? We might find something to our advantage.'

Bruno began jumping the steps two at a time.

'Way ahead of you, come on, let's get to the bottom of this nonsense for once and for all; I want to know what Evo is keeping here that he thinks justifies trying to kill us.' As they ran up the stairs Ava looked up and behind her onto the wall.

There on the wall, was one word that told her they were getting close to the truth. It was writ large in blood red vinyl lettering.

'Bruno, *wait… look at this.*'

CHAPTER 42

Matt had waited to give Ava and Bruno what he guessed was enough time to get to the entrance of the portal. When all was quiet for long enough and he assumed they were safe and unhindered; he decided he, Bella and Norton would head up to the road, find some phone signal and call the police. Matt decided he would make an anonymous 999 call, and report gunshots inside the portal. That should make sure the police took things seriously. Matt's thinking was that level of threat reporting should be too large for DCI Stimpson to thwart. They would have to come running.

'*Right*, let's all head up to the main road and find some phone signal; *then* we can head into The Portal, join the others, and wait for the police to arrive.'

'That's OK boss, Bella can stay with me; that would save us all traipsing up to the road, then all the way back.'

Matt thought back to the damning text on Norton's non-work phone and his generally poor behaviour since the case started.

'No Norton, *not happening*. We all go together like I said. *If that is OK with you*?'

Matt had headed out of the rhododendron followed by Norton, who was waiting to help Bella over the roots that needed navigating when leaving the tree-sized shrub's sanctuary.

'*No Matt, it isn't OK*. I think we'll start doing thing's my way.'

To Matt's utter horror Norton pretended to offer Bella help with one hand, and with the other, in one motion as if he had done it before, pulled a hypodermic syringe from his pocket, removed the cover with his mouth, and then plunged the needle deep into Bella's neck, fully depressing the plunger, draining the syringe's contents into Bella's body.

Bella looked first at Norton; then at Matt. It was a look of total lack of comprehension. She instinctively slammed her hand over the point where Norton had injected her, and had now removed the syringe. Again, Bella turned first to look at Norton, then to Matt. She fell, lifeless, to the woodland floor. A small cloud of old leaves blew upwards as Bella struck the ground.

Matt literally saw red; he saw nothing else but the colour red. His vision failed him. He charged and yelled in the direction he thought Norton was. He felt a blow to the back of the head, and he too fell to the ground. A moment or so later, his rage subsided, and he could see Norton; he had stepped out of the way. As Matt's vision fully returned, he saw Norton had a pistol pointed at Bella's head. He spoke in a cold, vicious and unemotional voice that Matt had not heard before.

'*Don't try that again old man*. If you do, I will

put a bullet in her, and you can explain to Max that because you failed to follow orders, his precious ex is dead.'

Matt needed to buy some time to think and plan, '*OK OK... fine.*'

'Now – *pick her up*. We are going to have a little wander into The Portal to meet my real employer. I am only going to say this once; *you try anything at all, and I will kill you both.*'

Matt was alive, he could deal with situations like this, he was trained for these. His PTSD subsided in a crisis; it was when all was mostly calm that he struggled. He would treat this like a mission. Norton was the enemy. To be taken down when he could. Questions could be asked later.

Norton was getting impatient.

'I said pick her up – *now.*'

Matt scrambled to pick Bella up and hoist her over his shoulders.

'So you haven't killed her then?'

'She's only asleep at the moment, whether she wakes up or not is up to you. Now *start walking, and no talking*. After all these years I can say out loud that I hate the sound of your voice. *God that feels good.*'

Matt's brain was calm, but misfiring, he could not fathom who this man was. Who this man had been? They had known each other since they were children, and yet he clearly didn't know this man at all.

Norton pointed his gun at Matt and waved it

twice in the direction of the portal.

'You are going to have to carry *Mrs Pain-in-the-Arse Stone* all the way into The Portal since your idiot friends have vandalised and drained it. We won't be using the bikes; you're too good a rider. I hope you are up to this. It would be a shame to shoot you both inside The Portal. I don't want the bullet ricocheting and hitting me.'

Matt decided to keep quiet and think. He was not sure he would be able to carry Bella nearly two miles into the portal; but he equally was not sure that if he failed, Norton wouldn't just shoot them both.

CHAPTER 43

Bruno stood looking at the blood red large letters on the wall that Ava had drawn his attention to. Two pieces of the puzzle now fell into place and made sense.

'Well spotted. So that is what Bella actually heard Pete say on those phone calls, CHARON, not SHARON. *The name for this place*, not a work colleague. No wonder we never came across any staff member with the name Sharon. Any idea what it means?'

Ava instinctively took her phone out to look it up. Then remembered she was deep underground in a tunnel. She was about to turn her phone off when the signal indicator caught her eye.

'I have full phone reception down here, *how is that possible*?'

Bruno looked pensive for a moment.

'Come to think about it, I noticed I had phone service when we were deep in the tunnel structure before. It must be Evo. They must have installed it for their own use. Since you already have your phone out, what does it say about Charon?'

Ava swiped and typed for a moment or two before coming up with an answer.

'What is it with Evo and this obsession?'

Bruno waited for Ava to continue, rather than answer her rhetorical question.

'I'm sure there are other things with that name, but the top search result is for the ferryman of Hades – or in other words the underworld; so I think that's probably the relevant one.'

Bruno nodded, 'That's Pete's calls fully explained, "See you at the underworld... sorry Charon." He was being corrected by, or joking with the other person about his use of name for this place, not joking with a work colleague called Sharon.'

Ava gave a small nod of her head.

'That's what the letters on the wall were, just another reference to the underworld. S-T-Y-X. They have named the canal after the mythical river in the underworld. Evo has a really weird sense of humour.'

'Or he's just really weird in general,' countered Bruno.

Eva tried to call Matt, then Joe, then Max. All their phones went to voicemail.

It was Bruno that eventually broke the moment's silence that fell between the two of them.

'Shall we go and have a poke about, and find out what this place is for once and for all; then we can find the others, and get the hell out of... well.... hell I guess. Creepy Evo's hell anyway.'

'Right behind you, lead the way.'

Keen to be on their way, they both bounded up the stairs to the landing.

They arrived in a cavernous hallway. The walls were unpainted concrete with all sorts of doors set in different walls. The space was formed in a hexagon shape. Four of the walls had very large doors and a large red number painted next to them. Clockwise they read 1 to 4.

Each door had a key pad on it.

Ava pulled the second key card from her inside pocket, 'Please do the honours.'

'*You sure?*'

'Yeah, then it's all on you if you trigger an alarm,' she added, smiling.

Bruno shook his head in a mock fashion, and held the key card to the panel by the nearest door, which had a large red number 1. He held the pass against it. The pass and the panel glowed green, and a word matching that on the wall flashed on the card. There was an electronic buzzing sound which ended in a click, and the door opened inward a fraction.

'OK,' said Ava, 'But what is this place, what is Underworld exactly?'

'Let's take a look.'

He swung open the door. Before them was another long corridor with many doors opening off it. As they stepped into the corridor, all the lights came on, making them jump.

'I guess they are automated; I thought for a second there was someone here with us.'

Ava was still taking in this new corridor. It too was warm, and had a concrete smell. It was reminding her of her school gymnasium, though here there was no smell of stale sweat, just an exceptionally clean, fresh, warm air.

'I would have expected to find someone here.'

'If this place is what I think it is Ava, it concerns me greatly that we are most likely not alone.'

They presented the key card to the keypad on one of the doors. The same green light display occurred and the door opened. They stepped inside, again as they did so the place lit up. This time though there was a dramatic change in air temperature, a cool air rushed at them knocking the warm corridor air out of the way; washing over them, flooding up their nostrils and reaching into their inner senses, as if they had just been transported to some high mountain top. They both stood there, light after light switching on, their mouths open. Even in their wildest dreams, they had not expected this, not here. What lay before them was still incomprehensible; how could something this size exist underground.

Ava was the first to speak, 'So it *is* a Freeport.'

'I think so. Evo has built a massive, illicit, private Freeport deep underground in the middle of the Gloucestershire countryside, its either genius or madness.'

Ava looked slightly concerned, 'I sincerely hope its genius, because if its madness… all bets are off. There is no telling what Evo could do. At least genius is based in reason.'

Bruno didn't want to go there in his mind, certainly not at the moment. Mentally processing this place and all its craziness was enough to be going on with. What lay before them was a vast store room. On one side of the wall there was a vast floor to ceiling store of wooden boxes containing fine wine all stored on industrial racking painted red.

Bruno had wandered over to take a look. 'There has to be over a million pounds worth of wine in here.'

'And what about this side?' Ava was looking at a large glass store room, with a humidity control panel fitted to the door. It was filled with different wooden boxes, a couple of which were over twenty feet tall.

Bruno wandered over.

'Those are paintings. I guess God only knows what is in there.'

'Whatever is in there,' said Ava, 'Something tells me that we are definitely going to have heard of the artist.

Bruno gave a small nod of his head, 'Yup, I agree.' He reached his hand out to touch another smaller box that was on the floor by their feet. As his hand made contact with the wood, an alarm started sounding in the roof space. Both Bruno and Ava were startled. They turned towards the door instinctively, and as they did so, to their horror, they saw the door begin to swing shut.

Without needing to say anything to each other, they both ran for the door. Just before they got there it clicked shut. Bruno panicked and lunged at the door handle. He pulled down with dread, expecting it to do nothing, but quite to the contrary, the door opened. He looked out into the hall, there was no one there.

'Bruno,' Ava's voice sounded very calm.

He wandered back into the room.

'I think we are OK. It was just a climate control alarm. We probably triggered it by leaving the door open.'

She pointed towards a control panel on the wall. It was flashing some text. HEVAC alarm. Climate parameters are outwith pre-set limits. Auto correction protocol initiated.

'That's OK then,' said Bruno, 'But that is likely to have tripped an alarm somewhere, there is no way in hell this place is not heavily monitored. I think we may have just shown our hand. Let's head back.'

They looked at the map schematic of the layout of the place that was on the wall. 'Look at the size of this place it has to be something like forty thousand square meters of floor space. Why don't we head over to the other side of the canal and look for the others? We could get lost here, and I am sure we will only find more of the same.'

'*Good plan.*' Suddenly Ava had a very real desire for everyone to be together; there would hopefully be safety in numbers.

They closed the door and headed off back into the entrance hall. As they passed through the larger doors, they encountered Evo waiting with four henchmen, all of them armed.

'Hello you two. Do you like my little secret? I really would have rather that you did as I asked, and left it alone. Now *what* am I going to do with you?'

Neither Ava nor Bruno felt like playing along, so let the silence linger. Evo seemed to be finding the whole thing quite amusing.

'Shall we go over to the other side of the tunnel, and join your vandalistic cohorts? I hope they are going to pay for the damage to my dam. Let's go.'

Two of the guards each jabbed a gun in the back of Ava and Bruno, indicating that they should start walking. The other two guards flanked Evo, who led the way up the stairs and towards an anonymous metal grey door with a large yellow and black warning sticker on it. It had some black wavy lines and just three words. Beware Deep Water.

CHAPTER 44

Max cautiously pulled back the grey metal door. To both he and his twin's relief, no water nor anything else tried to make its way through. Instead, they found themselves on top of a large concrete gantry, with some sort of enormous winching kit that rolled out across the rest of the chamber. Over the edge of the gantry was the rest of this enormous concrete chamber below, it was the size of a large warehouse. There was a large oblong hole in the floor that looked like it went a long way down. To the right, was a ramp or slide that slid down into the hole in the floor. Besides that, ran a staircase right down to the chamber floor. The only other noticeable feature was what looked like a vast round metal chimney that sat in the middle of the chamber; its top a good way off the ground. There was damp everywhere, and at various points on the walls, there were white and brown stains where the water was eating away at whatever was behind the concrete façade. Both Joe and Max stood in silence, taking in this strange place.

'The inside of this Portal is no less strange than the outside. What is this place? Do you have any ideas?'

'None.' Joe peered over the gantry railings.

There was a large raised concrete plinth below them.

'Shall we wander down those stairs and have a poke about. The floor looks wet, but if we take care we should be fine'

Joe was hesitant but agreed. They tried the most obvious door, and sure enough it led them to the top of the staircase beside the ramp that ran down into the floor.

'I'm in a building, and yet I am getting vertigo with the difference in distance and depth between where we are standing and the hole in that floor. Can you see how deep the hole is?'

Max took out his exceptionally powerful torch from the rucksack, and shone it down towards the hole.

'Nothing, the beam barely made an impact. 'It doesn't seem to end. Of course, it has to though. It probably just drops into The Portal.'

Joe nodded. They both descended the staircase until they reached the section where the last six steps headed off to the left, and took them down to the floor. There was a metal banister railing that Max shook violently to see how well it was connected. It held fast. Joe headed past Max down onto the floor. Max grabbed his brother by the arm.

'Let's not take any chances with this place. Here, I brought these.'

Max opened the rucksack and brought out a couple of harnesses, and two retractable metal wires. He set everything up and soon they were clipped in. As they walked, the wires unwound leaving them free to move forward. Max explained that if they were in trouble to hit the red button; the wire would lock in position then retract so they could get to safety. He didn't want them falling down the hole in the floor. He could not see how they would, but then neither Max nor Joe could explain why the floor was soaking wet. That was cause for concern.

They slowly made their way around the floor. First they looked at the plinth directly below the railings.

'Max, *look at this.* That's a blood spatter consistent with a fall from a great height.'

Max came over and looked, then took a photo. Both twins looked at each other at the same time.

'*Pete,*' they chorused.

Max nodded, 'It could certainly be where he fell from; if he did, there is no way Evo would reveal this place to anyone, he would move the body to somewhere he could explain away Pete's injuries. I guess Evo thanks God for the quarry.'

Question is though... did Pete fall, *or was he pushed.*

Max pursed his lips, 'That's the billionaire's question.'

They wandered towards the hole in the floor, making sure they moved about in such a way as not to get their wires tangled up. They peered over the small single wire rail around the hole in the floor. Max shone the torch again. They could still see no bottom.

'That doesn't make sense though; we haven't come up that far from the tunnel floor. It could just be black non-reflective paint at the bottom.'

Joe said nothing, but stepped back. They both set their eyes on the blue metal chimney; its scale and size only truly becoming apparent the closer they got. Its size was truly unnerving.

'That thing is giving me serious anxiety bro. You ever looked into truly deep water and got that nervous feeling and tingling in your fingers?'

'I have – I do. What are we afraid of though? It's a large metal tube.'

'Yeah, but it's a large metal tube on a scale we are not used to dealing with, so it's size and scale has got us on edge.'

Joe snapped his head towards his brother.

'*Did you feel that*?'

'The thump, yes I did. We've heard that before. It doesn't bode well. What's that other noise?'

'I don't know, it sounds like a rumbling, and a roar at the same time. I can feel the floor shaking. And there's suddenly a strong draught, I can feel it on my face, I can't tell where its coming from...It's getting stronger. It seems to be coming from the roof, but that can't be right, its solid concrete.'

Max suddenly looked terrified.

'*The draft*, it's coming from the chimney, I

think we need to get out of here, I think that's like a harbinger breath. I think it is being created by water coming towards this chimney from somewhere. Can you hear that?'

Joe listened. He could.

'*Shit*. That is the sound of a lot of water coming this way fast, *like a lot of water*. We need to go *now*.'

They both turned towards where they had come from. They began moving across the room, back past the hole in the floor to the safety of the stairs; the racing water sound was getting louder and louder. The sound was changing, both men could hear the sheer power of the water that was heading their way. There was a sudden sense of futility. The size and scale of this place and what was happening made them feel powerless, and yet they had to keep trying. They felt like a couple of ants trying to cross a football pitch in a hurry.

It dawned on them both at the same instant, this wasn't a room, this was a giant mechanism, a giant mechanism that created and unleashed a Shadow Tide; technically they were inside the Shadow Tide machine.

CHAPTER 45

They both began to sprint back the way they had come. When they saw what was before them, they were both pretty sure their time was up.

Rising out of the hole in the floor was a huge wall of water. Such was the power and force that the water seemed to hold the shape of the hole it had just risen from. Within seconds the wall of water that rose up was higher than the metal banister. The water then crashed to the concrete floor, spreading out in all directions.

'Mate, we are cut off, we aren't going to get back to the safety of the steps.'

'We have to, *otherwise…*'

They were now both having to shout, such was the noise of the water flooding across the floor. The sound was magnified as it reverberated around the concrete chamber. One word flashed across Max's mind; Tomb – he blocked it out.

Joe was looking around, panicking and wondering what their best chance was.

'*The chimney, maybe we can climb the chimney. Let's head for it.*'

'OK.' Max joined his brother in the run. The water was around their feet now, but still shallow, so they could gain traction.

They reached the edge of the chimney and realised the plan, like their predicament was totally futile; the rib that ran around the metal edifice that they had hoped to get hold of was at least twenty feet above them. They were trapped.

'We are going to have to just try and run back mate. *Oh shit... run. Look out.*'

They were both looking up as Max spotted what appeared to be steam rising from the top of the chimney. Steam? But the water was icy cold.

'Joe just run...now'

As they stepped back from the chimney in shock, a massive wall of water began to rain down from the top of the chimney. It crashed to the floor where they had just been standing, and both men realised, had they still been standing there, they would have been knocked to the floor with enough force to seriously injure them. The volume of water instantly increased tenfold, and as it hit the floor there was a loud crack that sounded like a massive rifle shot. Now the sounds were defining, the roar of water danced around the chamber. Max and Joe were just able to run through the tide of water that was rising up from the hole and coming towards them. Behind them the larger volume of water chased after them, and won against the lesser tidal power rising from the hole. They were both knocked off their feet. Having met a dead end, the water was now coming back from the far wall, which meant the depth was increasing dramatically with every moment that passed. It foamed and changed direction as if in search for something to attack, like some rabid beast.

Both men managed to take a massive gulp of air before they were pulled under and thrown around in the liquid torrent that had now formed around them. The last thing Max saw before he was pulled under was Joe being wrapped around one of the banisters, and being bent out of shape like a rag doll.

CHAPTER 46

Evo and the guards were escorting Bruno and Ava along a corridor that Bruno reckoned was directly over the tunnel, and connected the opposite sides. The door behind them flew open; they all swung round to see why. Bruno and Ava were dumbfounded by what they saw. Matt seemed to be struggling with carrying a lifeless Bella, and Norton – Norton appeared to be pointing a gun.

'Wait up Boss.'

'*Boss*?' Bruno looked to Ava for some help with understanding and processing what was going on. 'Matt's your boss…Norton what's going on?'

Evo smiled at Ava and Bruno, 'I'll explain everything in a moment. Mr Holland looks like he is struggling, would you like to give him a hand?'

Ava and Bruno realised they should have done that straight away. They were quickly at Matt's side; they took the lifeless Bella from him and carried her between them.

'Is she… *alive*?'

Matt was so exhausted, all he could do was nod.

'Come on everyone, we need to sort out what we are going to do with you; let's keep moving.' Evo was interrupted as the door swung open again. It was Eva this time. She looked shocked at seeing everyone here.

'Sorry Mr Evelyn, I was just coming to look for you, *what on earth...*'

'Nothing for you to worry about Eva, just come with us. It's OK.' Evo pushed her to walk with the others.

They moved off through another door, the noise inside this room was deafening. They moved to the far end. The Scott and Munro team all looked at the swirling raging waters below; trying to work out what this place was. Matt was trying to get his breath back when he noticed a body moving about in the water. Then another. He knew instinctively who the bodies belonged to. He scanned the room; on the wall was a large red button with STOP on it, and another with DRAIN. He ran to them hitting the STOP button first, then the DRAIN button. Evo took a moment to compose himself with what he was witnessing. This was not part of the plan either.

'Hold it right there Mr Holland. You move, and these men will shoot you, or I will. You can't help your friends now I'm afraid.'

The look on Matt's face made Evo very nervous, something about it said desperation, and he knew desperate people were dangerous people.

Matt started running for the open door that he reckoned led down to the water, shouting back to Evo, 'Well you had better fucking shoot me then hadn't you.'

The guards looked to Evo for guidance. He shook his head. Matt was gone. Evo motioned to two of the men.

'Go and help him recover the bodies.'

CHAPTER 47

Matt made it down the stairs in fast time; to his utter delight he saw Max come up for air. He couldn't see Joe though. As he got to the last step before the water's edge, he noticed the two wires clipped to the banister; he tried to pull on one, then the other. His feet and legs were soaked from the cold water as the waves smashed against the stairs. Each wire was tight with the weight of its user, and the wire was wet. Matt could not get a grip. The two guards appeared beside him. Their guns were holstered, and he realised from their body language that they were here to help.

Looking to make a plan, Matt couldn't believe his eyes. There right where Max was, a vortex appeared. Like the vortex you see in a plug hole only this one was the size of a large HGV. It whipped the water from a light blue colour to an angry foaming white. Matt knew there was nothing he could do. His heart sank. At least the water had stopped pouring in.

He was about to collapse, when he noticed there were four wet steps below him where there were none a moment ago, now five, six. The water level was rapidly dropping. As soon as he could he and the guards ran out onto the floor. They first rescued Max from the hole and then rescued Joe from being wrapped around one of the banisters. Both men were alive. In a state; coughing and spluttering and fighting for breath, but OK. The water was still running across the floor and dropping down the hole, sounding like it did when you stood close to an enormous waterfall. The sound was so loud, it hurt. They all sat for a few minutes catching their breath. When they could stand, and when Matt had uncoupled them from the harnesses that had saved their lives; he hugged them both. The guards motioned to start climbing the stairs.

Joe looked up at Matt, '*What's with Dumb and Dumber*?'

Matt shook his head and gave both men a look that didn't fill them with confidence.

'It turns out Norton is in cahoots with Evo. Bella has been drugged, but she is going to be OK apparently. If they can be trusted.'

Max just shook his head, 'Guess that all Figures.'

They got to the top of the stairs, and walked out onto the gantry to join the others.

Evo smirked, '*Well... isn't this nice*; quite the gathering. I think we need to talk, and we certainly need to make a plan.

CHAPTER 48

Max noticed that Bella was moving slightly, and she began to groan. He barked at one of the security guards to give him their jacket so he could make her comfortable with a pillow.

'*Use your own*,' snapped the guard.

'I'm soaking wet you *fucking idiot*. I am *trying* to help her, *not* make her worse with a wet pillow.'

Max glared at Evo, who in turn gave a nod to the guard that told him to give his jacket over.

Max gently knelt down and made Bella comfortable.

She managed the slightest of smiles.

Max could feel his entire body tense with anger. He stood up and walked towards Evo. Two of the guards blocked him.

'What are you planning for us then you *utter moron*?' He pointed towards Bella. '*She* needs to see a doctor now.'

Evo's face hardened, 'I wined and dined you, *yet* you still trespass on my private property. *None* of this is on me. I told you people to stay out of here, but you *didn't listen*.'

Max was still staring hard at Evo.

'*No*, you even sent your tame cop Stimpson around to warn us off.'

Matt imagined Max's remark seemed to throw Evo for a moment but, he then thought not.'

'It always pays to keep local law enforcement in your pocket. And to be fair, he was only asking a bunch of trespassers to stay off private property. He would be worried for your safety. Being a dutiful policeman, he would want to make sure no one got hurt.'

Max was a gentle soul at heart, but right now, nothing would give him greater pleasure than to punch Evo squarely in the face.

'Let's get on with this Evo; the police are on their way. I managed to get a text to Ollie asking him to make sure he didn't go through the local police office. I'd think twice before killing us all given they are on their way.'

'*Kill you*?' Evo gave a strained laugh, 'I'm not going to *kill anyone*. I want you off my property. *That's all.*'

'Your superiors told you not to kill any more people here I guess?' said Matt.

Evo was looking more perplexed.

'*My superiors*? I *don't have* any superiors, I'm the boss.'

'We know that to be total nonsense. We've spoken to a journalist by the name of James, he said you were a construct; someone else's puppet.'

Now Evo was looking angry. He threw a look at his housekeeper before answering.

'*A construct.* What is wrong with you people,

haven't you checked me out?'

'*We did*, we even had a nice call from a man at the government, who basically said the same thing, and I've seen it too. It's nothing that will stand up in court, but you constantly exhibit the wrong emotions for a situation. At first I just wondered if you were a sociopath or a psychopath; I'm no doctor of course, but then it dawned on me. Sociopaths and psychopaths tend to have no emotions as such. You on the other hand, have plenty; you just exhibit them at the wrong time. You're like a bad actor. You get the lines right, but your motivation is all wrong.'

Evo laughed.

'There we go again,' said Matt, 'This is a dire situation; you are looking at having to kill a great many more people than you already have, and yet you laugh. It's like none of this is really on you; that would only fit if this is all someone else's show.'

Evo's mouth dropped.

'*What do you mean killing more people than I already have*? *I haven't killed anyone.*'

Matt was being careful not to convey any of his own emotions in his face. The more he was pressuring Evo, the more Evo's emotions where coming into line with reality for the first time. He would keep up the pressure if he could.

Joe butted in with something he knew would help Matt out.

'You're *seriously* telling us, that *you didn't kill*

Pete? What, are we supposed to believe he fell over these banisters, and then somehow shifted his own dead corpse to the quarry where he was found?'

Evo was looking more stressed.

'Pete died in the quarry. As I have already told you; I have no idea what he was doing there or what happened. He *didn't* die here though.'

Seeing what Matt was doing, Max got out his phone, brought up the picture he had taken of the blood splatter on the plinth, and handed it to Joe, who showed it to Evo. An incredulous expression fell across Evo's face.

'*But... but he didn't die *here*... he didn't, *I had their word. – Wait* you said people, *what other people* do you think I have killed?'

'All the previous Shadow Tide deaths, *six* I think.'

'They were all accidents,' said Evo, following with a whisper to himself. '*They promised me.*' The team could see Evo was doing a lot of hard and rapid thinking.

Ava moved towards Evo.

'I assure you Evo, they *were not* accidents. *Those people were murdered.*'

A look of genuine confusion began to engulf Evo's face.

'But they *promised... they *assured* me, *no deliberate killing.*' He looked at Matt and the others like an eight year old child who had made a genuine mistake with serious consequences. There was an innocence on his face that made them all uneasy.

'*Oh come on Evo,*' said Matt, I saw the text Norton sent warning you that we were trying to get your housekeeper to roll on you, and incriminate you. So you must know she has agreed to.'

A moments silence passed whilst Evo was deep in thought.

'I always told them if there was any killing then *all bets were off*. Looking back now, I can see their mania was clearly getting worse, but I guess I just buried my head... *Well no more.*'

The team could see that Evo was doing some more serious thinking before committing himself to his next statement. He turned to make sure he was looking at them all.

'I never got any communication from Norton; *this is beginning to sound like a setup.*'

'OK. If they have broken their end of the deal, so be it. *I will not be party to murder.* I'll tell you; though what good it will do me I have no idea. I guess I just have to hold the memory I got to live a life well beyond anything else I could have achieved off my own back. The truth is I'm not very bright; left to my own devices I wouldn't have had half of this life. I only got this job because I look straight from central casting for a billionaire, and I can keep my mouth shut. Not much of a skill-set really.'

He paused for another moment. Gone was the bravado they had come to expect. Now before

them stood an incredibly sad and forlorn looking man, that had the body language of a scared
child; an innocent. None of the team could know
that Evo knew what fate awaited him.

'My name... *my real name* is Christopher ...'

Before Evo could provide them with his full
name, a thwack reverberated around the chamber, and he slumped to the floor with a thud. A
red spot formed on his forehead where the bullet
had entered his skull and passed into his brain.
There was confusion as to who had shot him. It
was a moment or two before all eyes settled on
Norton.

For the second time in the last couple of days,
words just fell out of Matt's mouth.

'Norton – *what have you done*?'

CHAPTER 49

Three unmarked four by fours pulled in to the edge of the road, close to the grey Audi A6 that had been tucked into a corner in the shade. DCI Stimpson disembarked and motioned to everyone to wait in the cars. He walked over and put his hand on the Audi's bonnet; cold. He walked round to the front. Pulled out his phone and pulled up some notes. He then looked at the registration plate fixed to the front of the car. FX56KTE, yes that was one of the Scott and Munro cars. He swore and headed off into the woodland in the direction of the portal entrance. After giving a complex whistle, two men rose out of the leaf-bed.

'*Alright* lads?'

'Yes boss.'

'SITREP?'

'Basically, two Scott and Munro lads turned up in a black Range Rover, destroyed the dam, drained the canal, and then reversed into the portal. They then...'

DCI Stimpson interrupted, '*They drove in?*' He swore under his breath again. '*And then what?*'

'Well boss, it's like their hosting a party in there. Another two went in, then another three, then a whole party with some armed guards went in somewhere over the top and vanished. Then a huge wave of water came out of the portal, and dispersed quickly through the broken dam. No bodies with it though.'

'*Damn it.*' Stimpson shook his head, 'Right lads, you're with me now, *come on*, let's get this wrapped up.'

Stimpson sprinted back to the cars. At his direction they drove up the track to park above the portal. A quick inspection of embankment allowed them to see how the Scott and Munro guys had got their car into the canal. Stimpson motioned to the two Land Rover Defenders to follow suit. Once down and in the canal, Stimpson radioed to two men to stay at the top. He then placed another two men at the portal entrance, and the rest he motioned forward to get into the two cars. They headed into the portal.

CHAPTER 50

Everyone was still trying to get their minds around what had just happened. The guards were not sure what was going on, and seemed unsure what to do now that Evo had been shot. Ava had managed to remove her phone from her pocket without causing concern. She opened a translation app, then selected Latin to English. Her stomach was churning, and her fingers were tingling; the truth was already filtering through, but she wanted to make sure. The killer had identified themselves sometime back, and she had missed it. It would be good to be able to show some sort of backup to her theory if needs be.

Ava punched the housekeeper's name into the translator app as it was given to them at the dinner party at Nalebury. Eva Veresum. She had thought at the time it was a stupid name, but was distracted with their role of watching Evo, and gathering as much intel as they could. The housekeeper had provided them with all the proof they really needed to unlock this case; but, however much people did not mean to, they often didn't pay as close attention to the staff as they did to the host and the other guests. It had been the perfect place to hide. Bruno may have been joking when they walked into the manor for dinner that night, but he wasn't far off the mark.

Ava's first attempt returned no results, so she tried a space. This time there was a match. As the results showed up, Ava carefully angled the phone so Matt could see what was on the screen. When he saw the text, he just closed his eyes and said nothing.

Eva Vere Sum - really am Eve

Matt was beginning to experience the same stomach churning that Ava had. Why had he not picked up on the name. Evelyn, a unisex name, so could be a man or a woman. The real Evelyn de Varley was still very much alive and standing next to Norton. Matt decided he needed the others to know this, and the best way he could think of doing that was by loudly accusing Eva so everyone could follow along.

CHAPTER 51

Matt walked as close towards Norton and Eva as he felt safe to; and a distance that she should still be able to see the phone's screen. Norton stood forward in a protective stance for Eva's benefit. Oddly that still stung Matt, despite what was going on and their predicament.

'So it's actually *Miss* Evelyn de Varley.'

In that instant, Eva's whole demeanour changed. It was like they were suddenly dealing with a different person entirely.

'*Well done Mr Holland*, took you long enough didn't it. I even gave you a couple of clues; so I think I played fair.

I always needed a proxy in business. A short, plain looking woman was never going to get anywhere in city life, even with my brain. I realised very early on that I was going to need a proxy if I was to succeed in the male dominated world of the City.'

By now Bella was sitting up, but feeling groggy, her brain was working though, and she was taking in the proceedings. Aided by Max she managed to stand.

'*So*... when I was – *was*...' she paused for a moment to steady herself, leaning on Max before carrying on, 'When I thought *I was playing you*

392

at the Tame Swan, and previously when I spilt my drink on my lunch, *it was you playing me all along.*'

'*Of course* it was my dear, *of course it was.*'

'*So you really do know your champagnes.*'

'I do; to be honest I thought that was perhaps a clue too far, but clearly not in your case. You were so focused on getting to Evo, and so sure he killed your husband you were blindsided. You couldn't see the whole chessboard. Speaking of which, I did even tell you Nalebury was mine, I enjoyed laying that little blatant clue that you totally missed. I told you your husband made me tea in my own kitchen. Like I say, I think I played the game fairly. You had your opportunities to work things out. You just weren't up to it. Don't feel too bad though.

'As soon as your husband met with his unfortunate end, I had my people watch you. The more fuss you made, the more I felt we needed to keep an eye on you, and control you to make sure you did no real harm to the important work I am doing here.'

Bella shook her head. '*Control me*? But you didn't, *did you*? I managed to find a superb competent investigation agency to get to the bottom of this, and they have.'

Eva smiled, 'You think that was your idea? *Have you not learnt anything yet*? Perhaps I have given you too much credit.'

Bella said nothing. Her face said it all; she was

lost. Perhaps if her system was not still full of drugs, she would have been able to follow Eva or was it Evelyn now?

An arrogant smile drifted across Eva's face and anchored itself firmly in place.

'I had Norton plant the fliers. It was his idea actually; and what a stroke of luck. We could lead you to an agency that you would implicitly trust, where I could keep an eye on you, and follow your every move. Always be several steps ahead of you. That way I could obscure the light the investigation was shining on things.'

It was Matt who was trying to keep up things in his mind now.

'But when I saw your phone in the field, you had warned Evo that we were interrogating his housekeeper. *I don't follow.*'

Norton also had a smug look across his face.

'*You were meant to find that.* If you remember it was written but not sent. We realised we needed to throw you off the scent, so thought that text would send you after... well after the wrong Evelyn. Our revised plan was to frame him for everything, but – well, we can't with everything that is going on here, it would all come out, and it mustn't.'

Six people realised their time was running out. There was no way they were going to be allowed to leave here alive.

'*Just what the hell is going on here exactly Norton?*'

'Shall we tell them?'

Eva just shrugged her shoulders, 'I *guess* we could.'

'*Hang on*, you have just shot Evo to stop him telling us everything... and now you're just going to tell us *anyway*?' said Matt who looked genuinely shocked.

'*Yeahhh*,' laughed Norton, 'I just wanted to kill him, I never liked him. *Any excuse really*. Guess that makes me a psychopath then?'

Bruno interrupted. He wasn't going to give these two people, if they could be called that any more self-aggrandising attention than he had to.

'We are well aware what this is all about. This place is an illicit Freeport. You are clearly storing vast wealth down here; it's probably ill-gotten gains from your gangster colleagues. You are a money grabbing psycho, who will stop at nothing to hoard as much wealth as you can, and all for what?'

Eva looked at Bruno with a genuine look of surprise that he didn't understand.

'I would have thought it was pretty obvious what it's for. The end of civilisation is coming, you do *realise* that? There are so many problems with the world. The gap between the rich and the poor is becoming an issue. If we get a weak government, they will only seize assets and redistribute them in order to get the populist vote; well, they'll have to find it first.' Her voice was beginning to sound quite manic.

Matt gave a shake of his head.

'This has all been about money?'

'*No Mr Holland*, it's *not about money*. It's about security against theft by lunatic governments. It's about the security, safety and freedom that money buys; it's not about the cash itself.'

'So you have spent God knows how much constructing an illicit Freeport in the middle of the countryside under some misguided thought that civilisation is coming to an end. Of course it isn't. *You're mad…*'

Eva's face went puce with rage. '*Mad, mad am I? I don't think so*. I managed to build my hedge fund from nothing to it being worth billions of pounds. I did that through cunning, guile and hard work. My ingenuity of creating a proxy with a tall good looking man with the same name to ease my path through the city; those are hardly the actions of a crazed lunatic are they?'

Eva paused for a moment. '*No one rumbled my proxy ruse did they?*'

'*Well, they had begun to actually.*' snarled Matt.

Joe put his hand out towards his brother, who instinctively took it, and they shook.

'Congratulations brother, you called it right. You said it was financial or madness, you were right on both counts. You just got the wrong Evelyn.'

By now Eva's eyes were wide, and she spoke faster than before.

'And you think hiding a Freeport in this place

is madness? Even after all the construction effort and alteration, no one knows it's here; it's hidden in plain sight for everyone to see. That's why I chose to put it here. It cost only five percent of my wealth to construct, so it's good value at twice the price. The portal is so much larger than a standard canal tunnel, so its associated infrastructure gave my engineers plenty of scope for building what I needed to build behind its façade. The original landscaping hides its true size; and for security, there is the Shadow Tide machine. As for its creation my dear Bella, you can thank your husband for that; it was all his own design and idea.

Bella screamed with rage at Eva.

'*No way, there is no way my husband would have any part of something that killed innocent people; you're a lying bitch.*'

Her obvious anger seemed to please Eva. 'Oh no, I concede I had to promise no one would come to any harm. I gave him my word, which is worthless of course, and we had long arguments about the previous deaths. As I had done with Evo, I assured him they were genuine accidents, but he was threatening to go to the police. I lured him here to be killed in his own invention.'

Max, like the others was deep in shock, and now cold, but his brain was still analysing, still trying to fill in the gaps.

'But you realise Pete guessed what you were going to do to him. He hid a clue of some replacement tattoo's, a stone and a handful of peat in some gloves at The Portal entrance.'

'He was a bright man, that doesn't surprise me, I wish he hadn't done that, and then you might all have been spared. We will blame him then shall we?'

Matt wanted to buy some time to try and work out an escape plan. He hoped the others were doing the same, and hopefully having more luck than he was.

'You say Pete built this, but what is *this* exactly?' He very much hoped the ego in Eva would love to explain and give him a chance to think. After all, it seemed to work in spy novels.

'He did, it's all his own work. I am afraid the story Evo told you about him working security was total nonsense. This was what he built for me. There is a massive manmade reservoir above us. When the water was dropped into the portal direct from there, it didn't have the momentum. Pete used his technology knowledge from working in hydro dams. This is basically a copy of a chamber that avoids water hammer damaging turbines. It gives the water somewhere to go. We adapted it here to get momentum into the water so that when it's released it has an awesome, unholy power and energy that created the effect I was looking for. We had to tweak a few things like lowering the water level before release and paint a low friction surface on the tunnel walls so as not to reduce the power of the Shadow

Tides when they erupted. Things like that. It worked. It kept people away, and the police could never find this room, so they took it to be subterranean waters or some sort of flooding anomaly, which was perfect. That made logical sense as there was no proof of what we were up to. I don't think anyone would ever have guessed... do you?'

Joe was beginning to shiver from his immersion in the water.

'*So that's why you invested in German hydro.*'

Eva nodded, 'Oh you know about that – you *have* done some homework then.'

Matt still hadn't come up with a plan, so he jumped to the first question that was in his head.

'There is a blood spatter down on that plinth, I guess that's where you killed Pete. How did you manage to recreate the blood spatter at the quarry?'

He hoped this pandering to Eva's ego was keeping them alive for now.

'That was improvisation at its best, would you believe the internet showed us how to do it? It's insane what you can find on the internet.'

'*So did you kill Pete?*'

Eva took a moment to consider what she had to lose. They were going to have to kill them all so she could at least give some closure.

'*I did*. It was more luck than judgement. We argued here by the railings. I pretended to drop my pen on accident, then managed to grab his ankle and upend him. Like everyone else in life he underestimated me and he paid the price. I guess I don't look like the sort of person who would go to the effort of learning combat moves that allow me to compensate for my size.'

So you and your people had Bella under supervision, you knew she had been up here poking about, that's why Norton was asking those questions at the interview. He already knew she had.'

'Indeed.'

'And the moving of the body, the mucking about with the concrete samples, the breaking into the pathology lab buildings to swap out samples etcetera; that was all you and your henchmen?'

'*It was.* It was our first time dealing with such things. We had no time to change his clothes and footwear. I might have guessed the Fullers Earth would get me in the end, its constantly trying to destroy the tunnel, *it has cost me millions.*'

Matt ignored the melodramatic remark. 'And the messing about with the padlocks and the concrete stairs? That was you lot as well?'

'It was. We were lucky it was so dry, that our vehicle didn't leave any tracks. It was too far to carry a body up there. It would have taken too long; we might have been spotted.'

'And you used another proxy to pose as Pete's boss during the inquest and to the police?'

'I did.'

Matt breathed a sigh of relief; he had no wish to die, but if they were about to meet their maker at least Bella had closure; they had managed to give her that at least. He was desperately trying to think of the next question to ask whilst leaving the other part of his brain to work on an escape, but was struggling with either. At that moment there was an enormous boom sound as the metal door that been ajar was thrown open, and in rushed several armed police officers shouting get down and pointing their weapons at everyone. Following behind them was DCI Stimpson with Alastor, who was already cuffed.

CHAPTER 52

The guards lowered their guns and everyone got down on the floor except Norton and Eva. Stimpson moved to quickly secure Norton's pistol. Matt looked at each of the team, and then at Bella. At each one of them he mouthed I'm sorry. He could not bear the look of despair on their faces. He began to close his eyes when he heard DCI Stimpson yell at the top of his voice.

'You two, I said get down on the floor, now get down on the floor.'

Matt looked across, Stimpson was coming straight for him.

'Mr Holland, are you OK? *Please*, you and your team should get up. I'm sorry we took so long to get to you, but I did specifically request that you stay out of here; which you and your team seemed to take as an invite to treat the place like a drive-thru. I assume that is your car parked in the Freeport loading bay?'

'If it's black, I suspect so.'

'*Well*, it looks like we have a fair number of prisoners to shift, so we may need to commandeer it for a few runs in and out; I don't think everyone will fit in ours. You and your team members may have to walk; those that can anyway.'

'Whatever you want, I'm just *glad* we are all alive.'

'*So am I.*'

Matt was delighted to see a friendly face. Stimpson motioned to one of his men who brought over a rucksack. Soon those that needed foil blankets had them, and the policeman with medical skills was tending to Bella as best he could.

'Eva confessed to killing Peter Stone.'

Stimpson shook what looked like an adapted mobile phone in his hand.

'I know, we got it all on tape. They were kind enough to leave the door ajar. I have been working with Serious Crime and Interpol, who have had their eye on Evo and this little operation for some time. We didn't realise he was a fake though, so thanks for that. They were watching someone else, a client of the Freeport here, and when Evo appeared on the scene and two of the items they were tracking ended up here; well, that is what brought this place to their attention. It's been under observation for months, in fact almost a year. Being a local man born and bred, I was their local liaison. That was why I was trying to persuade you lot to stay away, and appeared to not be interested in what you had to say. If we had done anything to jeopardise the investigation, it would have been more than my job is worth. I was watching out for you guys though.

'It is all to do with smuggling stolen goods.

Let's just say some of the owners of the artworks being stored here would like them hanging back where they belong. We don't think Evo, *sorry*, Eva realised they were stolen; but that aside, this is all nothing to do with Pete's case I'm afraid. I do promise to make sure his wife will get all the help she needs to see that justice is brought for him. I have to commend you guys; you don't give up, and you certainly got there when no one else did. I bet you are glad it's all over.'

'I think I can speak for everyone in saying we are glad it is all over. In respect of getting there, we had some luck along the way, and *ultimately* it was Bella who cracked the case open.'

'*Indeed*. If you'll excuse me.'

Once all the guards, Eva and Norton were cuffed and on their knees, Stimpson gave orders to find the control room and seize the CCTV; that would show evidence of who killed Evo. That would do for starters.

Matt motioned to Ava, I guess you or Bruno still have the second key card, we best give them both to DCI Stimpson.

'These will give you access to everywhere here. You'll work it out I'm sure.'

Stimpson nodded. '*Thanks*.'

Ava wandered over to Alastor.

'So Alastor – *sorry* – Jeff, I have one question for you.'

He didn't look up to meet with her eyes. 'Go on then.'

'Why did you try and scare us at The Portal that first day.'

He nodded in the direction of Eva. '*She* told me I had to try and put you off. She gave me no time to get down here and think of something plausible, so I just came up with the spooky stuff. Stupid I know, but it's what came to my mind. I'm an engineer, *not* a story teller.'

Ava shrugged, 'Fair enough. One last question if I may?' She looked to Stimpson for permission, he nodded. 'You are not exactly a young man; when you left us, I followed you up the road but you had vanished, how did you manage that? It's been bugging me.'

'Nothing impressive, I assure you, I rolled under the hedge and was lying in the ditch. Covered in mud and all I got for my efforts was a slight chill and stiff joints.'

'I appreciate your honesty.'

Alastor just stared at the floor, silent and forlorn.

Before he could stop himself, Matt wandered over to Norton, grabbing him by the chin and forcing him to look directly into his eyes.

'*Why… what* did *any* of us *ever* do to you that could turn you like this. What you have done is beyond comprehension. I cannot compute the level of betrayal you have shown towards us. *We're your friends*. We have been friends since we started school.'

'No Matt, *we never really were friends at school.*

You were popular, so I stuck beside you, but I never really rated you. *Nothing personal*, you're just not the sort of person I like.'

Matt looked shell-shocked at this revelation.

'*But* – but I liked *you*, I thought we were genuinely good friends. I know we lost touch on and off for years afterwards apart from the odd phone call, but after our meeting again, and you joining the agency; *I thought we were good*.'

'Sorry, I'm not really sure what to say. It was Eva's idea I join the agency. I read about your first case and told her. Another case of billionaire's seeing things so far out in front. She thought one day it might come in handy to have a tame Private Detective agency. I only joined because she felt it might be beneficial to her cause. She was right as it turned out, and more than she could possibly have imagined. She hadn't made the connection to Pete, Bella and Max when I signed up. When we discovered how lucky we were, we couldn't believe it.'

Eva butted in, 'I don't like to leave things to chance Mr Holland. I even had one of my men follow you on holiday.'

Matt bowed his head, shaking it slowly, 'Did your goon have a shaved head?'

'He did.'

'*I did spot him*, but I had no idea.' He then muttered under his breath, '*Well maybe I did*.'

'Yes,' said Ava, 'He mentioned you gave him an odd look on the shore of the loch, on the last day of your holiday.'

Norton butted back in; he seemed desperate for Matt's attention. 'I was able to plant the fliers knowing Bella would trust Max, and then I would be able to try to get you to doubt her honesty and decency, but you just wouldn't, would you. You kept giving her the benefit of the doubt and caring. It makes me sick. Every time I tried to plant some doubt, it was just ignored.'

Matt was getting more and more angry, and he was certainly done talking with Norton. 'How do you two know each other anyway?' he asked Eva.

'I knocked Norton off his bicycle when he was a teenager. He was shouting and swearing at me. I offered to pay him to keep quiet and he told me straight out, I could give him a job or he would report me to the police. I realised at once I had met someone who would be able to get things done. So I agreed. He became the family I never had, and I his. He's basically the only human never to betray me. All this will be his one day.

'He told me he had grown up without, around those with plenty, and it made him hungry. I was the same, and it terrified me, the thought someone could come to your door and throw you out for a defaulted loan, or not having enough to eat. I was determined to build such a robust empire to ensure that never happened. I knew some rules would need bending, and Norton would be fine with that. I'm not a nice person; I'm not a pantomime villain either though.

'I realised quickly that Norton was the same. He did talk of you Matt. Your always wanting to see the best in people, your naiveté in believing everyone is basically good at heart. We used to laugh at it, but I guess you won in the end. At least where I am going, money won't be an issue any more, I won't have to worry.'

DCI Stimpson gave a grave shake of his head, 'No, you won't have to worry about money in prison. At least seven death's, at your age, *you won't see freedom ever again.*'

For the first time, the team witnessed Eva smile.

'I... *we* have a contingency plan for that, don't we Norton.'

'*We do.*'

As he spoke, Norton lunged towards Eva. In one move he picked her up, flipped her upside down and dropped her headfirst over the railings. Initially there was no sound, then a loud crack of bone splitting wide open on concrete, and then the boom of a thud echoed around the chamber. Both Bella and one of the police officers, a young recruit on their first time out instantly threw up at the sound. No sound related to a human head should sound like a large stick snapping in half.

Stimpson and the other officers rushed at Norton, he backed up quickly towards the railings holding his arms out in the position to be cuffed.

'It's *OK*, relax, it's *all* good.'

As he reached the railings, he jumped up backwards, brought his arms in to his chest, crossed them and disappeared over the balcony backwards. Again, there was no sound except the crack and the boom. Everyone froze. Some time passed before anyone spoke.

DCI Stimpson just shook his head. Everyone was in shock, but he needed to secure the site. He looked over the railings, it was abundantly clear both Eva and Norton were dead. You didn't need any medical training to be able to tell that given the state of the heads.

'Right lads, get down there, *get those bodies covered up.*'

Stimpson turned to Matt with a quizzical look, 'How did you get to the bottom of all this?'

Matt pursed his lips and widened his eyes, 'Well, I have to say *we didn't really*. It both major breakthroughs were Bella. She turned up at the hotel when she wasn't supposed to, and one of the hotel staff recognised her from a photo Pete had shown them; things started to snowball from there.'

We kept looking because there were always too many coincidences, and you having done such a thorough job, left us free to look elsewhere. Obviously we are not constrained the same way you are.'

Stimpson gave an appreciative nod. 'And the other breakthrough?'

'Bella again, she would not let it drop, and as

I was getting ready to pull the plug and send everyone home, she pushed Eva into admitting Pete died in The Portal; the rest I think you heard.'

'Yes, pretty much. So a team effort then?'

'*Very much a team effort*; led by a seriously *determined widow*. There is no way that left to me; I would have let things run on as long as they did. We wouldn't have got there if it had been left to me.'

'Stimpson gave a wry smile, 'I think Bella may have missed her calling as a detective.'

Matt managed a small laugh, '*I think you might be right Edward*. But so have you; *missed your true calling, I mean*.'

'*I have? As what?*'

'An actor, you had me convinced you were in Evo's pocket, or at the least that you wanted an easy life. Clearly, you are seriously competent DCI at the top of his game. *Fair play*.'

'Thank you.'

Stimpson looked around at everyone, 'let's get you lot out of this place. I need you to do me a favour. Can you head back to Nalebury Park and secure it. Perhaps you would stay there for the night until we can get someone officers along to take over and secure it tomorrow? It is full of insanely valuable art, and we have no idea who knows about it being there, or who it really belongs to. It would be more than my job's worth if any of it goes wandering off into the night.'

Matt agreed they could, and Stimpson felt he was helping them. They could focus a little on a job and feel helpful, rather than just going back to an empty hotel room. They all made it to Bess and with some juggling managed to get her facing out of the portal. Stimpson's men had managed to turn the lights on now. They slowly drove out in silence, the lights casting a modern stark brightness that now replaced the inky darkness; showing this place to be nothing more than a pile of stone and concrete. Any suggestion of the supernatural or the mystical was completely dispelled.

CHAPTER 53

They collected the Audi on the way down the road, and it wasn't long before they were rolling up to the front door of the manor house. It was eerie, everyone had scarpered, even the butler. Matt, Ava, Bruno, Joe, Max and Bella were far too traumatised by the last couple of hours to care. Bruno managed to persuade the hotel to bring everyone fresh clothes, and to deliver some pizzas, which everyone picked at. It would have felt ghoulish to eat any of Eva's food. Bruno found the fridge full of food, bought with the expectation of being eaten, now sitting there redundant a little eerie. It was little practical everyday things that seemed to bring a death home in a brutally real manner. That loss of the normal stuff that had been planned for, and now would not happen, like eating.

Stimpson headed in and out of the house a few times. He was rifling through Evo's – Eva's office for various things, and the team helped where they could. He had found a set of diaries of Eva's going back twenty years. They would need to be studied in detail, but even a cursory glance showed a mania, that going unchecked over the years had developed into a full-on delusion. She had become more and more convinced the world was going to meet a cultural Armageddon, which seemed to be the reason for her labelling the portal with underworld mythology; and that had led Eva on her increasingly delusionary path.

Stimpson's mention of the study caused Bella to sit up and announce loudly, '*Oh no...* the bloody chair. *What an idiot I've been*. There was a clue right there at the start, and I missed it. *I'm sorry*.'

Stimpson looked at Bella, '*What chair?*'

'The one in Evo's office. When he took me in there on the evening we came to his dinner party, he sat me down, then he sat down in his own chair and lowered it. Being self-obsessed about myself and my husband, and being under the spell of Evo's charm; I assumed he lowered the chair to be courteous and not tower over me but...'

No one interrupted her sentence, so Bella continued it herself after a moment.

'But... he would have to lower the seat if someone much shorter had been sitting in the chair before. What would be comfortable for a woman of five foot or so, would not be for a man that was easily six foot. – What an idiot. I could have spared us all this heartache if I had been on the ball. The chair was set wrong because it wasn't his office.'

Stimpson shook his head in a matter-of-fact manner, 'You shouldn't feel bad Mrs Stone. I have training for that sort of thing, and I am not sure if I had been in your position, that I would have given such a thing any consideration either. Don't beat yourself up about it.'

Bella pursed her lips and gave a nod.

On the way out, Stimpson explained to Matt that it looked like Eva had been the one to activate the Shadow Tide machine with Joe and Max in it. 'I wouldn't lose too much sleep over her death mate, if I were you. Looking at her computer, it looks like she and Norton had decided to frame Evo and send you off in that direction. It looks like he genuinely didn't have a clue he was being framed. I suspect he didn't know about the deaths.'

In-between these visits, the team slowly began to face up to the initial trauma and shock of what Norton's betrayal meant to them. The consensus was that their biggest hurdle in dealing with the betrayal was that not only was the here-and-now wrong and a lie; but that every conversation and action with him over the last couple of years was also a lie. Not only was he not who they thought he was, they no longer felt they were who they thought they were. How had they missed the fact he was clearly a psychopath? This conversation would kick in and out throughout the night in the small chunks that they could manage, before the pain became too great, and they had to change the subject; or getup and continue to lockdown the manor, room by room. Window latches were shut firm, shutters were pulled to, curtains were drawn, power sockets where turned off, and doors were firmly closed and locked; the keys of the secured rooms then added to the growing bunch. Nalebury Park was no longer anyone's home.

At times, they briefly talked about how they were struggling not only with Norton killing Evo; but also Eva and then himself. It was on one of Stimpson's visits back to the house that he pointed out that whilst he didn't know about Evo; Norton and Eva clearly had a suicide pact.

Max looked surprised, 'A suicide pact. Who said that?'

'No one said, that's kind of the point.'

'*You've lost me.*'

'Well neither Eva nor Norton made any sound as they fell. They would have screamed or yelled if they had wanted to live; in my experience anyway. Their silence as they fell to their deaths speaks volumes.' Then he was gone again, back to the portal.

It was agreed with Bella that she would return to the hotel, pack and head home that night. The goodbyes were pretty emotional. Her adventure was at an end. She had spent nearly two years fighting the system, and against all the odds; she had won with help from these great and decent people. She hoped that now their professional relationship was over forever; it would be replaced with one of personal friendship. They would certainly come to Pete's wake and send-off along with Pete's friends from the hotel; she knew that much for sure. She must get on with planning that. She relished the thought of getting back to the normal mundane day to day of life.

Now that there was no longer any need to fight, Bella's body let go, and as she sat in the back of the taxi heading down the M4 towards her beloved London; the exhaustion began to consume her. She knew her husband's killer would never stand trial, but she felt a certain justice had been served. It was a justice she could live with. She would speak to the coroner's office as Matt suggested. For now though; Bella just wanted to get back home to her bed, the bed that she and Pete spent happy nights together in. She would cuddle up to his memory; right now she felt she could sleep for a month.

CHAPTER 54

In the morning, the team had handed the manor over to a fresh squad of police officers, then packed up at the hotel and said their goodbyes.

It had been a unanimous agreement to return to the portal for one last visit before they left the area. To say goodbye to the place that had changed their lives forever; not only their future and how they would see the world from now on; but as they had acknowledged last night, it had also changed what had gone before, thanks to Norton's betrayal. These were emotional scars that had been inflicted, and would be carried indefinitely by each of them. It really was not an exaggeration to say that life would never quite be the same again.

They got out of the cars and wandered over to the top of the stone balustrade where the staircase descended down to the portal. The grass on the edge of the stairs was all flat where vehicles had come up and down, collecting bodies and anything else the police had decided needed to be removed without delay. Several lengths of police tape were tied across the two posts that marked the start of the stairs. The tape was sagging, the slack allowing it to move about gently in the breeze.

Bruno walked along to the balustrade and peered over, his hands resting on the stone. Below he could see a couple of police officers looking back up at him. Bruno recognised them as two of the officers from last night. He gave a clear thumbs up to which both officers responded in kind.

'We have just come to say goodbye to the place,' Bruno shouted down to the officers, '*All the best to you.*'

'*And to you,*' came the shouted reply in stereo.

Bruno walked back to join the others.

Ava put her hand on the police tape to stop it moving. 'So many people tell you that the past cannot be changed, but it can; it has been here.'

No one said anything out loud. They were thinking about what Ava had just said. She was right. The past could be changed, Norton had proved it. Ava gripped the tape tightly in her hands.

Matt gave consideration to what Ava had just said.

'You're right. Norton has ripped the rug right from underneath us. In a heartbeat he has shown that an aspect of our life was not what we thought it was, and the logical thought is to question whether that is true of the rest of our world; but we have to hold strong and have faith. There are not really any words to fully describe what he has done, but we cannot let him destroy us. We are strong together, we are not like him, we are family, and we have each other's backs. The best way we can beat this and him is to have faith in each other. If we begin to doubt each other, Norton wins.'

Silence fidgeted amongst the team for a few moments before Matt concluded sharing his thoughts.

'Evo did tell us when we met him this was just a tunnel. *He was right*. It's just a building. It's all very clinical in the cold light of day. It was the people in this case that we had to be wary of, *not the buildings*.'

Ava had drifted off on a thought of her own. So, Evo was a construct... he was her construct – Eva's. Rest in peace Christopher whoever you are. She felt a sudden pang of sadness for a man who did not get to live his own life, had been lied to, then robbed of his existence. Her hand was in her pocket when her phone started to vibrate, which made her jump.

Pulling the phone out of her pocket and looking at it, Ava decided she would not answer it unless it looked important. The caller ID read DCI Stimpson. Ava took the call.

Ava walked away whilst answering the phone. Beyond her saying 'Hello,' the team could hear no more of the conversation. It was indeed DCI Edward Stimpson. Gone was the amiable tone from yesterday that Ava had come to associate with this now recognisable voice. Was that a very real panic she could detect in his voice? Ava was growing more unsettled as a panicked Stimpson almost yelled his information down the phone to her.

Matt had come to a decision. 'I think we have all earned a long weekend starting now, there is nothing in the diary for us work-wise for the next few days.'

Everyone nodded.

'*Damn right*,' said Bruno.

Matt was interrupted by Ava's return, and they all clocked the change in her demeanour.

'We actually need to leave.... now.'

'That was DCI Stimpson on the phone. He called us as a potential client this time. His sister has just been found dead at the foot of a waterfall called Boar's Cascade in the Forest of Dean.'

Ava paused for a breath.

'From what I could glean from that call, the investigation team and several eye witnesses are saying suicide; but Stimpson says that something his sister confided to him yesterday means he knows for a fact it can't be. Stimpson has little time before being removed from the crime scene because of the obvious family conflict. He is there now waiting for us.'

They turned and walked back towards the cars. If they took this new case, it meant the long weekend off was going to have to wait. They wouldn't be that far away if the police on the de Varley case needed to talk to them, and to be honest, they could all do with the distraction of a

new case whilst they continued to process everything in relation to Norton Graey; their friend…
their enemy.

AFTERWORD

Dear Reader,

The Determined Widow is the first in a series of books that follow the exploits of Matthew Holland and his team. Each book will be a complete standalone case.

I am working on the team's next case now, and it is due for release in 2022.

If you would like to receive notification when the next book in this series becomes available, you can keep an eye on Amazon or you can leave your email address with me at www.adammelrose.org and I will send you a notification around the launch date.

I will treat your email address with the same level of care and protection I would expect my own email address to be dealt with. It will only be used to inform you when the next book is available to purchase.

In the meantime, I would like to offer you a genuine thank you for purchasing and reading my first novel. If you enjoyed it, I would love to hear your thoughts. You can reach me via the above website.

I know there is a world of choice out there, and I am genuinely grateful you chose to give my

debut novel a shot. (Pun intended... well I am a thriller writer, I had to!)
Seriously though, thank you!

Adam Melrose

ACKNOWLEDGEMENT

I would like to begin by thanking my parents John and Jane and my superb junior school for introducing me to great books, stories and imagination from an early age.

I would also like to thank everyone who has supported me in the creation of this novel and for encouraging me to give it a go. Thanks to Alex for all the support, initial editing suggestions and for being a great sounding-board.

Thank you to my praise-shy editor for helping me get my word count down from 120,000 words to just over 95,000 and for all your guidance and understanding that I wanted to write a slow-burning thriller. Something that many think has no place in modern times.

I would also very much like to thank those members of my family who have taught me so much about life and how to live it that are the inspiration for Matthew Holland and four of his team members. You know who you are.

Thank you goes to Dr Brett Lockyer BM, BSc (Hons), FRCPath for taking time out of his already busy schedule, and for his putting up with my endless questions about how to kill someone, and the associated pathology and due process involved. Also for his keeping my plans within the realms of what is possible in reality.

Thank you also goes to John Giffard CBE QPM for being kind enough to talk to me about police procedure in relation to certain types of death and what relations might realistically be like between an investigating police force and a team of private investigators.

Finally, thank you to everyone else who has had a hand in helping to make this first book a reality. I am very grateful to you all. This book would not have happened without your help.

ABOUT THE AUTHOR

Adam Melrose

Adam Melrose grew up in the wilds of
Scotland and studied Agriculture.

He now lives outside London.

After many years working in systems design
and IT, in 2019 Adam took the plunge and
decided to see if he could write a novel.

He undertook online classes in writing,
including two with successful authors
who have been kind enough to share their
wisdom and expertise with beginners.

The first piece of advice he got
from both writers was...

"Write the book you want to read."

So he did.

Printed in Great Britain
by Amazon